Under One Roof

Stone Family Series
Book 1

Sophie Andrews

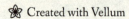

Content Note

Under One Roof has all of the emotion and spice you've come to expect from a Sophie Andrews novel, but Griffin and Andi have experienced grief, parental abandonment, and verbal/emotional abuse, all of which are discussed on the page. Though you can be guaranteed Captain Stone would NEVER give you a third act break-up.

For Andi J. Christopher for gifting us with the term stern brunch daddies.

And for Captain Von Trapp, the original stern brunch daddy.

Chapter 1
Andi

Four days, eight Red Bulls, and sixty-seven loops of my "I Am Woman, Hear Me Roar" playlist later, I have to call it.

I've let down Aretha, Alanis, Beyoncé, and my girl Kelly Clarkson in one fell swoop. Not to mention Helen Reddy. I'm not worthy to sing their songs, let alone roar.

I haven't showered since Albuquerque. My sleep hasn't been much better—a few hours at a time at rest stops off the interstate. I started getting punch-drunk somewhere in Indiana, and my car began smoking about five miles behind...wherever I am now.

Not Texas, that's for sure.

Ten years after I left my family's cattle ranch and everyone I knew in the dust, I couldn't go crawling back with my tail between my legs. So instead of making the turn off I-10, I white-knuckled the steering wheel and kept right on driving. Like if I went far enough, fast enough, I could outrun my shame and embarrassment.

Pulling off onto the shoulder of the road, I let my head fall back against the rest and close my eyes, accepting my current fate.

I inhale a few times, then grab my cell phone, the date and time on the screen.

April 12th, 1:37.

Write it on the death certificate. The day Andrea Halton's dreams well and truly died.

I put on my metaphorical big-girl panties and hop out of my Jeep, slamming the door to march around to the front of my hunk of junk. And because the universe hates me, not only is my car literally smoking, but it's raining.

Perfect.

Perfect!

I pop the hood like I have any idea what I'm doing and stare at the sizzling engine with wires and twisty things and boxes that look like they might be important. My big-girl panties quickly sag.

Turning in a circle, the pavement slick under my boots, I search for a sign to let me know where I am. I've been so bleary-eyed and haven't been paying much attention. Sorta just headed east.

As far as I could go.

Which is here, apparently.

I wipe my palms on my shorts and open the internet browser on my cell phone but stall out. What do I do next?

I have no idea.

All my life knowledge has evaporated.

Maybe it happened when I crossed the Mississippi. Everything I ever knew fell out of my head. Plunked right down into the river below.

Biting the inside of my cheek, I refuse to give in to the tears.

But it's really hard not to. So, I bite harder and sniff a few times, blinking away the evidence.

"Think. Think," I command myself. "Find a mechanic. Pull up the map. You can do this."

I start typing, but before I can finish, a big truck parks in front of me.

This will be my real time of death, 1:42.

Though it's the middle of the day, I tense up, ready to... fight. I guess. Or run. I've got little legs, but I can run pretty fast if need be. They didn't call me "The Flash" on my fourth-grade basketball team for nothing.

I attempt to keep my breathing steady as I stand as tall as my five feet two inches will allow and watch as a figure steps out of the truck.

It's a man.

I can tell from the sneakers that hit the pavement first, and then my gaze travels up the black sweatpants to the thick torso, and up farther, over the sturdy-looking shoulders to the face.

The face.

Sweet baby Jesus.

I actually whimper.

Because he looks like he should be wearing spandex and a cape, all swinging arms and muscles with a square jaw that could cut glass. With every step he takes, I take one back until I'm up against my Jeep, unable to do anything but watch this superhero approach me.

It's not until he's a few feet from me that I see his brow is furrowed under the bill of the hat he wears on his head, and he's got an actual dimple in his chin.

Slo-mo walking to me and everything, it's as if he stepped off a movie screen.

Or maybe that's all in my head.

Probably.

Because I don't even realize he's talking to me until he points to his ear. "Can you hear me?"

"Hm? Yeah." I straighten up. "Yes, I can hear you."

His gaze sweeps over me from head to toe. "I asked if you need help."

"Oh. Um. Y-yes. My car... It's smoking..."

Another full inspection with his dark eyes, and I shudder, my *You Can Do This* adrenaline taking a nose dive all at once.

"Are you all right? Do you need medical assistance?" the superhero asks, stepping so close, the tips of his sneakers touch the tips of my boots, and it's only now that I realize I must look ridiculous. My hair's plastered to my head from the rain, my Allman Brothers T-shirt is white, so it's become see-through, and I'm not wearing a bra.

I fold my arms over my chest in an attempt to warm up and cover myself. "I'm okay. A little lost and broke down."

Literally and figuratively.

His attention drifts past me. "Where are you headed?"

I swallow, my throat thick with humiliation. As if my life can't get any worse, the hottest man I've stumbled across in a long time is here to watch not only my car but my life break down in real time. I'm not sure what to say, so I shrug, biting my molars to keep my chin from wobbling.

The corners of his mouth tighten into a frown, and his eyes crinkle like he's angry. I'm not sure what about, but maybe rescuing a drowned rat wasn't on his to-do list today.

"I'm sorry, I—"

"Here." He unzips his hoodie and hands it over to me. "Put this on."

"I don't want to take your sweatshirt. It's—"

"You're freezing. Put it on." When I don't immediately take it from him, he drapes it over my shoulders, leaving me without a choice, so I slide my arms inside. While it's a little wet from the rain and three times my size, it's warm from his body heat. I wrap it tight around me and tug the soft cotton up to my nose under the guise of being cold, but really, I want to smell it. Breathe in his scent of earth and smoke.

"Go sit in my truck," he instructs. "You need to get warm."

"I don't think it's a good idea." I don't know him or where I am. I'm basically living the beginning of a *Dateline* episode.

As if reading my mind, he jerks his chin in the direction of his dark blue Ford. "My keys are in the cupholder."

Meaning, I could steal the thing if I wanted to.

"Are you sure?"

He curls his long fingers around my shoulder, tugging me away from my Jeep, and gently pushes me past him. "Go. I'll take care of this."

With one last wary look at him, I scurry to his truck, where I have to literally jump up into the passenger seat. As he promised, the keys are there, and I pump up the heat then turn to watch my rescuer work.

He's bent over, doing something with my vehicle's engine, his gray shirt now completely soaked through as the rain has picked up in the short time I've been enjoying the heated seats in his comfy truck. I feel bad. I shouldn't be letting him try to fix my Jeep or whatever it is he's doing, but before I can gather my courage to go out there again, he shuts the hood. Taking his cell phone out of his pocket, he leans against the Jeep, facing in my direction. I think his gaze is focused on me. I can't be sure with the rain and the whole truck between us, but I *swear* I can feel his eyes on me.

His conversation is quick, and he slides his phone into his pocket before jogging over to the driver's side. Then he slams the door, sealing us both inside with the heat blasting and rain pelting the windshield, and he's not only my rescuer. He's my prince.

Because now I know what Cinderella must have felt when she saw Prince Charming for the first time.

Like all the air was sucked out of her lungs and the noise everywhere went silent except her heartbeat in her ears.

Too bad for me, the clock has already struck midnight and my carriage has transformed back into a pumpkin.

My prince removes his fire and rescue cap and rakes his hand over his hair, the dark strands barely long enough to curl over his knuckles, with silver strands at his temples and some gray in the scruff that I can finally see around his jaw. I estimate he's in his late thirties or early forties, tanned and well-built, like a man who spends a lot of time working his body. I get caught staring at the tattoos covering his left arm. They're mesmerizing. The way the dark blue ink wraps and curves around his forearm, leading to the thick, fancy-looking watch on his wrist.

It's all so...masculine. Like, kill a mammoth and build a fire with only a stick and rock type masculine.

Maybe I've been around too many men who take more pride in their flat brims and spotless bright-white Jordans than in doing anything of value, but this guy exudes a type of get-shit-done attitude I haven't experienced in a long time.

He clears his throat, forcing my brain to ignore the loin-cloth-in-a-cave fantasies and start functioning in reality again.

I blink down to his hat on the seat between us and notice the emblem on it matches the one on his sweatshirt that I'm wearing, right above what I guess is his name. I assume he must be a firefighter and drag my fingertip over the stitching, quietly reading it to myself. "Captain Stone."

He answers with a deep, "Yeah."

I meet his eyes, heavy lidded and so dark brown they're almost black, with thick lashes that I'd kill for. So pretty. A stark contrast to the rest of him, stone-faced and carved from marble.

Even Michelangelo would be jealous of this work of art.

I gesture from him to the name on the sweatshirt. "You're Captain Stone?"

He nods.

"As in, fire captain?"

He nods again, and I exhale.

"Like Captain America."

He arches one thick brow at me, and I nibble on the inside of my lip, thinking I somehow offended him again.

"I didn't mean it as a bad thing," I rush out, yanking the sleeves of the sweatshirt down to cover my fists. "It's— You're rescuing me, and you have that kind of look about you and—"

"That's what my brother calls me," he says, interrupting my nervous rambling.

"Oh?" I give in to a small laugh. "See? Must be true, then. Captain America."

He pushes his air vents so they're all aimed in my direction. "Are you warm enough?"

I stick my covered-up hands between my knees. "Yeah. I'm okay."

"Don't lie." He shifts, stretching one of his long arms between the seats to retrieve a bag from the back seat, and pulls out a blanket, which he swiftly opens and drapes over me. "You're shivering."

I burrow into the warmth and push wet locks of hair behind my ears as he sifts through the bag again, this time retrieving a water from his emergency kit. I gratefully accept the bottle since I've been running almost exclusively on caffeine and beef jerky.

"Thank you for this," I say and slug back half of it before putting the lid back on, avoiding his gaze. "And thank you for stopping." Maybe if I stay still long enough, he'll forget about me, and I can continue on my merry way.

But he won't allow it. He takes hold of his sweatshirt on me with his bear-paw hands and zips it all the way up. Then he gives a playful tug on the strings with a quietly growled, "There."

The backs of his knuckles slide across my jaw, nudging my focus up to his steady gaze, lulling me into a sense of security. It's hypnotizing, how I can't look away from him. How it seems like he can see into my mind as his eyes drift back and forth between mine. "Appeared like you needed some assistance."

A lifetime passes before he finally removes his hands from me, and I can breathe again. Though the oxygen hasn't reached all the way to my brain yet. "I do. I mean, I did."

He ignores my Freudian slip. "Your engine's overheated because of a coolant leak. I called for a tow to take it to a mechanic shop. He'll be able to fix it for you."

After a decade in Los Angeles, I'm not used to a stranger being so helpful, and I reflexively reach for my bag, which, of course, I don't have at the moment. "I'll pay you."

"You don't have to do that. It was nothing."

"But..." I lift the blanket and water bottle, showing him how he helped me. I have to repay him somehow.

"But nothing," he snaps with a finality that rings through the small space we're both sharing, and I close my mouth, sitting up straight. The response is automatic, like my body knows it's a requirement to be at attention in his presence.

Next to me, Captain America breathes audibly, and out of the corner of my eye, I see him rub his forehead. "Sorry. I don't expect to be repaid." He sighs again, and when I turn to him, he lolls his head back against his seat, rolling to face me. "It's been a long day. I apologize for being short with you. Especially since you've obviously had a bad day too."

I nod, and I hate how my voice sounds so broken. "Bad week, more like."

Months, really.

He studies me with a shrewd gaze, and I know he can read me better than I can read him. Already, he's got one up on me, so I don't even try to lie when he asks, "What happened?"

I wipe at the wetness in the corner of my eye. "Small-town girl tries to make it big but fails and is afraid to go home and face her past, so she keeps driving until she breaks down in the middle of nowhere." I try for a smile. It fades quickly. "You know, the usual."

"The usual," he repeats dryly, though his face is soft. He extends his hand like he might touch me but changes course to point at the windshield. "You're not in the middle of nowhere. You're in West Chester, Pennsylvania. Not far from Philly."

I peer around as if the city is right outside the window. "Oh yeah?"

"About forty miles east." He gestures in that direction. "If you get back on the interstate, you'll hit New York City in two hours."

Not a bad spot to break down in, I suppose.

"After my car gets fixed, maybe I'll head that way," I say, more to myself than him, and he nods once, raising his arm to check the time on his watch that I guess must be a diving or military watch with more numbers and buttons than a person needs.

"The tow should be here in twenty minutes or so. I can drive you to the shop then."

I open my mouth to argue that he doesn't have to, but the words die on my tongue when he arches his brow again. He's apparently not used to being challenged, and I will not be the one to test him.

"I really appreciate you," I tell Captain Stone, and he waves as if it's no big deal. But it is. It's a very big deal.

And whether or not he meant to, he just made me fall in love with him.

Chapter 2
Griffin

"I'm, uh...gonna go grab my stuff," my roadside princess says and hops outside before I can answer one way or the other. By the time I move to open my door to help her, she's already halfway to her Jeep. With a perturbed huff, I step out of my truck. Thankfully, the rain has slowed to a drizzle once again.

I'd been looking forward to going home to a hot meal and a nap after my shift, but that idea flew out the window along with my goddamn good sense as soon as I saw her in those tiny shorts.

I would stop for anyone who needed aid—it's not in me to keep driving—but especially for a young woman in cowboy boots and a T-shirt that stuck to her like a second skin in the rain. It's a ridiculous outfit to wear at this time of year. We have weeks until summer, when she could wear those tiny shorts. Not in *this* weather.

And without a bra.

Killing me with those tight little nipples.

One look at her and my entire day was shot.

Because I couldn't rest until this soaking-wet slip of a woman was taken care of.

"Fuck me," I mutter as I reach her. She's got a duffel bag over one shoulder, a purse across her body, and a guitar case slung on her back. She jolts with awareness at my mumbled curse, and I stick out my hand. "Let me take those."

She hesitates for only a moment, and I try my best not to watch her small tits jiggle as she rearranges her bags, handing me her duffel, but not giving up her purse or guitar.

Smart girl.

Back in the truck, I set her bag on the rear seats then glance at my reflection in the rearview mirror. I run a hand over my hair and face then tug at my clothes as if I'm some young buck, vying for her attention.

Jesus Christ.

She's got to be more than a decade younger than me and in need of help, not some guy falling all over his damn self.

I'm such an asshole. But when she looks up at me with those big brown eyes and fixes her obscenely puffy lips into a pout that's half misery and half hope, I have to fight my instinct to take her in my lap and tell her I'll take care of everything from now on. All she has to do is say yes.

Instead, I shift my attention down to the guitar case she sets between her golden, tanned legs. Seriously. Why is she wearing shorts right now?

With a stiff shake of my head, I study the black case. It's well-worn. Well-loved, too, from the way she won't let go of it. She takes a deep breath and attempts to tame her caramel-colored hair, but it's a mess. She's a mess.

And so fucking cute.

I slant my gaze out the windshield, refusing to give in to any more of this middle school crap. I'm forty-two years old, a fire captain and a former Navy SEAL. I don't have crushes on girls.

Especially ones with sad eyes and stickers all over her guitar case, including but not limited to an *Awkward as Flock* flamingo, a trash bin on fire with the words *This Little Light of Mine, I'm Gonna Let it Shine* above it, and another which reads *Daddies Do It Better*. That particular one has me pinching the bridge of my nose.

Next to me, she clears her throat. "So, I guess..." She holds out her hand to me. "My name's Andi. Nice to meet you, Captain."

I stare at her hand for longer than socially acceptable and only take it when she giggles nervously. Her fingers are fine-boned with chipped polish on her nails, and a small, colorful hummingbird is inked on her wrist. I draw my thumb back and forth over it before letting go.

She skims her own thumb over the tattoo and offers me a quiet explanation. "For my grandmother. She loved them."

"That's...nice," I say because I'm a fucking idiot. "Are you close?"

"We were."

I wince. "I'm sorry."

She keeps her gaze on her guitar case, where she scratches at a rainbow sticker. "Thanks. It was..." Her throat works on a swallow as she gathers herself. I've never been a particularly patient person, but I am today. Or, at least, I am for her. Because I sit in silence as she licks those lips I can't stop staring at and takes a breath that makes her chest rise, and I force my eyes away from her peaked nipples.

An entire day passes before she finally says, "She was sick, and whenever I talked to her, she kept telling me to *stay, stay, stay, don't come home,* and then one day I called, and she wasn't there." Her chin trembles, voice cracks. "And now I can't face going home without her there." She shakes her head, still refusing to meet my gaze. "I'm sorry. It was a few months ago, but it feels...fresh. I'm sorry."

"Don't apologize." Before I even know what I'm doing, I catch the lone tear on her cheek with my thumb then stroke her jaw, gently prodding her to look at me. The tip of her nose is red, her eyes are wet, and it inexplicably kills me.

Feel-her-pain-in-my-own-chest kind of kills me.

And I fucking hate it.

Because I don't do this. I don't do feelings, and the few that I do have are secured tightly under lock and key, buried beneath the floorboards of my skeleton.

I can't give in to emotion, not with all the shit I've already been through and experience every day. If I did, I wouldn't have been able to last so long in the SEALs or put on my uniform every day to fight fires. I've seen more death than any person ever needs to and have been responsible for saving more lives than I can reasonably count up to, so I keep my mind tidy and the organ beating inside my chest on a leash.

Life is too short and too precious to fuck it all up with something so capricious as *feelings*.

Feelings make people do stupid shit.

But here I am, doing stupid shit.

I hand Andi a tissue and brush her hair away from her face. It's drying in waves that tempt me to weave my fingers into it, so I cross my arms, keeping myself from doing any more stupid shit.

Unfortunately, my mouth doesn't get the message. "I didn't come home for a long time after my mom died."

Andi lifts her head, her eyes full of compassion, her face full of understanding. Before she can say anything, I tell her, "It was a long time ago, and I stayed away until I couldn't any longer."

Until another untimely death forced me back to my hometown, I don't say.

But she surprises me when she asks, "Did you regret it? Not coming home before?"

I shrug. And then because I can't seem to shut my mouth, I confess, "I try not to think about my regrets."

That makes her release a soft laugh, and she may as well wrap her fist around my heart.

"That's a really good line," she murmurs, tugging her cell phone out to open up her Notes app, typing something. I try to get a peek at it, though she closes it before I can, and she turns to catch me spying.

"You a poet or something?" I can't believe I used to be good at this. I used to be able to have a conversation with a woman. Albeit, that was a very long time ago, but I think learning to speak Russian was easier than this.

Although I can't be too embarrassed by my ineptitude because she smiles at me, faint as it may be, displaying two shallow dimples on either side of her mouth. A playful glint shines in her eyes. "Or something."

I lean forward into her space. "What's that mean?"

She squints, and a moment passes when I think she might not tell me, but she gives in with a shy shoulder shrug. "On my better days, I like to think of myself as a songwriter."

The guitar makes sense, and I nod, interested. More so, captivated.

I have been since I pulled over and saw her face. I always thought love at first sight was bullshit, and this certainly isn't that. Although I did feel...something in that moment.

And the longer I sit here with her, the more it settles into me.

Not an electrical current or euphoria, but something like familiarity. Which is impossible. We're strangers to each other, and yet I can't stop wanting to talk to her, wanting to know her, wipe her tears, and make her smile. Because it feels like we've done all this before, like her sitting in the cab of my truck is exactly where she's supposed to be. Like I'm the one supposed to be tucking her hair behind her ear, so I do, and I'm the one supposed to be taking care of her, so I do.

When the tow comes, I tell her to stay put and get out to direct the driver to take her Jeep to Matthews Mechanic. I wait until he's on the road then sit back behind the wheel of my truck. That's when Andi thanks me again, and I shake my head. Making sure she's safe is the least I can do.

I turn on the radio, and it's a song I don't know, so I move to change it.

"No, leave it." Andi catches my wrist, her cheeks going pink, and she releases me like she burned herself. "Sorry. I mean, please. Please leave it. I love this one."

It's the easiest request she could make, and I raise the volume a couple of clicks. While I drive, Andi's head bobs slightly, her voice barely above a whisper as she sings along to Billie Eilish, and I could not name one of her songs if someone paid me a million dollars, but I might download her album to check it out.

At a red light, I steal a glance at the woman in my passenger seat, noting the few small hoops around her earlobe and those lips she purses. She must not realize what she does to a man with that mouth, because if she knew the depraved fantasies they've already stirred in my brain, she'd run far from me. Not to mention, the dewy shine of her skin that calls to be touched. I'm not sure if it's natural, from the rain, or lotion, but I tighten my fist around my steering wheel so I don't place my hand on her thigh.

When we arrive at the shop, we don't have to ring the bell for service, because Dylan Matthews is already at the desk. He's my son's baseball coach, and while I wouldn't exactly say we're friends, we're acquainted enough that I bring my truck here when it needs an inspection, and I've recruited my siblings to become customers as well. The guy does good work.

Andi introduces herself and explains what happened. I fill in the information about the leaky coolant, and Dylan nods.

"It's not a difficult job, but I'll have to order the parts, so it'll be a day or two before I can get to it."

Next to me, I feel Andi's little body tighten with tension at that news, so I try asking, "There's no way to overnight it?"

He studies me then Andi before flicking his gaze back to me. "I'll see what I can do, but I make no promises."

I nod my thanks as Andi knots her fingers together, another problem surfacing. "Would you be able to tell me how much it'll be? Approximately?"

"A few hundred."

She sucks in a breath. "A few hundred, like two? Or like eight? Because I might have to split it between credit cards." Her face flushes red. "Or do you have payment plans?"

Once again, Dylan slants his eyes toward me, and I give an imperceptible shake of my head, hoping he understands what I'm saying. That I'll take care of it. Just don't fucking make this worse.

"I can't be positive until I get under the hood and have the parts in my hand, but I'm sure it'll be closer to two."

I blow out a relieved breath and stick my hand out to him. "Thanks."

"Not a problem." I'm grateful he says no more. He keeps it uncomplicated. How I like it.

With my hand on Andi's back, I usher her out of the shop,

where she pauses outside the door, turning her face up to mine. "I guess I'm staying in West Chester for a little while, but I don't know of a place to stay."

"I do."

Chapter 3
Andi

As we pull up to The Nest Bed-and-Breakfast, I take in the charming exterior. A big Victorian, painted a soft yellow with white trim. A wide wraparound porch spans the front, complete with rocking chairs and potted plants. It's like something out of a postcard.

Captain Stone, aka grumpy Captain America, parks his truck and gestures toward the house. "It's not usually full this time of year, and it's within walking distance of downtown. Should suit your needs while you're here."

Between the coming mechanic's bill and this unexpected stay, I'll be emptying all my savings and hitting the limits on my credit cards, but I don't have time to worry about it because he's opening my door, offering me his hand to help me down. Standing next to him, I can't help but notice he's more than a foot taller than me and feels twice as wide with biceps the size of my head. He handles my duffel that I have packed to bursting like it's no heavier than a feather. I have a few boxes and one large suitcase still in the back of my Jeep, but my essentials are in my bag, including clean underwear, makeup, and my vibrator.

Which just so happens to power on from Captain handling it.

We both hear the buzzing at the same time, and my eyes must bug out of my head as I try to tackle the big guy, reaching for my duffel. He sets it on the ground before shoving his hands into his pockets and turning away from me, granting me some sense of modesty, I guess. But he's already seen me at my lowest; why not bury myself under another six feet.

I nearly tear the bag open in my haste to shut it off, but because I can always go lower, I have to pull the bright-pink thing out of my bag to find the power button. With flaming cheeks and embarrassment coating my skin, I shut it off then shove it far down the duffel, hoping to dive right in after it.

Behind me, Captain clears his throat, and I wipe a clammy hand over my face. "I... That was, uh..."

He doesn't utter a word, only carefully zips the bag back up and carries it like a grenade waiting to go off. Then he nods for me to follow him, and I dutifully fall in line, silently cursing the author of my life.

He leads me up the creaky wooden steps to the front door of the B&B. Inside, the foyer is warm and welcoming. White wainscoting lines the lower half of the walls, contrasting with the dark damask wallpaper above. A chandelier hangs from the high ceiling, bathing the space in a soft glow. To the left, a sitting area with carved wooden chairs and velvet chaise longue, straight off the cover of a romance novel, creates a welcoming atmosphere in front of the fireplace.

Before I can explore any further, a tall white woman with a long bob and most excellent balayage greets us, but not in a way I'm expecting.

"What are you doing here?"

I open my mouth to answer. What? I don't know, too taken aback by her tone, but Captain steps in.

"We need a room." He points to me. "*She* needs a room."

"And you brought her here?" The woman flicks her gaze between the two of us, and my good Southern manners keep my lips zipped, but if she works here, she's got terrible customer service.

"Her car broke down, and she needs a place to stay."

"Just for a night or two," I add, and the woman's eyes land on me again. They're familiar. The shape of them reminds me of my rescuer's, along with her mouth. Maybe that's because she's frowning. Like he does.

"Family discount," he says, and the woman cants her head back, as if ready to argue, but a silent communication passes between them, and she relents after a few seconds.

At my evident confusion, he tells me, "This is Taryn. My sister."

"Oh." I smile. "Hi, nice to meet you. I'm Andi."

She motions for me to follow her to the check-in desk. "I thought it's our brother who takes in the strays."

I freeze, unsure what she means. "Huh?"

"Knock it off," Captain grumbles from behind me, and I realize her words were meant for her sibling when she smirks at him. And my shoulders curl in.

Stray. I'm the stray.

She's making fun of me.

And after the day I've had, I don't have the energy for a Bless Your Heart comeback. Instead, I reach for my duffel bag from Captain Stone's shoulder and turn to leave.

He catches me around the waist. "Ignore her," he whispers in my ear. "She's just pissed I'm showing up unannounced. My sister doesn't handle surprises well."

"I am showing up unannounced," I correct, but he shrugs

and keeps his arm around me as he circles us both to face Taryn once again. She keys something into her computer and, a minute later, hands me a key.

"You don't need a credit card?" I ask cautiously, and she looks to her brother, as if for the answer.

"We'll take care of it when you check out."

I'm not sure how I'm going to repay this man for all he's done for me, but I'll start a list to make sure I do before I head out of this town. He insists on carrying my bag upstairs as Taryn informs me of breakfast times and places I can visit, but I can barely listen with the heat of Captain America's hand on my back, his fingers spanning what feels like the whole of it, his pinkie resting just above the curve of my butt.

"This one's yours," Taryn says when we reach my room. It's covered in flowered wallpaper that I think would give me a headache if I stared at it for too long, but there's a bed and a shower, and that's all I need.

"This is great. I really appreciate you fitting me in."

"It's not a problem," Taryn replies, though she's glaring at her brother, who ignores her to set my bag down on the quilted comforter.

I do the same with my purse and guitar then pivot, intent on thanking him for his help, but he lifts his cell phone from his pocket and reads something on it.

"Fuck," he grunts, and Taryn steps closer, reading whatever it is that has him suddenly so upset, and she shakes her head. Quietly curses, too.

"Everything okay?" I ask, and he raises his gaze to me. He shifts, taking one step toward me then stops suddenly, rocking as if he's hit an invisible wall.

"I have to go. I need to take care of this."

"Is it a fire?" When he shakes his head, I try again. "Is it something I can help with? I'd love to pay you back for everything you've done for me today."

His dark eyes sweep over me, jaw tight, his hand balling into a fist at his side. "I've got to go."

"Okay. I...hope it all turns out okay."

He nods. "Nice meeting you, Andi."

"You too," I get out, but he's already on his way down the hall, leaving me alone with his sister, who barely spares me a cursory glance.

"I'm here until five, if you need anything. The robe and slippers are complimentary." Then she's out, too, and I wait only a few seconds to close the door and belly flop onto the bed.

Rolling to my back, I blow out a long breath.

It's been a day.

A week.

Months.

Making a fool of myself in front of Captain America is the cherry on top.

But it's over now, and I can relax for a night. I stand to strip out of my clothes, and that's when I realize I'm still in his zip-up. I bring the too-long sleeves up to my nose, smelling him again. The scent calms me, and I smile to myself even as I hang it up. I don't know if or when I'll see him again, but I can at least make sure the sweatshirt's dry.

After I'm undressed, I turn the shower on hot and step under the spray. It feels amazing on my sore muscles, and as I lather up with the floral-scented soap provided, I think back over the last ten years of my life.

How I left home with stars in my eyes and big dreams in my head, only to arrive in LA alone and without much support besides a monthly check for fifty dollars from Mimi. She'd been the one to teach me how to play the guitar and the only one who wanted me to go when everyone else wanted me to stay.

She'd been the only one I regularly talked to, and she'd been the only one to tell me not to give up, that my day would eventually come.

I thought it had when I lucked out by getting the job as Ryder St. James's personal assistant. I assumed it would be my big break—that *he* would give me my break. Problem was, he turned out to be the male version of Miranda Priestly, except worse. He might be brilliant, but he has the maturity of a fourteen-year-old boy.

And the way he fired me after everything I'd done for him? It was humiliating. Not only in what he'd said, but in whom he'd said it in front of. It had been my last straw.

I couldn't face the possibility of failure anymore. The fight had gone out of me. So, I packed up what was left of my dignity with the idea of going back home, ending up here instead.

No job, no prospects, and no more support because Mimi is gone. My grandmother passed, and I never even got to say goodbye. By the time I cobbled together enough money for a last-minute flight, I could only stay long enough for the funeral and dinner before hopping right back on the plane because Ryder needed me to take him to an emergency appointment. The idiot had crushed up Viagra with his coke, and his erection lasted a lot longer than a few hours.

It's always a penis that ruins everything.

I turn off the water and step out of the shower. The plush robe and slippers provide some small comfort as I towel-dry my hair, and my mind drifts back to Captain America.

I bet his penis wouldn't ruin anything.

In fact, I bet his penis would solve a lot of problems.

One of my favorite romance authors coined the term *Stern Brunch Daddy*, and I don't think I really understood it until now.

Until this man showed up with his handsome frown and

23

stately grays, taking over the situation like he could handle anything thrown at him. Like it was his pleasure to rescue me.

And, honestly, it felt nice to be rescued.

Felt even nicer when he put his hands on me.

I can't deny the instant attraction, and I'm positive it wasn't one-sided. I'm sure he thought he was being smooth, but almost every time I slanted my eyes to his, they were on my mouth first before darting up to mine. And I don't think I imagined the way he seemed to hesitate when he left, his hand outstretched to me like he meant to hug me.

I would have happily obliged. Starved of affection for too long.

But clearly, the man has bigger issues to deal with right now than some random stray he plucked up off the side of the road.

And I need to figure out my own life—get my Jeep fixed and come up with a plan, starting with finding my vibrator from where I buried it in my bag.

Might as well relieve some stress while my Captain's face is still fresh in my memory.

Chapter 4
Andi

My brain slowly switches on, and I arch beneath the sheets, stretching my back and arms. For a moment, I don't know where I am, still half in a dream. Then it all comes flooding back...the smoke pouring from my Jeep's engine, the handsome stranger who came to my aid. Captain Stone.

Then I remember the days spent in my car and Ryder's cruel words said to and about me at the worst possible time. Ryder was at a dinner with a bunch of producers, people who had power and money in the industry, and he called me to bring him his baggie of party favors that he forgot. While I was there, I got to talking, attempting to make my own contacts since he hadn't helped me in the three years I'd worked for him. But he didn't like me taking any of the spotlight away from him. So, he put me down with a few words and a smarmy smile.

He dug his elbow into his friend's side, raising his voice so everyone heard as he made it obvious to the entire party who I was to him. Insinuating I was nothing more than a paid blow job. Even though I'd *never* touched him.

"Her face is plain, but she's got those cock-sucking lips. 'Cept even those can't help her get her shit together. Worthless. Consider this your notice, Halton. Unless any of you wants to put those lips to good use."

I know I'm not worthless, but it still hurts. To be degraded and demeaned.

And the fact that I'm currently stranded with no idea of what I'm going to do with my life doesn't make me feel any better.

Lifting my phone from where I have it charging, I read the time, a few minutes after eleven. I suppose I needed the sleep since I haven't slept in like this in a long time, and my first instinct is to think that I need to do something. When I worked for Ryder, my schedule was not my own, constantly at the beck and call of his mercurial whims. If he wanted a special-order smoothie at six a.m., I got it for him. If he needed me to kick a woman out of his house at three in the morning, I did it.

And now that my life is my own once again, I'm at a loss.

So, I pull up the contact of the one person who I know will understand and FaceTime her. She answers immediately.

"There you are, mama! I miss your face already!"

I smile at my best friend of six years. Dahlia Ruiz let me live in her house rent-free for the last year, and she's the singer who gives life to my words. "I miss you and your cuddles."

Dahlia always let me snuggle her. Over the years, we've spent hours playing with each other's hair or scratching each other's backs, and I especially miss it first thing in the morning, when she'd come into my bed. Then Vic would almost always join us, the three of us like a pile of puppies.

The thought of never having that again makes my heart ache.

On my phone screen, Dahlia pouts. "Vic misses you too. We don't know what to do with ourselves."

I snort a laugh. I'm sure that's not true. I've been the third wheel in their relationship for a long time. No matter that he's like a brother to me, I know I was starting to cramp their style. He all but told me so when he said he planned on proposing to Dahlia soon. The puppy pile had to end at some point.

Yet another reason for me to pack my bags. Usually, a person needs only one or two signs to make a decision. I got, like, seven to know Los Angeles just wasn't for me anymore. If it ever was.

"So, when did you get home?" Dahlia asks, and I roll over to set my chin in my hand as I hold my phone up to keep myself in frame.

"I didn't."

Her eyes widen, and I turn the camera to show her my room. "I'm at a bed-and-breakfast in West Chester, Pennsylvania."

"Where's that? Why are you there?"

I recount the story of what happened, and by the time I finish, she's practically frothing at the mouth. "Andrea May Halton. You were rescued by an actual hot firefighter and didn't get any more information from him? How can you finally break your dry spell without knowing how to find him?"

"Ma'am." When she eyes me critically, I try on my best scowl. "First of all, it's not a dry spell—"

"Your cuca's drier than the Mojave," my best friend says, and I scoff.

"You are so rude."

"Is it rude if it's true?"

"To point it out, yes."

"So, you agree?" she says in her best impression of Regina George, eyeing me with a smile. "You need to get fucked."

I don't answer. I was raised in a conservative small town, going to church on Sundays and attending bible camp during the summers. I was taught to believe sex before marriage was bad, and while I may have removed myself from that world a long time ago, I haven't ever been able to dig myself out of the hole I'd been shoved into when it came to sex. Even with Dahlia's influence.

But when I tell her about how my vibrator went off while Captain held my bag, I have to wait almost a full five minutes before she calms down from her laughing fit. "Oh, it's too good. I'm sure he went home and fantasized about that all night." She points her finger at me. "You need to find him. Mission one while you're there."

"I would have no idea where to start."

She shrugs and suggests, "With a fire?"

I can't keep the amusement from my face, even as I try. I bring my phone into the bathroom with me, and we talk about her upcoming gigs while I pee and brush my teeth. On her end, Dahlia makes breakfast, and it almost feels like I'm still in California and not 3,000 miles away. When I'm fully dressed, Dahlia moves closer to the screen, like she always does when she has something important to say, speaking almost nose to nose.

"Seriously, what're you going to do?"

I flit my gaze to the windows of my room, where the sun shines outside. Something tugs inside me to follow it. "I'm not sure," I tell her, "but I think I'm gonna stay here for a while."

"You know you can always come back," she reminds me, and I nod, although I'm not so sure that's true. I don't have anything to go back to anymore.

"I love you," I say, and she blows me a kiss.

"Te quiero."

I tuck my phone away and loop my purse over my shoulder to go exploring. West Chester is a quaint and quiet town, more walkable than I'm used to. I pass a few parks, a university, and eventually find myself downtown with cobblestone sidewalks and boutique shops. I check out the pet store with homemade dog treats, browse around the record store, and try on but ultimately decide against buying the super-cute bell bottoms in the secondhand store. I need to save all the money I have to pay for my car and the bed-and-breakfast.

Even so, I wander into a lingerie shop called Lux & Lace, drawn in by the colorful window display.

"Hello, there," a bubbly voice says, and I turn to find a woman about my age with a Sabrina Carpenter vibe. "Can I help you find something today?"

"Oh. No, thank you. I'm just looking."

She flicks her hand. "That's what they all say."

"It's actually true for me. I'm sort of checking everything out around here," I say, motioning behind me, to the whole of the town.

She leans her elbow on the rack. "Oh yeah? You here visiting or...?"

"Or..." I trail off and then laugh at myself. "I'm not really sure. My car broke down yesterday, and I've suddenly found myself here. I think I might be staying for a while."

"Well, hi!" She lights up, introducing herself. "I'm Clara, one of the owners here, along with my wife." She points to a Black woman behind the counter, who is busy on the computer. "That's Marianne, and we'd be so happy to give you a tour and answer any questions you might have."

At her name, Marianne lifts her attention. "What are you volunteering me for?"

Clara drapes her arm around me protectively. "Helping our new friend."

Marianne sets down her pen and crosses over to shake my hand. "Don't let her steamroll you."

"Oh no. I'm fine. It's nice, actually. Great to meet y'all since I don't really know anyone."

"Good thing we know everyone," Clara stage-whispers, earning a playful eye roll from her wife.

As Clara fills me in on where to buy coffee and that I need to try a cinnamon bun from Sweet Cheeks, Marianne continues her business, and I relax in their presence, enjoying the easy rapport with each other, not to mention how helpful they are. I find myself answering all the questions they ask, about where I'm from, how I got here, and what I do for a living.

"About that," I say with a hopeful smile. "You aren't hiring, are you?"

"No, sweetie, sorry." Clara frowns then she sets her hand on her hip, tossing a look I can't read to Marianne, who turns to the front windows in thought.

I follow the direction of her gaze to the shops across the street. "Are any of them hiring?"

"I don't think so," Marianne says before pivoting to me again. "But we happen to know someone in need of a nanny."

"A nanny? Of children?"

"Yeah. Nanny of children." She laughs and moves to stand next to her wife, both of them eyeing me curiously, as if mentally saying to each other *Are you thinking what I'm thinking?*

I have no idea what they're thinking, and I lean into them for a clue.

"It's a bit of an emergency. The last one up and quit yesterday," Clara tells me.

I wrinkle my nose. "Without notice?"

They both nod, and while I've never exactly had a nine-to-five, I know that's not very professional. Just like it's not professional to fire someone in the middle of a party with important people everywhere, embarrassing your employee.

"I'm sure the parents aren't very happy about that," I say, and Clara nods.

"Would you be interested in the position? It pays well, and we know he's looking to fill it quickly."

Am I interested in being a nanny? I like kids fine, but I don't have experience working with them, unless you count some babysitting I did when I was younger. And Ryder.

Who is basically a child. I think about his temper tantrums and ridiculous demands. I controlled his schedule and booked all of his meetings and appointments, not to mention the odd housekeeping chores I did here and there, picking up after his messes and smoothing over the waves he made when he threw a fit. Hell, if I opened my purse right now, I'd find a couple packs of his favorite snacks, Dunkaroos—the chocolate ones with chocolate dip, which were very difficult to acquire—and orange Starbursts, because he truly is the devil. That's along with Flintstone vitamins because the man couldn't swallow pills—though he could snort them just fine—and a notebook that I kept handy because he liked to order me to write down random thoughts of his like they were brilliant nuggets of information or inspiration, even though he never referred to them again.

If I could handle Ryder St. James, I can certainly handle a kid or two.

I tell Marianne and Clara I'm interested and exchange cell phone numbers with them so they can forward me the information. An hour later, after I've sent off a bit of a padded résumé and letter of interest to Griffin at GS1982@xmail.com and bought myself a cup of coffee, I'm surprised to receive a reply.

Griffin informs me that Clara and Marianne are vouching for me, and while my résumé is a bit atypical, he's impressed with my first aid and CPR certifications. I'm glad he noticed because I took it seriously. After a scare at a party Ryder threw that involved broken glass and the pool, I immediately signed up for classes. While I thankfully never had to use those skills, I wanted to be prepared for anything after that.

Griffin tells me he is a single dad with two kids, and that this is a live-in position. He explains that he's away for entire days at a time because of his work, and the nanny would be responsible for essentially keeping the kids watered and fed, which I can easily do.

Although I find his question at the end of the email funny.

What would you do if you were locked out of the house with the kids inside and you didn't have access to a phone?

With my experience, I don't think there's a test I can't pass with these left-field scenarios, so I give him an honest answer.

Well, I suppose it depends on the ages of your kids and their abilities. If they couldn't unlock the door, I'd try to communicate how to open it, and if that didn't work, I would pick the lock. I learned how to do it during my previous employment when my ward was left incapacitated in a house that he'd inadvertently locked himself in. Google and YouTube are amazing resources for learning new skills.

A few minutes later, his reply arrives in my inbox with an invitation to come to his house to meet. I happily agree.

Chapter 5
Griffin

When the résumé from Andrea Halton showed up in my email, I was hesitant to read it because it didn't come from an online service. But then I remembered the last few hires came from "professional" agencies and not one of them could hack it, so this one couldn't be worse. Her accompanying references from Clara and Marianne —my sister's best friend—let me know I could trust her.

Besides that, I liked her answer to my question about being locked out of the house. Because my kids had done that...twice. To separate nannies. I need someone who won't lose their cool, and this Andrea seems to be someone who can think on her feet, which I appreciate.

I have a couple days off work to get my home situation sorted, even if Logan and Grace begged me not to hire anyone and promised I could trust them.

I don't believe them.

Because they've repeatedly shown me they are not to be trusted.

So, here I am again, opening the door to yet another possible nanny.

But what I don't expect is to find Andi on the other side of the stoop. We both jolt back.

"Andi?"

"Captain?"

"What are you doing here?" I ask as her eyes dart around.

"I think I might be at the wrong place. I'm looking for 1035 Marshall Drive."

"This is 1035 Marshall Drive," I tell her, and those lips of hers—the ones I thought about being wrapped around my cock as I stroked it last night—open wide.

"You're Griffin?"

I nod. "You're Andrea?"

She bites into her plump lower lip. "Andi...short for Andrea."

And for a moment, both of us are quiet, gazes frozen on each other, the crackling tension we'd found in the cab of my truck simmering between us once again.

I'm stunned, to say the least, but I finally grab hold of two brain cells to rub together. "So, you're not leaving?"

She lifts one shoulder. "I thought I'd stick around for a bit."

"And work for me?" Images of *working her* flood my mind, and I squeeze my eyes shut, shaking my head to rid them.

"I didn't know..."

When I lift my lids again, she's staring at me with a mixture of wonder and curiosity. She's barely as tall as my shoulders, and she's close enough that I could reach out and wrap my arm around her waist, pull her to me, press her face to the middle of my chest.

I don't touch her, but I do clear my throat, drawing her attention briefly below my chin before she blinks a few times.

Then her eyes meet mine, and she winces. "I didn't know it would be you. If it's weird, I can..."

She vaguely motions behind her, and there is no way I'm letting her escape again. Not when I wasn't sure I'd see her again. "No, come in."

She does, and when I close the door behind her, I see she's wearing my sweatshirt. I'd been too stunned to notice before, but I do now. Which makes her realize too, and she begins to unzip it.

"Keep it. Looks better on you." What I mean to say is, *I like my name on you*, but I keep that sewn up tight. I motion for her to follow me. "I'll show you around."

When I understood I'd need full-time help after the babies were born, my siblings helped me remodel the basement to make it a little apartment. It has a small bathroom, even smaller kitchenette, but there's also a bed and enough room for other furniture if she wanted.

Andi helps herself to looking around, dragging her fingertips along the counter, and I help myself to taking in the shape of her legs. Thankfully, she'd swapped out her cotton shorts for more suitable jeans, but they're just as tempting with the way they hug the curve of her ass. She still wears her cowboy boots, and with her hair pulled up, showing off a few necklaces, there's something about her that makes me think of country music, sticky floors, and neon lights.

"Where are you from?" I ask, and she turns to me, her pretty pink lips tipped up.

"A little town in West Texas."

So that's the faint twang I hear.

"My family owns a cattle ranch there."

And that explains the cowgirl vibe.

Not that I needed an explanation because, either way, I'm in. She had me from the start.

"And you're from here?" she asks, closing the distance between us.

"Born and raised."

"But you said you left."

"I was in the Navy for a while."

Her gaze openly tracks down the length of me, and I hold my muscles taut, standing at attention as if I might impress her. Like a fucking chump.

But the rise and fall of her chest speeds up with her breathing, and she obviously likes what she sees, so maybe I'm not so stupid after all.

Especially because her tongue flicks out to the corner of her mouth, a flirtatious slant to her lips, and I don't remember the last time I wanted a woman so badly.

And she's here to be my kids' nanny.

Fucking son of a bitch.

I stuff my hands in my pockets and inhale, hoping to clear my thoughts. All it does is fill my lungs with her scent, flowers and coffee, and I'd like nothing more than to bury my face in her neck.

"So..." I cough. "You want to tell me more about your background?"

She toys with the zipper of my hoodie, the one that's hers now. "There's not a whole lot more to tell than what you already know. I'm from Texas and moved to LA to be a songwriter. I've been there for the last ten years, and I worked with a temperamental but exacting boss for the last three years. I'm adept at managing schedules, and I think I'm a quick learner, efficient."

Efficient. Like how quickly I'd be able to have her stripped naked in front of me.

Which is not exactly what I need to be thinking about right now.

In an attempt to move on, I ask, "How old are you?"

"Twenty-eight."

Good Christ. I'm lusting after someone nearly fifteen years younger than me.

She looks even younger when she asks, "Do I get to know how old you are?"

"Forty-two." And because I need to pull back, I tell her, "My schedule can be a bit chaotic. I typically work twenty-four-hour shifts, but they can sometimes be longer, depending on the call volume and emergencies we face."

She nods along, her smile teasing. "And you're the boss?"

"I have a team to manage, yeah."

She steps toward me, so she has to tilt her head back to keep my gaze. "That's a lot of responsibility."

"Nothing I'm not used to."

She arches her brow in a silent question.

"I wasn't just in the Navy. I was a SEAL."

Her mouth drops open, eyes widen, and I love how sweet she looks when she's startled.

"Wow. That's... You really are a superhero, huh? My friend's brother tried and didn't make it."

Only twenty-five percent of candidates make it through BUD/S training. They don't call it Hell Week for nothing, but then again, when Andi reaches her fingers up to my bicep and traces the tattoo on my arm, I have to close my eyes at the sight of her small hands on me.

Hell Week is nothing compared to this, keeping my will in check and not touching her.

"Thank you for your service," she says quietly, her fingertips following a vein on my forearm.

For once, my usual reply stalls on my tongue. Instead of "Serving my country was worth it," I say, "You were worth it."

While her cheeks pinken and silence descends between us,

I don't want to take it back. Because it's true. Yes, serving my country was worth it. Serving and protecting the country that is the home to this woman is beyond worth it.

"Did you like it?" she asks after a while, and I force myself to look down at her once her hands are back at her sides.

"I wouldn't say people like being a SEAL."

Her brows furrow, worry lining the creases of her mouth. I can read her emotions like the back of my hand, and she thinks she said something wrong. She didn't.

I drag the tip of my finger over my name on her chest. "It was the most difficult thing I've ever done in my life. The scariest. Also, some of the best times I've ever had with men who are my brothers."

Her jaw moves as if deciding how to respond for a few seconds before she finally says, "Are you okay, though? How long have you been out?"

I avoid the former and answer the latter.

"I've been out since my kids were born. It was hard at first, for a lot of reasons, but I don't get swept up in the past. I stay present and run a tight ship here...so to speak."

"I see what you did there," she murmurs with a smile as she wraps her hand around my wrist, her fingers cool against my pulse point. "But, really. You're okay?"

She eyes me carefully, and I hate that I can't seem to keep my goddamn mouth shut with her. "I'm okay. Promise."

Nothing a few years of therapy and antianxiety meds couldn't fix.

She doesn't let go of me, and I don't try to shake her off. "So, Captain, what do you need me to do?"

"Keep my ship running."

She grins, dimples appearing. "Really milking this metaphor for all it's worth, huh?"

I ignore the way my chest tightens and the growing pull to

give in to my own smile. "I need someone who can keep my kids in line when I'm not home. I need someone who will give them structure, set boundaries, and make sure they stay on track with schoolwork and chores. Think you can handle that?"

"Sounds easy enough."

I huff. "That's what you think."

"I know I may not look like it, and we didn't meet under the best of circumstances, but I'm tougher than I appear."

"Though she may be but little, she is fierce," I quote, and she finally releases her hold on my wrist. I miss it immediately.

"You know Shakespeare?"

"Days were long when we weren't deployed."

"So you read Shakespeare?" she asks with a laugh, and I shrug.

"The library wasn't very big. There were only so many books to go through, so a lot of them got reread."

"Handsome and smart." She clucks her tongue coquettishly. "Remind me why you aren't married?"

"I was. She died from complications after giving birth to the twins."

Andi inhales sharply. "I'm so sorry to hear that."

"Thank you, but it was a long time ago," I say, maybe a little too curtly, but I have a hard time reining in my feelings around her, and I'm not interested in divulging pieces of my past I'd rather not linger on.

"Still." She frowns up at me. "You've lived three lives in one lifetime."

I consider her words, hating that she's making me feel these fucking emotions. I lock them down tighter, especially when her eyes round. "There hasn't been anyone since? You never wanted to remarry?"

"The opportunity never came up."

She hums like this is fascinating to her. Some kind of mystery to uncover. There isn't. It's simple.

I'm an asshole, and so are my kids. But she doesn't need to know that. At least, not yet.

I bring us back to the issue at hand. "You think you can handle my ten-year-olds?"

She rolls her shoulders back, unflinching in her answer. "Yes."

I should probably be more discerning in who I hire. More careful about their experience and ability to take control of a situation, but I'm tired.

I'm tired of not being able to trust the person in my house or my kids. I'm tired of stress, and I'd really like to be able to come home and relax. Maybe even enjoy myself for once.

"You'll be able to take care of my kids and the house?"

"Definitely." Her smile is pure confidence. *Though she be but little, she is fierce.*

"So, you'll take the job?" I ask, extending my hand.

She glances at it, then back up at me, before sliding her palm against mine. We shake. Her grip is firm but her skin is soft, and neither of us lets go. I brush my thumb over the hummingbird on her wrist again, the rapid beat of her pulse like the flap of its wings.

I don't know how long we stand like that, but it's long enough for Cat to skulk into the room, meowing at our feet. Andi screeches happily, bending down to scratch behind his ears. "Oh my gosh! Who is this?"

"Cat," I tell her.

"Yeah. What's its name?"

"Cat."

"You named your cat Cat?"

When I nod, she tosses her head back and laughs. The

sound is infectious, filling the room, filling me. I love it. I want to hear more of it.

The corner of my mouth tugs. "I found him a few years ago when he was a kitten. We were going through the debris of a fire, and he was the only one left. The others didn't make it. He wouldn't leave me alone, so..."

"So, you took him in," she finishes, lifting Cat into her arms. He immediately rolls to his back and relaxes, his paw flopping out to the side.

"More like he demanded I take him home."

She pets his belly, and it's the first time I've ever been jealous of an animal. "That's really sweet."

I shift side to side, uncomfortable with the praise. "It's what anyone would do."

She shakes her head. "No, not anyone. But you did."

Our eyes meet again, and I want nothing more than to pick her up in my arms, hold her like she's holding Cat. But it's impossible.

Not when she's going to be my kids' nanny.

I've lost so many already. Fantasizing about fucking her, let alone doing it, would cost me yet another one.

"Do you want to see the rest of the house?" I ask, and she nods, setting Cat down.

Upstairs, we tour the kitchen and living room. I point out the calendar and the kids' schedules. Andi asks questions, and I can tell she's taking mental notes, remembering details. I like that. I like that she's serious about this job. We move up to the top floor with the kids' rooms and the bathroom they share, before we end up in my bedroom. I didn't need to show her, but I hadn't thought about it.

And now she's admiring my corners.

I don't imagine tossing her on my bed to mess up the meticulous sheets. She pivots to me, stating the obvious. "This is your room."

"Yeah. It's...where I sleep."

Brilliant, you fucking idiot.

She smiles, like she knows what I'm thinking. Like she can read my mind. And maybe she can, because she takes a step closer, her eyes never leaving mine.

"It's a nice room," she says, all soft and pillowy. "A nice house."

"Thank you." My voice grates like a goddamn rusty nail.

We stand there, neither of us moving, neither of us speaking. The air thick with something unspoken, something unnamed. Yet I can't act on it. I can't cross that line.

It's time to stop acting like a jackass and get my head on right. So, I take a giant step back. "Should we talk logistics?"

"My favorite," she jokes and follows me downstairs, where we make plans for her to move in and start her job as the nanny. Both of us living under one roof.

Fucking brilliant.

Chapter 6
Andi

I set my duffel bag, purse, and guitar down on the floor in
Griffin's mid-size Colonial as he carries in the rest of my
belongings. From the outside, it looks like the rest of the
houses in the small development, with a two-car garage, stone
walkway from the sidewalk to the front door, and rows of
shrubs on either side. It's cute.

The inside? Not so much.

The entryway is stark white and meticulously clean. I take
a deep breath, the scent of lemon cleaner and something
distinctly Griffin filling my lungs. I'm not sure what I expected,
but this place is so...sterile. In the brief time I spent here two
days ago, I didn't notice any family photos or school art projects
like I'd assume there would be in a house of two ten-year-olds.
No sneakers out of place or bikes in the yard.

Behind me, the door closes, and I turn to find Griffin with
his arms full, bags hanging from his shoulders and elbows, two
boxes stacked in his hands. I tried to carry some, but he insisted
he had it. And he does. Not a hair out of place.

His biceps look mighty fine straining like that.

The veins running along his forearms and the ink...

I force myself to stop staring. "Thank you."

He ignores my appreciation, as per usual, and steps around me to set my boxes and bags down before sticking his index and middle fingers in his mouth to whistle. It is both a shock to my eardrums and my nervous system at how hot it is. Before I have time to wonder about what a weird new kink I have for whistling, two sets of feet patter down the staircase.

I'm not sure what I expected since the idea of being a nanny to a set of ten-year-old twins was sort of nebulous. In my mind, I pictured them as faceless paper dolls, but now that they're in front of me, I'm both surprised at how big they are and a little disappointed that they're so old. When I thought of activities we could do, they were crafts and sing-alongs and Chutes and Ladders... things these prepubescents would obviously not be interested in.

Griffin moves next to the staircase and gestures to his kids standing side by side on the step. "This is my son, Logan, and my daughter, Grace." Then he motions to me. "This is Miss Andrea, your new nanny."

They both stare at me, unsmiling. Logan has the same brown eyes as his father, while Grace's are a warm hazel behind her glasses. Her dirty-blond hair is pulled back in a ponytail, while Logan's dark hair is cut short, a mini-me of his dad, even down to his straight-back posture.

I smile brightly. "Hi. It's so nice to meet y'all. You can just call me Andi."

When neither of them responds, Griffin clears his throat, and the two march down the remaining steps, stopping in front of me.

"Nice to meet you," Logan mumbles, holding out his hand.

I shake it, taken aback by the firmness of his grip. "Nice shake you got there."

Grace copies her brother, shaking my hand as well. "Welcome."

"Thank you," I say, wanting to wrap her up in a hug, but the stiffness of her posture tells me she wouldn't like that.

Griffin's voice cuts through the awkward silence. "All right. Each of you, help Miss Andrea and grab a bag to bring downstairs."

They both immediately reach for one of my bags without complaint and head to the basement. Griffin hoists my boxes back up and carries them downstairs as well, so there's nothing left for me to do but follow. By the time I get downstairs and place my guitar on the bed, Logan and Grace are standing by the steps as if waiting to be dismissed.

It's strange, but I slap on a this-isn't-weird-at-all smile. "Thanks so much. It's nice to have it all moved in one trip."

They don't reply, and I glance to Griffin for help, who tips his chin to his kids. "Dinner's in two hours. I'm back to work tomorrow, so make sure all your chores are done."

With terse, mumbled acknowledgments, they take off, leaving Griffin and me alone in my new little apartment.

I turn to him, eyes wide. "They seem very—" Disciplined? Rigid? "—respectful."

Griffin's face remains impassive. "As they should be."

I don't know what to say to that, so I force a smile and let my gaze wander about my room before meeting his again.

"After dinner, I'd like to go over the schedule for the week and show you a few more things."

"Uh, yeah, sure."

His eyes trek down the length of me, his jaw ticking in that way that makes me think he'll explode at any moment, but of course, he doesn't. Captain Stone is nothing if not in control at all times.

He nods once. "I'll leave you to get settled. Make yourself at home."

After I'm alone, I let out a long exhale and sit down on the edge of the bed, absently tracing the geometric pattern on the comforter, my mind spinning. The kids' distant politeness, the sterile house, Griffin's no-nonsense demeanor, it's all so jarringly different from the easy rapport he and I have shared. I feel off-balance, like I walked onto a movie set and everyone knows their lines except for me.

I shoot a few texts to Dahlia and spend a good long while contemplating if I should call my mother before deciding it's a no from me, dawg. I unpack my clothes, making a mental note to buy a few things to make it feel homier once I get my first paycheck. In the bathroom, I set up my toiletries and find hiding spots for my curling iron and hair products before checking my reflection in the mirror above the sink. "You can do this," I tell myself. "You're smart and capable and have really great eyebrows."

Running my finger along said eyebrows, making sure each hair is in place, I mentally repeat my mantra. *You're smart. You're capable. You're smart. You're capable.*

Because if there is anything I learned from my time in LA, it's if you tell yourself something long enough, you might just start believing it. Fake it till you make it and all that.

Then I go upstairs to begin this new job.

Dinner is about as odd as our meeting in the hallway. Griffin asks the kids questions, which they give yes or no answers to, and everyone pretty much ignores me. Griffin explains that when he's home, he doesn't expect me to stick around the house, but if there is an emergency with the firehouse, he'll be on call—ergo, I'll be on call. I notice Logan roll his eyes and tuck that away for later.

After we eat, the kids do the dishes as Griffin takes out the garbage, and I feel terrible sitting there twiddling my thumbs so I brush off imaginary crumbs from the table until the kids are finished loading the dishwasher.

"Can I hire you two to clean up my room?" I joke, and the twins turn to look over their shoulders with the same bland expression.

I force a laugh. "Or not."

They stalk off, shoulder to shoulder, and I thump my forehead on the table, trying to remember what it was like when I was ten. Working on the ranch. Running around. Learning to play the guitar with Mimi.

"Feeling okay?"

I lift my head at the sound of Griffin's voice. "Oh yeah. Fine. I'm fine. Just tired."

"I get that." He drops into the seat next to me, his forearms on the table, his right hand over his left fist, and some of that intimidating veneer fades away to reveal a dad. A hot dad. But a dad, nonetheless. One who's exhausted and in need of help.

"I'm glad you're here," he says quietly. A secret. And when he hits me with those magnetic eyes of his, we're suddenly back in the cab of his truck, and I have an overwhelming desire to put on his sweatshirt. The one that I have draped over the small dresser downstairs.

The one that's mine now.

I try to bite back my dopey smile, keep it from growing, but I can't. He raises his hand to my face, his fingers barely grazing my jaw, the tip of his thumb skating back and forth below my mouth until I release my lower lip from under my teeth. That's when he places the pad of his thumb there, pressing down on the roundest part of my lip, dragging it down. Unconsciously, my tongue follows.

Without thinking, I wrap my hand around his wrist, keeping him in place so I can taste the salt of his skin. Except he tears his arm away from me like I've burned him, and the whiplash has me frozen with my hand in midair, rejection slithering along my skin until I feel like peeling it off.

I sit back slowly, tucking my hands under my legs, chastened, and he shakes his head like the surfers I used to watch at Topanga Beach. Like he fell off his board.

Or maybe I did. Maybe I'd been aiming for too big of a wave, and I needed a dose of reality. A crush of cold water.

"I'm sorry," Griffin mutters, not meeting my eyes as he stands abruptly from the table. "I shouldn't have..." He trails off, repeatedly opening and closing his fists at his sides. "I need to maintain professional boundaries."

"No, you're right," I say immediately, my voice brittle. "I overstepped."

An awkward beat passes before he reaches for a drawer in the corner cabinet, pulling out a manila folder. He slides it across the table to me. So he doesn't have to risk touching me, I guess.

The thing about shame is that it's invasive. Once it's been introduced to you, it's impossible to completely ignore. That brand can't ever be hidden or cleaned off. It can't be cut out or thrown away. And my father's voice rings in the back of my mind.

Whore.

Slut.

No man will want you now.

Ryder's words echo.

She's got those cock-sucking lips.

Worthless.

I know it's not true. And yet...that scarlet letter is not only stitched on my shirt. It's in my blood. I stand to refill my glass of water so Griffin won't see me wipe my tears away.

"I made copies of everything you might need," he tells me

in his no-nonsense tone that must have served him well in his career. "Copies of insurance cards, basic medical history, contact information for doctors, and some authorizations you'll need to fill out for the school."

I nod. "Okay. I'll do that tonight."

He doesn't say anything else, but neither does he leave, so after a few awkward moments, I turn to find him rubbing at the back of his neck.

"Anything else?"

He lifts his focus, resting his hands on his hips. I don't know how someone can be so paradoxically imposing yet obviously uncomfortable.

"Did I do something wrong?"

"No." He shakes his head once, his five-o'clock shadow catching the light above us, highlighting the grays along his jaw. "You didn't do anything wrong, Andi."

I start to speak, tell him that he doesn't have to worry. I'll be professional. No more daydreaming and fantasizing. I'll keep my hands to myself, though he clears his throat before I can get any of that out, and he informs me that he's going in to work a few hours early. I assure him that everything will be fine and the kids will get on the bus Monday morning.

He nods. "That's all for tonight."

I'm dismissed. I very nearly salute him, but I keep my hands at my sides, taking the folder on my way to the basement.

Downstairs, I collapse on the bed, ignoring how it probably would have been easier for him to fire me. Because now I'll have to pretend as if our first meeting never happened, and that I never felt an instant connection with him. And how it didn't seem as if he wanted to kiss me that day in his sister's bed-and-breakfast. And how he didn't break my heart minutes ago in the kitchen.

Yes, packing my bags would have been much easier than this.

But I carry on. The following day, he leaves with nothing more than a wave, and I reread the schedule for Sundays even though I already know it's for grocery shopping, Logan's baseball games in the afternoon, and changing the bedsheets in the evening. The kids file into the kitchen, and I turn to them with high hopes.

"So, it's just us now."

They don't answer.

"I was thinking I could make brunch. Maybe French toast and bacon and a fancy mocktail?"

With how they're sneering at me, I might as well be the mean girl in *Addams Family Values* at Camp Chippewa before Wednesday lights the whole place on fire.

"Or we could hang out and watch TV while we make the grocery list."

"Dad makes the grocery list," Grace says, pointing to the magnetic pad hanging on the refrigerator. Everything is itemized already in Griffin's neat block handwriting.

"We don't hang out with the nannies." Logan spits out the word "nannies" with the same ire I might say I don't hang out with spiders.

"Okay, well—"

"No, thank you," Grace interrupts, and the two pivot on a dime, stalking out of the kitchen. Headed for anywhere I am not, I would estimate.

Great. Really great.

Chapter 7
Griffin

I f I thought a shift at work would get my mind in the right place, I couldn't have been more wrong. I knew the way I left things with Andi was shitty, and I felt bad about it. So bad that it followed me around. Made me sloppy.

Exactly why I needed to avoid feelings.

Because that's how people got hurt or worse.

Pulling into the garage, I kill the engine of my truck and stuff down the gurgle of satisfaction that rumbles in my gut at the sight of her Jeep parked next to mine as I head toward the back door.

Dylan Matthews sent me the bill after he completed the work. I paid 80% of it, then told him to make up an excuse about why it only cost her $120. I don't want to hurt her pride and certainly don't want to make her feel indebted to me, so I hoped she didn't know much about auto work and let it slide. Which she did.

Thoughts of taking care of her are still on my mind when I walk into the house to find her bent over the dishwasher, emptying it. To avoid staring at her ass in those tiny shorts, I turn to take off my shoes and accidentally knock my arm into the wall. I grit my teeth to hold in my curse while my bag slides off my shoulder and hits the floor.

She startles and spins around, removing her AirPods. "I didn't hear the door open. I was— Are you okay?"

I nod, but she sets down the plates in her hand and immediately crosses the kitchen to me. "What's wrong?"

"Nothing. Got a little bump today, is all."

She scans me from top to bottom. "Where?"

"My arm. It's fine. Andi, stop. It's fine." She doesn't listen, too busy yanking up the long sleeve of my T-shirt to reveal bruises and cuts all up my forearm. Some bigger than others, and I swipe my palm over them.

"Oh my god, Griffin!"

"It's nothing, really."

"How did this happen?" She gazes up at me with a frown, an angry little divot between her eyebrows. "Aren't you supposed to wear gear to keep you safe?"

I feel the corner of my mouth curve in amusement. I can't help it. It only makes her more annoyed.

"Yeah, sweetheart, we wear protective gear." I hate that I love how she's fussing so much. "This is no big deal."

"You're bleeding!" She snatches a towel from the counter to wrap around my forearm, using the ends to tug me to the hall. It's cute, all this worry. If this weren't her fault, I might enjoy all the attention.

But the reason I'm scraped up is because my head isn't in the right place. It's on Andrea Halton, the nanny, instead of where it should be. Focused and aware of the goddamn broken glass from the window I had to crawl through.

"Come on," she says, guiding me into the bathroom, where she digs out the small first aid kit from under the sink. "Let me look at this."

When I don't move to help her or twist my arm to show her, she huffs like *I'm* the one making a big deal out of this. We stare at each other in a standoff, and that attitude reminds me of another Shakespeare line, one from *Taming of the Shrew*. "If I be waspish, best beware my sting."

This little thing does come with quite a sting.

Fucking took me out with it already.

Though, I'd never want to tame her. If anything, I'd want to set her free.

Giving in, I sigh and lift my arm. That's when she tugs on my sleeve, revealing the bloodstain. "How far up do these cuts go?" she asks. And then she almost absently says, "Take this off so I can see."

I grab the back of my shirt and slide it over my head, careful when I pull my arm out, but it's no use. I smear more blood on the cotton. As if she can read my mind, she waves her hand, swatting away the problem. "It'll come out in the wash. Here, lemme..."

We both realize at the same time that I'm in front of her with my shirt off, and her head is even with my pecs. A room has never felt so small. The entire house has never been so silent.

I can hear every single one of Andi's inhales and exhales. Can practically feel the air between us, like right before a storm. Hot and heavy and electric.

I swallow, my throat dry.

She licks her pouty lips to a shine, her eyes never lifting above my collarbone.

It's torture.

Easier to pull myself through that window again than stand here and not touch her.

"You, uh..." She blinks a few times and steps back, forcing a laugh that sounds manic. "Just, like..." She waves her hand in front of her face and whirls around to riffle through the kit. "Took me by surprise."

"You told me to take it off," I say, as if I didn't like her looking at me. As if I didn't wish she'd do more than stare.

But it's a long time until she slants her gaze to me again. "Do you have any cuts anywhere else?" When I shake my head, she points to the closed toilet lid. "Why don't you have a seat?"

I do, and she finds the hydrogen peroxide and cotton balls then turns to me. She gently takes my hand to place on the sink, forcing me to extend my arm, her eyes drifting to my chest, over the tiger tattoo there, and up to my shoulders. Eventually to my face.

I'm not sure if she's disturbed to find me watching her, but the only reaction she shows is a pinking of her cheeks and biting into her lower lip. Maybe embarrassed she was caught again.

As if I haven't been watching her this whole time. As if I haven't studied every goddamn thing she's been doing. Every breath and bend of her spine. I've spotted the few freckles dotting her legs and counted the number of hoops lining the shell of her ears. If someone asked me what color her eyes are, I'd tell them they're a swirl of gold and brown to create a color close to how I take my coffee.

That's what Andi is—a hit of caffeine. Comforting yet strong, pumping through my veins, a jump-start to my heart.

She pours the hydrogen peroxide over the cotton and cleans off all the cuts on my forearm, wincing to herself when she gets to the biggest one. The one that keeps oozing blood. "How did you even do this?"

I lift my shoulder, ignoring the burn. "Things happen."

She shoots me a glare. One that I think is supposed to intimidate me into telling her the truth. It doesn't, but I want to anyway. Because I think I'd cut my chest open and hand over the organ she kicked into gear if she asked. "I was climbing through a broken window, and..."

"Things happen," she fills in, and I nod. "You should be more careful," she chides, and the laugh I let out shocks not just Andi but me too.

"I'll do that."

She presses her lips together, fighting a smile. "Good. You can't be coming home banged up like this all the time."

But I will be coming home. To her.

And I like that idea.

More than I should. More than I have any right to.

She applies some ointment to my cuts then sticks on large bandages and closes up the kit with a snap. "Okay. All done."

I don't move.

Neither does she.

In fact, she shifts closer, leaning her hip against the sink and folding her arms over her chest, pushing up her breasts under the tank top she wears. She has on a sweater, a long knit cardigan that falls off her shoulder. She's sexy in an understated way, with her hair thrown carelessly up in a loose ponytail. Her shorts and top are simple cotton, and I'd probably think the sweater is ugly if not for it being on her body.

I reach up to fix it, settling it back over her shoulder, my knuckles skimming her collarbone. I shouldn't, but I do... I let my fingertips glide over the base of her throat, her skin soft and begging to be kissed. She inhales deeply, her chest rising, and it's enough to bring me back to earth. Back to the fact that I can't be acting like this.

I can't lose my fucking head.

"I'm sorry," I say, removing my hand from her, and she dips her chin, her eyes on her socked feet.

"I don't understand you."

I grunt. I don't understand me either.

I've never had this problem of dissociating. I'm so good at compartmentalizing, I should have a degree in it, but for some reason, I can't with this girl.

This fucking girl who is too young for me.

Too good and sweet and my children's nanny.

"I'm sorry," I say again because I don't know what else to say.

She shakes her head and lifts her gaze, those eyes that will haunt me tonight—and maybe every night—round in a way I know means she's upset. I've upset her.

She mumbles something too quiet for me to hear, and I unthinkingly pull her to me, my palms around the backs of her thighs. I spread my knees, making room for her. "I can't hear you, sweetheart."

She tilts her head back and huffs out a frustrated sound. "I said..." A few seconds pass when she takes a deep breath then clamps her hands to my bare shoulders and meets my eyes. Hers blaze with anger, and seeing this fight in her stirs something in me. I appreciate her standing up for herself because I have a feeling she doesn't do it enough, and I'm happy to be the outlet if she needs it.

"I said I don't know what to do, Griffin. I don't know what to do with you, with this, with my job. I don't know what to do."

I get it. I'm an asshole who can't make up his own mind. One who wants her and can't stop himself from giving in, permitting touches and moments like this. Only to turn around and ignore her because I'm too chickenshit to give in, yet completely unable to stay away.

So, I go with the simplest truth. "You scare me."

Her fingers dig into my shoulders. I never want her to let go of me. "I scare you? Why?"

I skate my hands up and down the outsides of her thighs, letting my mind briefly drift to a different place and time. One where I could tug her shorts down and grip her ass, drag the tip of my nose over her stomach and between her legs.

"I don't do emotions," I tell her, and she outright laughs at me.

"This is you being emotional?"

Her incredulity stings. It shouldn't because I don't do emotions. But for her...

For her...

I lick my lips, readying myself to offer her another truth. "That's why you scare me. You make me feel things."

Her palms smooth circles over my shoulder blades and back, to my bone frog tattoo. She traces it, a reminder of why I compartmentalize. Why I need to.

"I don't know what to do," she repeats, and I shrug because I don't know either, but I know I'm not quite ready to let go of her yet either.

I squeeze her thighs and drop my forehead to her stomach. Her hands come to the back of my head, her fingernails scraping along the column of my neck and up to my scalp. It sends goose bumps down my spine, and I groan into her middle.

"You should be out with someone your own age. Having fun. Not...here. Tending to me. Some guy who's so much older than you with kids."

"It's the middle of the day," she reminds me, with enough sass that I think it's supposed to be a joke, but it doesn't quite land. Because there is something else in her voice, too. Something that begs me to listen. "There is no guy. And even if there were, I doubt he'd want to take me out at one in the afternoon."

I'd take her out at one in the afternoon. I'd take her out anytime, anyplace. Wherever she wanted to go. Because she deserves to have whatever she wants.

And it's a problem.

"I can't do this," I say once I'm able to lift my head away from her. "We can't do this. I never have an issue following through... Not until you."

She sniffs a laugh that sounds more sad than humorous. "Sorry."

"You have nothing to be sorry for."

"I'll...try to stay out of your way."

I swallow the lump in my throat. "I'll keep my hands to myself."

She bites her lower lip and steps away from me so my hands drop from her legs and her fingers fall away from my shoulders.

I hate it.

Her fake smile guts me. "I'll get out of your hair and go finish cleaning up the kitchen."

I stand, my fists at my sides, and let her go.

Chapter 8
Andi

I let out a relieved breath as the sound of Griffin's truck fades down the driveway. Ever since our moment in the bathroom the other afternoon, things have been...delicate between us. If we're not deliberately avoiding eye contact, we're accidentally bumping into each other in our attempt to run away. Neither one of us can get out of the room fast enough if the other is in it.

The last two days have been nothing but replaying our conversation in my head.

You scare me.

You make me feel things.

I'll keep my hands to myself.

It's everything I don't want.

I don't want him to be scared of me or to keep his feelings shut down, and I especially don't want him keeping his hands to himself.

What I do want are his hands on my thighs, his eyes tracking my movements, his mouth turned up as he fights a smile.

I want his gruff voice and his callused palms.

I want him.

But I can't have him.

And I need to get it together, remember why I'm here—for this job. For two ten-year-olds who don't like me.

So, I decided I would break protocol tonight and bribe them. I learned they love Thai food. They're pretty adventurous eaters, according to their father. A factoid he told me while studiously scrubbing the counter so he didn't have to meet my gaze. And I figured I'd use that to my advantage.

After school, I followed the usual schedule of picking up Logan from the bus stop, homework for him, then drop-off at baseball practice, so that I could drive back to the school to get Grace from her science club before swinging around to the Thai place. I ordered a bunch of different things, hoping I could impress them with a buffet.

"I heard you love pineapple fried rice and drunken noodles," I say, catching her gaze in the rearview.

She reluctantly agrees, and I turn to smile at her. "I ordered pad Thai and two different curries. I know your brother likes spicy food, so I got one spicy and one mild for me."

"You don't like spicy food?"

I shake my head. "I'm a wimp when it comes to spice."

She nods and flicks her gaze out of the window. I take it as a win. A conversation that was more than one word.

I pick up Logan from practice, thanking the baseball coach, the mechanic who fixed my car so quickly. Like Griffin, he shrugs off my appreciation before gesturing to whom I assume are his wife and kids, a cute little family that suddenly has me wondering if I'll ever have that.

A man who throws his arm around her shoulders and spins his hat backward to kiss her.

A woman who has kids who obviously love her with smiles and hugs.

They walk back to the parking lot, all physically connected by holding hands.

It makes my heart ache.

Not that I expect the twins to love me, but I would hope they don't hate me.

Though they clearly do, because as soon as I open up the driver's side door, they immediately stop talking from their seats in the back. Logan had run ahead to the car while I watched his coach's family for a few seconds—time that feels important.

Like I'm walking into something. A trap.

I ignore the bubble of nerves in my stomach and slap on a grin. "Okay! Let's go home and eat. Logan, I told your sister I bought your favorites from White Orchid, so I hope you're hungry."

When neither of them answers, I do what I've done since I arrived at Griffin's house and carry the conversation. I blabber on about the funny Instagram reel I saw and this new album I downloaded. I ask what music they like and if they ever thought about playing instruments. I offer to teach them how to play the guitar or piano, if we could find one...maybe convince their dad to buy a keyboard. And when none of that works, I up the volume of the music and enjoy the ride with the windows down.

I've never lived anywhere with four seasons, and over the last week, I could actually see spring blooming. Today is the first really warm day since I arrived in town, and even though it's been a rough start for me here, I can't help but hope I'll have a new spring, too.

Words pop into my head, lyrics I can't quite grasp about life and love blooming in harsh conditions, a desert flower, a winter rose, and I'm a little distracted as I dump all the food into bowls when we get home, hurrying to write them down before I forget while the kids set the table.

For once, they're animated, thanking me for the food instead of following the menu.

"I'm just glad y'all are happy," I say, and Grace meets my eyes with a small frown.

"You're not like the others," she says quietly, and Logan elbows her.

I don't understand the silent communication between them, but I laugh anyway. "Is that a good or a bad thing?"

Grace digs into her food instead of answering.

"This smells so good," I say before popping a heaping spoonful of what I think is mild curry into my mouth, but as soon as I swallow, I start coughing. My eyes water, and for a moment, it feels like I can't breathe. I avoid spicy foods because they don't sit well with me, and I'm not used to this spice. I cough a couple more times then chug down my water as the kids giggle.

"You okay, Miss Andrea?" Logan asks, grinning.

"Yeah, it's..." I cough a few more times. "It's hotter than I expected."

I eye the curry, then look at them. I swear I dished out the mild one for myself. But the kids set the table and... No, I'm being paranoid. They wouldn't mess with my food, right? Especially because Grace offers me some of her fried rice, which is really nice of her.

I push away the thought of them playing a trick on me and enjoy the rest of my non-spicy meal. Afterward, the kids complete their chores and then scatter, leaving me to my own devices. I play guitar for a while, FaceTime Dahlia, and double-check the locks after I've made sure the kids are asleep.

Downstairs, I decide on some self-pampering to keep my

mind off what Griffin might be doing at this very moment. If he thinks about me at night, the same way I think about him. If he imagines me touching myself, like I imagine he touches himself. Because even though it's been tense between us, I still use that vibrator every night with the picture of him in my mind.

I take it out now, drawing the tip over my stomach, tickling my skin. After I moved out to LA and realized I had the time and space to explore what I liked, I found a small female-owned boutique off Santa Monica with a woman who kindly walked me through the store, asking what I was interested in. I stammered nervously and told her I wasn't sure, so she introduced me to my bright-pink boyfriend, the one who's been with me for a long time, and taught me that I didn't have to be ashamed of my desires. At least, not alone in my bedroom.

I close my eyes and think of Griffin. Of what his fingers might feel like on me, rough and solid, how his breath would feel on my neck or breasts before he took my nipples in his mouth. I slide off my shorts and underwear then turn on the vibrator, teasing my upper thighs with it before pressing the tip against my clit. It doesn't take long for me to get wet, and I push it inside me, groaning, pretending it's Griffin's cock. Fantasizing what his weight would feel like on top of me, the best kind of pressure. He's so big, he'd cover all of me, completely cocoon me, and I like that. I like that he could protect me, shield me, be tender and strong.

Yet somehow I know he'd be the exact right amount of unrestrained with me. Take me how he wanted.

I come, thinking of his hips pistoning, rubbing exactly where I need, and when I'm done and open my eyes, I spend a few seconds being sad that it's not real before standing and shaking it off.

In the shower, I squirt a dollop of shampoo into my palm and start lathering up, but something's off. It's too thin, and the smell... I bring my hand to my nose and sniff. It's not my shampoo. It smells like...dish soap?

I rinse it off quickly, cursing under my breath. I don't know when they could have done this, but it had to be the kids. With dinner and now this, I know it's not paranoia.

Especially when I think about the questions Griffin asked before he hired me. What I would do if I were locked out of the house? That's like when people or businesses put up warning signs not to do something dumb because someone did the dumb thing at some point. Well, I guess Griffin asked me because the kids have locked nannies out of the house before.

I hurriedly finish rinsing off and wrap a towel around myself to think this through. I recall all the ridiculous tasks Ryder had me do, and while giving me spicy food and switching out my shampoo with dish soap aren't exactly pleasant, they're also not the worst problems I've ever experienced. These little tricks are their way of hazing me, testing my boundaries. I can handle it.

Like a bully, I figure the best way to deal with them is to ignore it. Show them they can't get to me. I'm not going to quit or leave just because of some literal elementary school stuff. It would take a lot more than that to make me sweat. I throw on my pajamas and tuck into bed, falling asleep, not to thoughts of Griffin but of his rascal kids.

The next morning, when my alarm goes off on my cell phone, I roll over to shut it off then curl back up under the comforter until Cat paws at me. The last few days, he's found his way downstairs so that he's next to me when I wake up.

I pet his head. "The kids will get you breakfast. That's on their chore list."

He obviously doesn't understand and steps on top of my chest, kneading me.

"Fine. All right. I'll get up," I tell him and lift him off me so

I can sit up. Still half asleep, I stretch my arms over my head and yawn, rolling out my joints before standing. I shuffle toward the bathroom, but I recognize a second too late that I've walked into some kind of wire.

Which sets off a nightmare.

A blast of cold water dumps over my head, and in the midst of my confusion and astonishment, there's a loud pop of a balloon. I shriek as a cloud of glitter explodes all around me. Completely disoriented and dripping wet, I blindly take a step forward but trip over something furry.

Cat darts between my feet, setting off another spray of water from a contraption rigged to the floor. This time, I manage to shield my face, but my pajamas are soaked. Catching my breath, I turn in a tight circle, taking in the war zone around me, studying the mess of string, glitter, and water guns rigged up in my room. This is no kid's prank. This is some *Home Alone*-level type shit.

Parent Trap times a million.

Logan and Grace aren't just mischievous kids—they're evil masterminds.

And it takes me a full ten minutes to accept who I've been hired to take care of. Another twenty to clean everything up, refusing to let their antics get to me. No way am I giving them the satisfaction of seeing me crack. Once I've dismantled their elaborate traps, I take a shower, but I think I'll be finding glitter in my ears for days to come.

I dress, pretend the glitter that wouldn't come out of my hair was put there on purpose, and add a bit of extra makeup this morning, aiming for a Kesha circa 2010 effect.

Upstairs, I make sure the kids are awake and getting ready for school. They greet me with innocent smiles I don't buy for a second.

"Morning, Miss Andrea!" Logan chirps. "You look nice today."

I force a smile. "Thank you, Logan. And how are you two this morning?"

"Great," Grace says sweetly. Too sweetly.

I won't let them see I'm rattled, even though my mind is racing, trying to figure out how to get back at them. If it's war they want, then it's war they'll get.

We make it through breakfast, and they get on the bus without incident, but as soon as I'm back, I start scouring the house for supplies. No way am I letting them best me. Time to fight fire with fire. Or in this case, glitter with glitter.

I used to handle the biggest diva in the music industry; I can handle a couple of kids. Even if they are supervillains.

Chapter 9
Griffin

I push open the door to Cuppa Jo to see Taryn and Ian are already tucked into our usual booth, coffees steaming in front of them. I slide in next to my brother, who hands me my coffee order with a "Hey, Cap."

"Thanks."

Taryn blows over the top of hers. "How was work?"

"Same old."

Ian slaps my back. "It's all saving cats from trees and little old ladies from breaking hips, huh?"

"We can't all be like you, barely working."

Ian stretches out his legs beneath the table. "What can I say? I'm good at my job."

It's true. Ian's tattoo shop is popular. He has waiting lists months long and can make his own schedule.

"What about you?" I ask my sister. "How are you?"

Out of all of us, Taryn works the hardest. She's always on the go, conquering the world, a single mom and manager of the bed-and-breakfast. Her ex-husband is a piece of shit, refusing to lighten an ounce of her load, and the only thing I'd love more than punching him in the throat would be for her to take a nap.

"I'm all right," she says, as always.

"How are the kids?" Ian asks, as always. He's our older brother, with eight years on me and nine on Taryn, but in a lot of ways, he's more of a dad than our own ever was. Even now, when we're all coming up on middle age, he's the one who makes sure we meet up for coffee and checks up on our kids. For holidays and birthdays, he's the one who gets us together as often as possible.

"Kids are good," Taryn says after a sip of her coffee. "Jake's been working hard, training for soccer, and the school musical is coming up for Maddie."

"Right." Ian taps his finger on the table a few times. "I want to make sure I get tickets."

"Me too," I add, and Taryn flips her cell phone around to type something in.

"I'll send you the link. Seats are first come, first serve."

Ian drags his hand over his graying beard a few times. "My kids will be there too, so I'll make sure to go early and save everyone seats."

Ian's kids are all in their early twenties, and between his biological ones and the "strays"—as Taryn so aptly puts it—he's picked up along the way, he's got half a dozen or so. I can't keep track, but I can say I love spending time with the entire family. Especially if it's to support one of the kids. We make sure we all show up for them since we know what it's like to grow up with a single mom who scrimped and saved and struggled to make it work. In her honor, we try to be better for our children.

Which is why I feel so bad about mine.

Their whole life, they've only ever had me, and I sort of hate that for them. I'm not the best dad. I'm better than my own, but I often doubt my own abilities. It's why I need a full-time nanny, because my kids need more than I can give them. And I know I'm hard on them, but I don't know how else to be.

Our dad was a drunk, in and out of our mother's life, and because of that, I crave stability and order. Didn't need the VA's psychologist to tell me that, but he did make me realize I had to do something about it.

I need my kids to know I will always provide for them. I will always keep them safe. I would quite literally die for those I love before I let anything bad happen to them.

I try to shake off my dark thoughts as someone calls out, "Well, if it isn't my favorite family."

We all look up to find Clara walking toward our table while Marianne orders their drinks at the counter.

"How are we today?" The three of us mutter some type of greeting, and she laughs. "Just rays of sunshine, you all are."

Ian lifts his coffee in silent salute.

Clara pops her hand on her hip and tips her chin to me. "I know you have that fundraiser for the fire department next month, and I had a thought. What about a calendar?"

"A calendar?"

"Yeah. A sexy one, you know? Oil all of you up, and I could take some pictures. I bet you'd raise a lot of money."

Taryn snorts. Ian slaps his hand on my back again. "How 'bout it, Cappy? Or should I say, Mr. July?"

Clara beams. "Oh my god! That would be perfect for you. With your face and background? It's perfect for July Fourth."

I slice my hand through the air. "I don't think so."

Clara sighs in time for Marianne to appear with their coffees. "Here, babe. Why are you pouting?"

"Our esteemed fire captain shot down my calendar idea."

"Surprise, surprise," Marianne says, not at all surprised. She and Taryn have been friends since they were little. At this point, she and Clara are basically part of our family.

"Come on, Griffin," Clara goes on. "You're hot. Make some money off it. Get a couple of your buddies. The ladies will love it."

"You're gonna make my brother self-conscious," Taryn deadpans. "He's real shy."

"Shut the fuck up," I grumble and take a sip from my coffee.

Marianne gestures to me with her to-go cup. "How's it working out with Andi?"

"It's good."

Clara and Marianne both wait for more.

"It's fine."

"It's good. It's fine," Clara parrots with an eye roll. "I thought there would be more to say than that. Or, I don't know..." She shrugs theatrically. "Maybe, thank you so much, Clara and Marianne, for finding the perfect nanny for my kids."

I repeat her words flatly. "Thank you so much, Clara and Marianne, for finding the perfect nanny for my kids."

"And you?" she urges, curling her hands. Clara's a huge gossip. "Do you like her?"

I play off her question, skating my gaze out to the windows, looking toward Aster Street. "Yeah, she's great."

Taryn, the goddamn traitor, speaks up. "Don't try to hide it. You brought her to my B&B and paid for her room."

Marianne whistles quietly, playacting at wonder, but she won't be winning any awards any time soon.

Ian wrenches his head back. "You didn't tell me that."

I don't tell my siblings much of anything, particularly about my personal life. "Why would I tell you that?"

"Because you made it seem like she was just a stranger you were helping out."

"She was a stranger I was just helping out," I say, and Ian

shakes his head at me then looks to Taryn, Clara, and Marianne, in turn.

"How many of you have rescued someone from the side of the road, paid for a hotel, and then hired them to be your nanny?" When none of them answers, my brother raises his brow to me as if it proves a point. It doesn't prove anything besides he's an asshole.

And, yes, I rescued Andi from the side of the road and made sure she was safe with a roof over her head before I knew anything about her, but our mother always said, "When you can be anything, be kind."

"I was just being fucking kind," I say, earning smirks and snickers from everyone. If they ever found out I'd paid for her car to be fixed, I'd be boxed even more into a corner.

As it is now, I don't have much of a leg to stand on. Nothing to say in self-defense.

"We thought she'd be good for you," Marianne tells me, and her wife winks.

"Real good for you."

I scowl at her. "Stop trying to set people up."

She smiles like she's cute. "Never. It's my life's calling."

"To get into everyone's business?" I ask, folding my arms across my chest.

Clara pokes my shoulder. "I will have you know I have an intuition about these things."

At that, Marianne rolls her eyes. "That what your horoscope told you this morning?"

"No." Clara wraps her arm around Marianne's waist. "But, heads up, Jupiter and Uranus will be in alignment next week. This only happens every fourteen years, so it'll be huge."

Marianne huffs and takes Clara's hand. "All right, enough of cosmic energies. We have to get back."

Clara lets herself be marched away, smiling as she tells us, "It'll be a new cycle for creativity or rebellion!"

"Hear that?" Ian squeezes my shoulder. "It's rebellion time for you, Cap."

I rake a hand through my hair. "Doubt it."

Taryn studies me with her dark eyes, the same ones we all share.

When she doesn't say anything, I push her. "What?"

She lifts a careless shoulder. "Nothing. I just think it's interesting. You meet this girl, are kind to her—" she adds air quotes to her words like an asshole "—but you've never treated anyone else like that before. You never brought anyone else to me, demanding a room."

Ian inclines his head. "You also texted me to ask if you should hire her. Never done that before."

"Because I've never hired anyone outside of an agency before." Then I turn to my sister. "And what did you want me to do? Leave her on the side of the road with no car?"

"No, she's an adult. I'd let her fend for herself."

"Cutthroat," I say as Ian huffs an amused sound.

"Our sister, the fucking gladiator. Only the strong survive."

Taryn drops her gaze to the table, though I'm not sure if it's to hide a growing smile or to shake her head in dismay. My sister is a warrior and has very little patience for anyone who can't keep up.

Which only makes me think of Andi and her gentle spirit and sweet smile. I don't want her to be a warrior. Not if she doesn't have to be. I don't want her jaded. If anything, I want her to remain soft and tender. I'd protect her, if I had to. If I could.

I'd keep her safe. Do all the fighting for her.

"Just watch it," my sister eventually says, her eyes back on mine. "Be careful with her, okay? Your kids need someone to stick around. Don't do anything to screw it up."

I know that already. I'm trying my best.

"Hey." My brother elbows my side for my attention. "You're a good dad."

I don't believe him, but I thank him anyway, and we all get up to say goodbye. Ian has a tattoo appointment in a few minutes, and Taryn's lunch break is over. Since she walked from work, I follow her across the street to where I'm parked.

"Before you go," she says, catching my arm with one hand, her coffee, keys, cell phone, and wallet in the other. I've always been amazed at how she can carry fourteen thousand things in her hands without dropping any of them. Claws of steel. "I've got everything planned for Ian's party, but I'm putting you in charge of getting hold of Roman."

"You're kidding me." I drop my head back to my shoulders. I should be grateful that Taryn is planning our brother's surprise 50th birthday party, but chasing down our little brother is the last thing I want to do.

"No. I'm not. I did everything else. You can do that."

"He won't show, so why do we have to invite him?"

"Because Ian would want him there."

It's not because he's our sibling and we're family. It's because Ian wants him there. Not her and not me. Our eldest sibling has always had a soft spot for our youngest. I don't fucking get it since the guy's a selfish prick, but... "Whatever."

"I'll see you later, brother," she says, and I briefly tug her to me for a hug.

"See you, sister."

She fights a smile and punches my arm before heading in the direction of The Nest. Taryn and I are only a year apart and have always been close. Closer to each other than to Ian, our protective big brother, and Roman, the baby. We stuck to each other as kids and continue to as adults. And while I appreciate Ian, it's Taryn's words that follow me home.

Don't do anything to screw it up.

Which is really fucking hard when I step into my house and see Andi in the living room in a skimpy little top and leggings, doing yoga with one arm out in front of her and the other holding her foot up behind her.

I loudly thunk my keys on the counter so she knows I'm home, which causes her to pop up to standing. And that's worse. Because she faces me with pink dimpled cheeks on either side of her wide smile and nipples beaded beneath the thin light-blue material covering her tits. It's basically a bra, revealing her toned and tanned stomach with a belly button ring. I remember back in high school, all the girls were trying to be like Britney Spears and getting them pierced. I didn't realize it was still a thing to do. But now that I've seen the small jewel, I can't look anywhere else.

My sister's voice rings in my head. *Don't do anything to screw it up.*

"Hey, sorry. I've been doing this in my room, but it's hard to do all the stretches and poses, so I came up here. I hope—"

"It's fine. Do whatever you need to do. This is your house too." I force my eyes up to hers. "How did everything go yesterday?"

She smiles, but something is off about it. "Good. Great. Really good."

I eye her, and she smiles brighter. Faker.

I'm sure whatever the problem is, I'll find out eventually, but first, I have to take care of the problem stirring to life in my sweats. I tip my chin toward her mat and laptop, playing a yoga video. "Are you going to be long?"

"About thirty more minutes."

"I'm gonna grab a shower." I already took one at the firehouse, but another won't hurt when I've got this new image of Andi to yank it to.

I move to the steps, her voice trailing behind me. "Okay, have fun!" Halfway up, I hear say to herself, "Have fun? What is that?"

It's cute how she's tied up. Because even though I promised to keep my hands off her, there's no way I'm not thinking of her while I take care of myself.

Every fucking day with her being here is Hell Week.

And it's no fun at all.

Especially when I'm underneath the spray of water, washing the ropes of my come down the drain.

Chapter 10
Andi

Griffin was home for forty-eight hours. The longest forty-eight hours of my life. But as soon as he drove away, I started setting up Logan and Grace's payback. I only spent half of that time thinking about their dad and how he had a hard time keeping his focus above my neck when he walked into the house while I was doing yoga. As I filled the water balloons, I thought about how he doesn't shave at home, growing two days' worth of stubble on his jaw that I imagine would feel good to run my palms over. While I placed the bucket of colored powder up on the board, I thought about how capable and hot he looked grilling dinner of salmon, vegetables, and potatoes. I was astounded to learn the kids ate salmon, but then again, Griffin would never deviate from his schedule or menu. Making sure everyone eats the appropriate amount of protein is super important to him.

Never would have guessed Captain America has Thanos's spawn for children.

I stand at the corner now, rocking back and forth on my heels, impatiently waiting for the school bus to arrive. I don't know what Griffin would think of my battle plan, but I highly doubt he'd sanction my revenge. Let alone what he would say if he ever found out about the kinds of tricks the kids play. I'm sure he knows some of it, but maybe not the extent. He doesn't seem like the type to ship them off to military school, yet I don't want to test that theory.

I need to figure out why these little criminals want to run off every nanny they've ever had. And to do that, I need to show them they won't be doing the same to me.

When the yellow bus rumbles to a stop, the twins stroll out at different paces, as usual. Grace is first off, her backpack high on her shoulders. Logan is last, yelling something to a buddy as he gets off, his smile immediately falling when he spots me.

"How's it going?" I ask the twins once they're together, studiously avoiding me. "Learn all kinds of stuff? I can't remember much about fifth grade besides a field trip we took to this museum in Odessa, and this kid wouldn't stop bullying my friend, so I punched him."

The twins gaze up at me with wide eyes.

"That's right," I say. "Popped him right in the mouth. Sometimes, you have to stand up to bullies. Not just ignore them."

My two underage nemeses put their heads down and take off down the sidewalk to get away from me, so I have a perfect view of when they walk into the garage, setting off a volley of water balloons. They sail through the air, hitting both Logan and Grace in the face.

"What the..." Logan splutters, wiping water from his eyes with his forearm.

Grace steps back, fixing her glasses, and pivots her shocked face to me.

That's when I tug on the rope pull I set up, flipping the 2x4 above them upside down so the bucket I nailed to it upends all the colored chalk powder I dumped inside it. The evil twins stand there frozen, covered from head to toe in a rainbow.

For a moment, they stare at each other in disbelief. Then they both look to me. I shrug with a smile. "Gotcha."

It's quiet for another moment, and then, to my surprise, a grin slowly spreads across Logan's face. "That was epic!"

Grace starts to giggle, and before I know it, all three of us are doubled over with laughter at the rainbow mess I have made of them. I pull out my phone and snap a quick photo to memorialize my victory over them.

"I can't believe you did this," Grace says when I hand her a towel.

"I can't believe you two booby-trapped my room."

"That was nothing," Logan admits, rubbing purple and pink off his face. "Grace blew up the last nanny."

"You *what?*"

Grace shrugs. "I didn't blow *her* up. I blew up her drink in her face. Like a volcano."

Gobsmacked, I wait for her to continue. All she does is wave me off like her dad.

"I'm good at science. I like blowing stuff up."

I shake my head at them. "Truly, you are on a whole other level."

Logan's proud, and he nods. "Right?"

"But why?" I pick up their backpacks from the ground. Neither of the twins says anything when I hand them brooms and wet wipes. They know we need to clean this mess up.

After a few seconds of sweeping, Grace confesses, "We hate having nannies."

"Obviously." I grab a roll of paper towels and start wiping down the wall where most of the powder ended up. "But making my life miserable isn't going to change that. Your dad still has to go to work."

Logan pauses in sweeping. "Yeah, but whenever we run off a nanny, he has to take time off to interview new ones. So we get him home—for a little while, at least."

I toss the soiled towel in the garbage and tear off a clean one. "You're really doing all this for his attention?"

They nod, not meeting my eyes.

"Have you tried telling him that?"

Grace scoffs. "He's too busy. He's always at work or doing stuff around the house. He doesn't have time to play with us."

"We're not little kids, you know," Logan says defensively. "We just want to hang out with him sometimes. But he's so..."

"Captain Stone," I fill in, and they both nod again.

Griffin runs his house like I assume he commands his fire squad or how the military worked. It makes sense that the kids would act out for attention and connection.

"I get that," I say gently. "But maybe there's a better way than tormenting me. I'm sure your dad would make time if he knew how you felt."

The twins exchange a skeptical look.

"It's worth a try, right?" When they frown at me, unconvinced, I continue, "Besides, I'm not going anywhere. So you might as well figure out a different way to get your dad's attention."

At this, Logan smiles. "I kinda like you, Miss Andrea."

"Andi," I say, holding up my hand for a high five. "Call me Andi."

He hits my palm, and then I offer the same to Grace.

"I'm on your side with all of this, all right?" I tell them, and they both seem pleased with this new truce.

We finish cleaning the garage in thoughtful silence. I can tell the twins are processing, realizing their tricks have been misguided. I feel for them. Griffin, too. He's a good dad, just busy and overwhelmed at times. He's parenting the best way he knows how, and no one can blame him for that.

Later, when I call the kids for dinner, the energy in the house feels different. Calm and happy. I trust that I won't wake up to any more glitter, and I hope they know they can rely on me. I'm here to help.

I set down their plates of spaghetti, along with the small salad I made, and both of them dig through the noodles as if searching for something. I laugh. "I wouldn't be cruel enough to put something in your food. I'm not like you."

"Sorry about that," Logan says.

"Me too," Grace adds.

I accept their apologies. "It's okay. I mean, it's not okay, but I understand now what you were trying to do and why. Although, I think we can move on and get to know each other. What do you think?"

They agree, and they actually answer my questions about what they enjoy. Grace loves school and wants to be a scientist like someone named Emily, who makes YouTube videos, and I mentally file that away so I can find out more about this person. Logan tells me he loves playing sports, and his favorite is basketball. I inform him that I used to play, up until high school.

"But you're so short," he says, and I splutter a laugh.

"Yeah, but I was fast, and I had a pretty good free throw."

"Really?"

I nod. "We should play sometime. I saw you have a hoop outside."

"Cool, yeah."

Grace slurps up some spaghetti before wiping the sauce from her mouth. "Did you really grow up in Texas?"

"Yes, ma'am. On a small cattle ranch. Me, my brother, my parents, and a whole lotta cows."

Grace smiles, twirling her fork in the noodles. "What was it like?"

My first instinct is to say lonely, but instead, I give them the easier answer. "Fun. Cows are like giant dogs. They're nice to cuddle with."

Logan chuckles. "No. Really?"

"Yep. My favorite was Mini. She was spotted white and brown, and I'd go out and lie with her, play my songs for her."

"I saw you have a guitar," Grace notes. And when I nod, she asks, "Are you, like, good?"

I toss my head back to laugh. "I hope so. I used to live in LA. Once upon a time, I thought I'd make it as a songwriter, but..." I shrug, hoping I don't sound too forlorn. "Now, I'm here, getting glitter bombed instead."

When the twins quiet from giggling, Grace asks, "Do you think you could teach me?"

"Of course. We can start tomorrow if you want."

"Yeah. There's a talent show at the end of the year, and—"

"What? You want to be Taylor Swift," Logan teases, and I shush him, waiting for his sister to go on.

"Sometimes girls make fun of me, and, I don't know, I thought if I could do something different, they wouldn't see me as just a nerd or something."

"First of all," I start, sitting up straight so she knows I mean business. "Nerds are awesome, okay? Nerds grow up to make a ton of money and run the world, so you don't worry about people calling you a nerd. You should take it as a compliment. And secondly, I will definitely teach you to play guitar, but you have to be confident in yourself. Don't do it for other people. Do it because you want to."

They're both quiet at this, and I take a deep breath. If I open up to them, I think they'll open up to me in return. "You know, when I was your age, I felt like no one really saw me for who I was. It's hard, especially when you're young, to feel like you're not getting the attention you want or need."

They both look up at me, their eyes wide. I can see the recognition in their gazes, the understanding that I get it. I get them.

"Fifth grade is hard, right?" I lean my elbows on the table, shifting closer to them. "You're trying to figure out who you are, what you like, who you want to be. And sometimes, it feels like no one understands you. Like no one sees you."

Grace's eyes shine with unshed tears behind her glasses. "Yeah."

I reach across the table, squeezing her hand. "I want you both to know that I'm here for you. Whatever you need, whatever you want to talk about, I'm here."

Logan drags the tines of his fork over his plate a few times before he finally mutters his quiet question. "Even if it's about girls?"

"Even if it's about girls," I promise.

His cheeks flush slightly. "There's this girl, in my class... I don't know what to say to her."

I set my chin in my hand. "Well, what do you like about her?"

"I dunno. She smells good and is really nice to everyone."

"Then tell her that," I say. "Well, don't tell her you think she smells good right off the bat. That'll come off creepy. Start with a compliment about something. Like, hey, I like your backpack. Or, hey, nice job getting that good grade on the test. Or, Isabella, I really like how you treat everyone nicely."

"Isabella?"

I wave my hand. "I took a stab at it. I feel like every girl is named Isabella or Amelia these days."

"I do have two Isabellas in my classes," Grace says. "But Logan likes Valentina."

"Shut up," he hisses, and I smile.

"Valentina? I love that name."

"Me too," he murmurs, and I could die at how cute he is when he's embarrassed.

"Just be yourself," I instruct. "That's the best way to get someone to like you." I point to Grace. "You too."

She nods, and I sit back in my seat, feeling like I really did something today. I made a difference.

And as we finish our dinner with lots of laughs and conversation, I know we'll be all right.

Chapter 11
Andi

I'm in the middle of putting groceries away when Dahlia FaceTimes me. We haven't talked in a few days, and I prop my phone up against the toaster before answering with my face close to the screen. "Where the hell have you been, loca?"

My best friend cackles with delight. "Hanging with a sparkly vampire."

One of the things we often liked to do was play drinking games with movies. The *Twilight* series provided hours of drunken fun. Vic hated it, but he'd eventually give in and play with us. Two Christmases ago, I bought him a Jacob cardboard cutout. A few weeks later, he put it in my room in the middle of the night, and when I got up to pee, it scared me so bad, I went in my pants.

"I miss you and Vic," I say, peeing my pants notwithstanding.

"I miss you too. How are you? Fill me in. Have you fucked the daddy yet?" she asks while making herself tea, and I snort.

"No. I told you. I'm not having sex with my kids' dad."

"That's cute," she says, arching a dark brow. "How you call them your kids."

I toss the multigrain bread onto a shelf in the pantry. "What else am I supposed to call them? I'm taking care of them."

"But it's going good still?"

I texted Dahlia after my breakthrough with Logan and Grace, and while it's only been three days, it feels like it might as well have been three months with how well we're getting along now. Grace has taken to playing guitar like she completes her schoolwork, with single-minded focus and determination. Logan and I have played a round of basketball, and he's been allowing me to wrap my arm around his shoulders as we walk back to the house after getting off the school bus. It's not quite the cuddles I'm used to with Dahlia, but I'll take it as a start.

"Everything is going great with the twins," I say.

"And firefighter daddy?"

"I really need you to stop calling him daddy."

"Why? Because you want to and need me to step off your man?"

I roll my eyes. "I can't with you."

She grins and pours her steaming water into the big mug I bought for her birthday a few years ago that reads *May you have the confidence of a mediocre white man*. Then for my birthday, she bought me one that says *Little Miss Doesn't Get Paid Enough for This Shit*. I have it downstairs, to hold all my loose odds and ends since I don't think Griffin would like me adding it to the shelf with his oddly beautiful matching ceramic mugs. They're stonewashed blue and brown and look home-made. My Little Miss cup wouldn't fit with the vibes.

Moving on from her obsession with my boss, I ask, "You ready for the gig tonight?"

She nods, sipping her tea. "I was about to go over the setlist. Want to help me?"

"Of course." I finish up with the groceries as we go back and forth on the best order of songs she'll sing, a mix of covers and originals we wrote together. I wouldn't consider Dahlia a powerhouse singer, but she has a throwback vibrato that always reminded me of 1960s rock and roll. When we first started jamming together, I convinced her to sing the classic "Hey Lover" by Daughters of Eve. It was one of Mimi's favorites and the first song I learned to play. Incidentally, Dahlia still sings it. Brings the house down as her finisher. She has an interesting intersection of music: the history of Tejano, a love of folk-rock, and a dash of country because of me. Put it all together, she's like a Mexican American Brandi Carlile. Not to mention one of the most beautiful people I've ever seen in real life with perfect bronze skin, black hair down to her butt, and the height of a supermodel.

I never necessarily wanted the spotlight, satisfied with playing guitar and writing music, so when we found each other, we instantly clicked in our aim for the business, as well as on a base level of friendship. Which is why I'm so happy to hear she's been getting some interest from record labels lately, including from one she's had her sights set on for indie folk-rock artists.

"You think you'll ever come back?" Dahlia asks once we finish with her setlist.

"I don't think so." I plop down in a chair at the kitchen table. "After everything that happened with Ryder, I feel so defeated. All those years of working my ass off, writing songs constantly, going to open mics and sending demos. And for what? To be told I'm worthless."

"You are *not* worthless."

"I know, but..." I look off into the distance, recalling the night he fired me. Making fun of me in front of everyone, dismissing me like I didn't practically keep him upright for three years, because I dared to have a conversation of my own about my songs. God forbid, I take a small advantage of the situation.

"Some days I feel like I'll never write another song again," I admit, and Dahlia gasps.

"Don't say that. You just need time to heal and rebuild your confidence. You'll be creating in no time."

I meet her gaze on my screen, knowing she's right but still feeling raw and dejected. "It's hard not to feel like a failure."

She narrows her eyes in answer, lip curling when she growls out, "I could actually kill Ryder. Fuck it, kill your parents too."

I sniff a pitiful laugh. While Ryder was the one to put the nail in the coffin, my parents were the ones to build it. No matter what I wanted, it wasn't what they wanted, therefore a terrible idea. My dad wasn't very good at compliments. Aside from calling me a whore, telling me no man would ever want me after he caught me with my high school boyfriend, he was quick to inform me I'd never get anywhere in life with my attitude and lack of work ethic. All because I preferred daydreaming and playing my guitar to wanting to stay on the farm and marrying that same boyfriend he caught me having sex with. The day I left, he told me I'd never amount to anything.

So, while I think keeping such strict schedules with Grace and Logan may not allow them to truly express themselves or their desire to spend time with their dad, I know Griffin loves them. He's never once raised his voice or demeaned them. Besides, they wouldn't want his attention so badly if he were anything like my father.

"I don't have enough bail money," I tell Dahlia. "So, thank

you for the offer, but please do not commit murder on my behalf."

"I will do it." She huffs. "You really won't come home?"

I shake my head, not sure where home is at the moment. "I'm liking it here for now. I'm having a good time."

She relents. "Okay, but whenever you're ready to start writing music again, I'm here. We're a team, remember?"

Her words make my heart swell with gratitude and affection. "I don't know what I'd do without you."

"You'll never have to find out," she promises. "I've got your back, now and always."

I feel myself tearing up a bit at her unwavering support and belief in me. It's exactly what I need to hear right now. "Thanks, Dahl. Love you."

"Te quiero mucho." She blows me a kiss through the phone, and we hang up in time for the back door to open. Griffin's home.

He's in sweats and a firehouse T-shirt, but today, he's got a cap on, like the day I met him, and he takes it off to run his hand over his hair a few times before tossing it on the counter. Then he lifts his gaze to me, and as always, I melt under those eyes of his. It's like he can see right into my head, past all my smiles, to my heart.

Which is why I guess he frowns at me. "You okay?"

I nod, waving at my face, hoping I'm not red from the conversation with my best friend. I hate that my first reaction to any kind of emotion is to cry. If I'm sad, I cry. But also if I'm mad or embarrassed. Or even if I can't find something. I'll cry. My tear ducts were born in overdrive and have yet to let up.

"I'm fine," I say, standing, which only allows him to crowd my space.

I don't hate that he is mere inches away, towering over me, but I hate that I can't touch him like I want to. Put my head on his chest and curl my hands into his T-shirt. This close, I can feel his body heat. I'd like nothing more than to wrap myself up in it.

And burn.

"What happened?" He studies every inch of my face. "Did the kids do something?"

"What?" I squeak, hoping he didn't somehow find out about what they did to me or I to them in retribution. It's our secret. "No."

"What *did* happen?" His nostrils flare, exhaling heavily from his nose. I might find his irritation on my behalf humorous, if not for the emotion clogged in my chest.

I cross my arms and lean against the counter. "Nothing. I was talking to my best friend."

"What did she say?"

I force a laugh. "What's this interrogation about?"

"You look like you were crying."

I turn away from him. "I was."

That's when he reaches for me but stops himself, his fingers millimeters away from my chin. I tip it up anyway to find him peering down at me with a steady, comforting gaze. I'm not sure what he reads in my features, but he nods a few times. "Why?"

"I miss her. I miss..." I bite my bottom lip to keep my chin from quivering when it hits me just how much Dahlia means to me. "She's my family, my support system, and I miss having that."

Griffin sets his hands down on the counter on either side of my waist and bends, lowering himself so he's almost at my eyeline. "Someday you'll tell me about why your best friend is your support system and not your actual family."

I sniff a watery laugh at his order. "Okay."

"My family means everything to me," he says. "My brothers and sister. My kids. They're my world, and I hate that it's not the same for you. I hate that you're crying in my kitchen because you miss your best friend. I hate that you ran away from something in LA, and I'd like to hear about that, too. But I want you to know that while you're taking care of my children, while you're in my house, you're a part of my family. You have my support for whatever you need."

Before I can stop it, a tear slips from my eye, and he knuckles it away. I blink a few times, clearing my sight, careful not to let go of the tight hold my arms have around each other. I can't give in to the overwhelming pull to bury my head against his neck. Or worse, jump on him, cling to him like a koala.

My well to be touched and petted and soothed needs to be refilled, but like he said, our relationship has to remain professional. So, I smile and say, "Thank you, Griff."

His gaze lingers on my mouth, and in a poor attempt to escape these close quarters, I blurt, "I have to talk to you about the kids."

This makes him stand up straight and back away from me, all the way to the island so there are a few feet in between us. He braces himself, and I assume it's because he thinks I'm going to quit or tell him about some awful thing the twins did. Now that I've been let into their evil mastermind plans, I learned they once placed a fake tarantula on the pillow of the nanny that came two before me, and when she woke up, she flew out of bed, hitting her head, giving herself a concussion. There was also the male nanny who liked to go running, so they put Cat's turds in his very expensive running shoes.

Really, I got off easy.

Though there's no telling what they would have moved on to next if I hadn't shown them I could play their game. A fake tarantula would most definitely make me pee myself again.

Griffin waits, a little impatiently, if how he checks his

watch is anything to go by. The man lives and breathes by seconds.

Under his intimidating stare, I take a breath and set my shoulders, mentally reminding myself of my affirmations. *You're smart. You're capable. You have really great eyebrows.*

"I wanted to suggest that maybe you could ease up a bit on the rigid schedule with them."

He frowns. "What do you mean?"

I twist my fingers together nervously. "I know you run this house like a well-oiled machine, but they're kids. They could use a little more...fun. Spontaneity."

Griffin's jaw tightens, and he slants his attention to the side. I hurry to continue so he doesn't get the wrong idea.

"The structure is good for them, but they're desperate to hang out. Play some basketball in the driveway, watch movies together, whatever. They want to spend time with you, that's all."

He's quiet for a long moment, his expression indecipherable.

"I want what's best for them," he finally says. "I've had to be both their parents, the disciplinarian and the good guy, and still, I have to make sure things run smoothly."

I nod in understanding. "I know. And you're doing an amazing job with them. I can tell how much you love Logan and Grace. But I think, maybe, they'd appreciate the time you spent relaxing with them. They know Captain Stone as their dad, but what about, like, just...Dad. You know?"

He considers this in silence. An entire day passes before he meets my gaze. He seems like he might snap the marble top right in half for how hard he's gripping it. Then again, that's not much different from his normal appearance.

That's the thing about Captain America—he's strong as hell, but he only uses his power for good.

"Thanks for letting me know," he says and stalks off. I make myself scarce and stay downstairs even when I hear him and the kids come home from the bus stop. Although I don't catch every word, I specifically hear my name and "told me" and "hang out" and "more time."

An hour later, about when dinner would usually be getting started, Griffin calls down to me. "Andi? You want to play some basketball with us?"

I'm caught so unaware I drop the laundry I'm folding.

"Really?"

He pads down the few steps, enough to bend down so he can talk to me. "Logan told me you two have been playing together."

"Only twice," I reply, as if we've been naughty.

"Come on." He juts his chin up to the door. "Meet us in the driveway."

Then he marches back upstairs, and I don't waste any time. I throw on his sweatshirt and lace up my sneakers to head out to the driveway, where Griffin's dribbling the basketball with an ease that makes my skin heat. His hands are big, his legs long, and he arches his brow in a challenge before tossing the ball to me.

Logan bounds over to my side. "It's you and me against Gracie and Dad."

Although I know Grace isn't much for sports, I love that she's grinning. So is Logan, both of them openly happy to be out here with their father. When I turn to him again, butterflies take off in my stomach at the way he tilts his head, studying me, "Time's ticking, Andi. Are you in or out?"

"I'm so in," I say with a laugh then proceed to do the complicated handshake Logan and I came up with the other day. After, I throw the basketball back to Griffin, who catches it with an audible breath, surprise crossing his features at the power behind it. "Losers get the ball first," I taunt. Trash talk is half the game.

Griffin shakes his head and dribbles right up to me, a full, heart-stopping smile curling his lips. "That's tough talk for someone who was born in the Keebler Elf tree."

"Yeah, I was born sweet."

He looks me up and down lasciviously. "I'll bet."

And I go weak.

Absolutely lose my place in time and space, unable to intercept the pass when he tosses it to Grace. But it's worth it when she takes a shot on the basket, missing by a mile, and Griffin tells her, "That's all right, sweetie. We'll get it next time."

Dead.

Died.

Gone to heaven

Chapter 12
Griffin

ROMAN

Sorry. Won't be able to make it tomorrow.

I roll my eyes at my brother's message. After days of texting him, that's what he responds with? I scroll back through the thread, reading everything I sent him.

We're having a surprise party for Ian's 50th next Saturday. You should come.

I don't know why you refuse to answer, but I know he'd want to see you.

If you don't come, Taryn will kill me.

Come on, man. What the fuck? You can't take two seconds to text me back. Like I don't have my own shit to deal with.

ROMAN

Sorry. Won't be able to make it tomorrow.

I stab at the keypad, having to delete multiple times because my thumbs are too big and I'm too ticked off.

> At least fucking call him and say happy birthday to him tomorrow.

With a huff, I hit send, knowing he won't respond, and smack my phone on the table with more force than necessary before snatching it back up to check I didn't crack the screen or scuff the table.

But, fuck.

I understand addiction is a disease, but at some point, you have to take responsibility for your life. Roman has been wallowing in self-pity for over a decade now. Enough is enough.

What makes it worse is Ian blames himself for the way Roman's life has turned out, but it's not his fault. He's done everything he could to help, even paying for multiple stints in rehab. Roman just doesn't seem to want to fix his life.

I don't have time or patience for him, but Ian has a soft spot for our little brother. Always has, and now the little shit isn't even coming to his birthday party. For all of Ian's bluster, he wears his heart on his sleeve, which leaves him vulnerable to people like Roman who're happy to take advantage of his kindness.

And it pisses me off.

Because Roman has to take some personal responsibility and get his shit together. Ian deserves better than silence. We all deserve better.

To my utter amazement, Roman responds.

ROMAN

> I will, and it's not that I don't want to go to the party. It's that I can't.

What do you have going on that's so important?

ROMAN

It's not for a text conversation. Sorry, man. I'm trying.

ROMAN

I swear.

I close my eyes and rub at the back of my neck, trying to roll out the knots of tension, but it feels like they've been there my whole life. The stress I carry in my muscles won't be going anywhere anytime soon, so I stand, intent on heading upstairs, when notes of music drift up to the kitchen. I stop to listen.

After the helpful advice Andi gave me last week, I spent hours thinking about it. Thinking about how I was letting my kids down, and with how she seems to be bonding with them, I took her words seriously. I never thought my children would want to spend time with me. After all, I never spent much time with my own dad. The good memories I have of him can be counted on one hand. The rest are of him drinking and throwing temper tantrums before he left for good, leaving Mom to take care of the four of us on her own.

I've been raising my kids the best way I know how. Possibly a little too militaristically. Since that conversation with Andi, I learned Grace and Logan really did want to hang out with me. It was actually quite simple, though I'd been nervous to ask them about it. More nervous than they would ever believe I could be.

But since then, there's been a seismic shift. My kids are smiling more. They're laughing. Hell, I'm laughing. And we're playing together. I've loosened the reins on having such a tight schedule for them and tried to relax more around the house, inviting them on a run with me, which turned out to be a long walk where I got to know my children, and they me. Grace informed me that Andi has been teaching her how to play the guitar for the talent show, while Logan and I have played basketball together every day I'm home, even if for only a few minutes like today because it was all we could fit in.

It's been... Well, it's been amazing. All because Andi had the audacity to tell me the truth. I'll never be able to repay her.

With the kids asleep, I quietly make my way to the basement door and lean my ear against it, listening to Andi playing. I don't recognize the song, but I do recognize her voice, quiet as it is. She told me she was a songwriter, but I don't know why it never occurred to me that she sings too. Maybe because I've been so wrapped up in my physical attraction to her that I couldn't imagine her level of talent.

Curious, I silently open the door and sneak down a few steps, enough that I spot her sitting on the floor, her back to me. She's wearing my zip-up again, and it never fails to hit me hard. That she has a piece of me with her. *On* her.

I sink down to sit on a step, sure to stay quiet so I can enjoy the show, the way she rocks back and forth, the neck of the guitar sticking out on her left side, her head bobbing along. I wish I could see her face, know if she is smiling or has her eyes closed. I imagine both.

I assume this is her first love, playing music, and I don't know shit about it, but she's good. She sings about broken dreams and heartache, and though her voice cracks on a high note, it's the most beautiful song I've ever heard. I suspect anything she played would be the most beautiful song I've ever heard.

She finishes singing then strums a few chords. I don't move, wanting to hear more, and Cat joins me, nudging at my leg for a pet. I try to shake him off, but he continues, and I glare at him to leave me alone. I'm busy. When he continues to paw at me like he doesn't get enough attention, I silently call him an asshole yet give in, petting him, which earns a purr.

Normally, it wouldn't be a big deal, I wouldn't mind, but in the quiet of the basement, he might as well be screeching. Andi swings around, startled.

So much for stealth mode.

I lift my hand. "I, uh...heard you upstairs and came down to listen."

Her cheeks turn pink. "I'm sorry, I didn't know I was so loud. I won't play at night anymore."

"No." I stand quickly and practically jump down the rest of the steps to get to her. "It's okay. Please, play whenever you want."

"It's a little late for you to be awake," she notes, and I like that she's learned my schedule. Although, I guess she had no other choice with how I wanted her to do her job, run the house like I would. But that's changed now.

I shrug. "I was texting with my brother."

"Ian?"

"No, Roman. He's my younger one. He's in New York... doesn't talk to us much."

She opens her mouth, like she wants to ask a question, but stops herself. Good. Because I wouldn't know the first thing to say about my relationship with Roman. Still, I'd tell her all of it. Whatever she wanted to know.

She sets down her guitar before bending to pick up Cat. He burrows into her arms, rubbing it in my face with a rattling purr that he's able to touch her and I can't. She sits on her bed, all comfy and cute-looking, and I feel like I'm intruding on her space, but I also don't want to leave. So, I ask, "Was that one of your songs?"

She nods. "I wrote it forever ago."

"It's pretty."

She blushes even more than before and mutters a quiet "thank you" then glances to the spot next to her on the bed. I don't waste the silent invitation and plant myself close enough that my thigh rests against hers. She draws those big eyes of hers up to mine, biting her lip shyly, and I've never been more fascinated. Such an interesting little creature she is. A mix of insecurity and confidence, modesty and pure sex. I can't get enough.

"When did you start playing guitar?" I ask, reaching out to pet Cat, which annoys him. He only wants Andi's attention, and I get it. She sets him on the bed, and he flicks his tail—I think in a flip-off to me—then jumps to the floor to slink back upstairs.

Andi shifts to face me, sitting cross-legged, and I can't help but admire the smooth expanse of her legs, the way the material of her shorts bunches at her hips, and how the hem of my sweatshirt covers her so it's almost like she's not wearing anything except that.

"About thirteen or fourteen. My grandma taught me. She started playing because of Janis Joplin. She wanted to be just like her."

"And you?" I settle my right knee on the mattress so I'm facing her too. "Who did you want to be like?"

She taps her hummingbird tattoo. "My grandmother."

The girl is so goddamn sweet, it makes me ache listening to her speak.

Andi's smile takes on a faraway glint. "It sounds weird to say, but she was my best friend. We were kindred spirits, both of us born into a time and place I don't think either of us was meant to be in."

"Why do you say that?"

She lifts her gaze, skirting it around the room, where she's settled in quite nicely. It's not as tidy as I keep my room, but it's not a mess either, merely lived-in. She has picture frames on the dresser and a wicker laundry basket that's full to the brim. Her sneakers are next to her cowboy boots, lying on their sides.

I picture her sneakers and boots next to my shoes upstairs in my closet, but I quickly shake that idea from my mind. Especially because she clears her throat. "I was a bit lonely growing up. I have an older brother, but he's four years older. He was okay with life there. I wasn't. I never felt like I truly fit in. And Mimi—my grandma—she was an old hippie chick. She didn't fit in either, but she came to live with us on the ranch when my grandpa died. And my dad..."

She slants her gaze to me, her brows drawn down. "My dad could be a real son of a bitch," she says on a sad laugh. "He tolerated Mimi because she was my mom's mom, but he didn't have the same...restraint with me. I was his daughter, so he could discipline me how he saw fit."

I instinctively curl my fingers into fists. "He ever hit you?"

She bites into her bottom lip, her eyes going watery. My tenderhearted girl. "No," she whispers eventually. "He never hit me. Sometimes I think that might have been easier to take. A slap over his words."

I shake my head, my voice close to a rumble. "No child deserves to be abused in any way. Full stop."

She sniffs and nods. "That's why I was so close to Mimi. She supported me. Loved me when it sometimes felt like no one else did."

"Fuck, sweetheart. I'm sorry you had to go through that, but I'm glad you had your grandmother. I'm glad she was there for you."

"That's why it was so hard for me when she passed. It felt like..." She picks at the zipper of the hoodie as she finds her words. "She was the last person to believe in me, and she's gone."

I can't sit here and listen to her heartbreak and not touch her, so I place my hand on her bare knee. When she glances at it, I'm quick to remove it, but she hits me with one of her soft smiles. The shy one that makes me want to pull her into my lap and keep her tucked up safe against me. "It's okay."

So, I let my palm cup her knee, fingers extending up her thigh. "You said you have a best friend, though, right?"

"Dahlia, yeah. She's there for me."

"And you have me and the kids."

She catches my eyes, cheeks dimpling. "And you and the kids."

A moment passes between us when I imagine the four of us all curled up on the couch, watching a movie together, me on one end, Andi on the other, with the twins between us. My arm on the back of the cushions, playing with Andi's hair. Her smiling at me.

It's too good of an image, and it takes me a lot longer than I'd like for me to push it out of my head.

I'm not sure when my fantasies went from thinking about her lips wrapped around my cock to spending family time together, but I feel like this is so much worse.

Wanting to fuck somebody is a passing fancy.

Wanting to bring someone into a family is something totally different.

And as hard as I'm trying to ignore all these bubbling feelings, I can't.

"We're having a party for my brother tomorrow," I say, and she nods.

"I know. It's on the calendar."

"It's a surprise party."

"That'll be fun."

"I think you should come," I blurt out.

The shock on her face melts into something that looks a lot like fondness. "You want me to come to your family's party?"

I try to cover myself. "I think the kids would really like it if you did."

Her coffee-brown eyes search mine, drifting back and forth, and I hope she can't find my lie. I don't know if she does or not, but her answering smile settles deep in my chest, warming my cold, weary heart.

"Yeah, okay. I'd love to come."

Forcing myself to stand, I offer her a tip of my chin. "Have a good night, Andi."

"You too, Griff."

Then I take the stairs two at a time and head straight to my shower, the lingering scent of her stuck in my nose and the picture of her staring up at me with those plump lips curved in a sultry pout as she strips naked for me. As soon as the water is warm, I step inside and fist my hand around my erection, pretending that coming while imagining her riding my cock will solve all my problems and leave no room for wanting more.

Chapter 13
Andi

I'm not sure how much of a surprise this party can be with it all out in the open like this. Griffin pulls into a spot in the lot in front of the park, lights and streamers strung all over the pavilion. Already, over two dozen or so people are here. I recognize Taryn, though my only interaction with her wasn't the best. I wouldn't say I get nervous to meet people, but being the new girl on the block is a bit intimidating.

I check my hair and makeup in the visor's mirror, but the kids are impatient and run off before I even have my seat belt unbuckled. Griffin shouts directions at them as he comes around to my side, extending his hand to help me out of the truck. In a cream-colored polo shirt and jeans, he has no right to look so good. He got his hair trimmed yesterday, the sides close-cropped though the grays still shine through, and I'm moving before I think better of it, reaching up to sweep my fingers through the longer strands on the top of his head.

He stays very still, his eyes cataloguing every inch of my face, and I don't know what else to tell him besides, "You had a hair out of place. Didn't think you'd like that, Captain."

He shakes his head, nudging my hand down to palm his cheek, and he leans into it for a moment before shifting away, so I lower my hand to my side. Even though we promised each other weeks ago we'd keep our relationship strictly professional —boss and employee, nanny and single dad—I can't help it.

I don't think he can either.

"You seem nervous," he says, and my stomach flutters at his observation.

It's both immensely pleasing that he can read me so well and a little frustrating that I can't hide anything from him. "How'd you know?"

"You wear all your emotions on your face." He presses his hand against the small of my back, guiding me through the crowd. The warmth of his touch calms me. "I'll introduce you to everyone. They'll love you."

I inexplicably hope they do.

Just as I can't explain meeting Griffin for the first time, my immediate and undeniable infatuation with the guy who rescued me from the side of the road. The man who has never made me feel anything less than safe and secure. This mature and considerate father who needed someone to look after his children. Whom I have no business falling for, but every time we're together, it's like swimming upstream.

It would be so much easier to let go, to give in to the current and be drawn to the ocean. I'm sure he could and would save me.

As we weave through the throng of people, Griffin rattles off names. I meet Ian's kids, Jasper, Jaybird, and Juniper. There is Eloise, the owner of Sweet Cheeks, the bakery next to Ian's tattoo shop. Marianne and Clara are here, as well as Taryn's two kids, Jake and Maddie. Unlike the day she and I met, she appears to be in a better mood. In fact, she tells me she's heard I've been doing a wonderful job with Logan and Grace. Which means Griffin has been talking about me, and I'm infinitely giddy about that.

Especially when Ian shows up to a chorus of cheers. Griffin's older brother is... Well, he's hot. A silver fox with a beard, muscles, and tattoos all over. When he finally makes it through the crowd to us, he grips Griffin's shoulder with a gruff, "Cap."

"Happy birthday," Griffin says before hugging him, a few more words I can't hear exchanged between them. Then Ian turns to me with a raised brow. "And who is this?"

Griffin gestures between us. "Ian, meet Andi. Andi, this is my older brother, Ian."

"Ah." Ian takes my hand, his grip firm and warm. "This is the infamous Andi." His eyes are just as dark as Griffin's, and he sweeps his gaze over me. Not in any sexual way, more out of curiosity. "I've been looking forward to meeting the woman who has my brother upside down and inside out."

"Fuck off," Griffin grumbles.

"So defensive." Then he winks at me, and it kind of...it makes my heart stutter. Ian doesn't notice because he's on to greeting the next person, but Griffin certainly does, scowling at me like I've offended him.

"What?" I laugh, and he scowls harder. "Your brother is really good-looking."

"No, he's not."

I like jealous Griffin. Ruffled Captain Stone.

"You're jealous." I knock my hand into his thick shoulder, and he stares down at me like he doesn't mind my teasing. Likes it, even.

He opens his mouth to reply but is interrupted by someone calling his name. He glances over his shoulder to acknowledge them then murmurs to me, "Be right back."

He lightly pinches my wrist before he marches off, and I watch as he effortlessly carries bags of ice from the trunk of

Taryn's car to dump them into a cooler. They have a short conversation, and he tosses his arm around her shoulders, an action that warms my heart. Since I'm not close to my family, it's nice to see the Stone family interact.

Although I don't know any of them all that well, I can tell they love and care for one another. A vague notion of being accepted into their circle filters through my brain. I have no idea how I would do that or if I'd even be welcome, but I stand off to the side taking in the party as a whole. Lots of laughter and smiling faces.

It's a home.

"Andi, do you want to play with us?"

I spin around to find Logan, Grace, and their cousin Maddie. They've got a frisbee, and I shrug.

"Sure." I follow them out to the grassy area and throw it around for a while, learning Maddie is twelve and has terrible aim since I'm constantly running to grab the plastic disk until I'm out of breath.

"All right," I say, laughing. "I need a break. Let's go grab something to eat."

The kids agree, and we help ourselves to plates of food then settle at one of the long tables. Logan shovels macaroni salad into his mouth while Maddie and Grace chat about some TV show. My own plate is piled high, but I'm too distracted by the woman I notice with Griffin. She's standing awfully close to him, smiling about something.

"Who's that with your dad?" I ask, all casual-like.

Logan pauses long enough from eating to follow my line of sight. "Ugh. That's Elsa."

"Like...*Frozen*?"

Grace shakes her head. "Yes, but she's nothing like that Elsa. Except they're both blond."

"She's Dad's ex-girlfriend," Logan explains around a mouthful of food. "She's the worst."

I raise my eyebrows at that. This Elsa woman is tall and willowy with long, straight blond hair. Even from here, I can tell she's gorgeous in an intimidating way that highlights all my own insecurities.

"How come?"

"We overheard her talking on the phone one day, telling someone that if she ever married Dad, she'd send me and Gracie to boarding school."

My mouth drops open in shock. "Seriously?"

Not that the twins couldn't be terrors, but boarding school is not the answer. Obviously. I mean, I solved the puzzle of their bad behavior. It wasn't that hard to understand.

"It always felt like she didn't like us, but we never even played any tricks on her," Grace whispers to me. "So she didn't like us for no reason."

And *that* is reason enough for me not to like her.

"Did your dad know that?"

"We never told him," Logan says after chugging half a can of Coke.

"But he broke up with her?" I guess, and the kids shrug. I turn back to Griffin and Elsa, irritation simmering in my gut. The thought of him with someone so clearly awful makes me want to march over there and tell her off. But that would be ridiculous, right? I have no claim over him.

I force myself to finish my food, even though I've lost my appetite. The kids are done eating too, and since I'm in need of a distraction so I don't do something stupid, I tug on Logan's arm. "Come dance with me."

There's music playing, a ska band from the '90s, I think, and he makes a face. "What? No way!"

"Oh, come on!" I stand, pulling him up with me. "It'll be fun."

He fights me the whole way as I drag him to a little open space under the pavilion. "Dancing is not fun."

"Yes, it is." I hold his hands, urging him to move. He doesn't. Merely stands there, glaring at me like I'm embarrassing him.

But it's a rite of passage.

"I don't know how to dance," he grumbles, and I grin.

"Good thing for you, I do. Your future girlfriends will appreciate that I taught you. Now, look, all you have to do is find the beat. Stick with this side-to-side motion. Yeah, like that."

He keeps his head down, following me as I lead him, step-touching right to left.

"You can get fancy, like this," I say, opening our arms out wide and then pulling them in between us, forcing him to step toward me, and he crashes into me. I laugh. "Not like that."

"This is so dumb," he mutters.

"No, it's not. You just have to avoid stepping on my feet."

He fights a smile and starts to loosen up, so I make a suggestion. "Can I teach you a two-step? It's super simple." When he shrugs indifferently, I show him how to hold his arms, and for once, I'm glad I'm so short. There isn't too much of a difference between us when he reaches up to hold my right hand. I explain that he should lead. "You're going to guide me with a little bit of pressure to show me what direction to go in."

He listens intently as I show him how to take two quick steps to the side and then one slow to the other. "Get it, two-step?"

"Ha-ha," he says, with a roll of his eyes like he's too cool for this, even though I can feel how damp his palms are.

"Let's try it. You lead, 'kay?"

He nods and all but shoves me to the left. I laugh, trying and failing to make this simple two-step work. Even though he's smaller than me, it doesn't feel great when he keeps stepping on my toes. I playfully shriek whenever he does, earning a mumbled apology and half smile. I want him to have fun. Which he seems to be having, especially when he attempts a spin move.

"Look at you!" I toss my head back to laugh when he smashes into me again, and that's when I notice Griffin watching us, his gaze hot on me, even as Elsa is still talking to him. My steps fizzle out as I'm unable to tear my gaze away from him. Logan tries to pivot us again, and he steps on my foot, hard this time.

I bend over, hissing in my pain, and he immediately jumps away. "I'm so sorry! I didn't mean it."

"I know, buddy. It's all right. It's—"

"Mind if I cut in?"

Both Logan and I look up to find his dad next to us, and Logan eagerly hands over the reins. "See ya!"

"Thanks for the dance," I call after him as he runs off. Right into Ian's daughter, Juniper. From the little I know of her, she's in college and the apple of her father's and brothers' eyes.

"Not so fast, Romeo," she says, pulling him into her. "Dance with me. I love this song."

"Not you too!"

I bite back a laugh then sweep my attention around, noting how others are joining in dancing, so it doesn't feel like all eyes are on me when I take Griffin's hand.

His are the only eyes I want on me.

Those unblinking dark pools remain on me as his warm palm engulfs mine, his other hand on my lower back. And I fall into him, easily letting him take control and walk me in a circle, his eyes never leaving mine. It's unrelenting and hard to breathe with this force between us. Pushing us together.

Both of us pretending we should stay apart.

But we have this. A dance.

A moment.

His feet leading me, and my heart in his hands.

He surprises me into a giggle when he circles our arms up above our head, spinning me around in a move that is not for beginners.

"I never took you for a dancer," I say, but instead of answering, he swings me around him, his hand trailing over my middle, his fingers skimming along my stomach. When we face each other again, I ask, "Where'd you learn?"

"I was stationed in Virginia. One of the guys on my team was big into line dancing. We used to give him a lot of shit until we learned how many girls he pulled with it."

"So, you learned?"

"So, I learned," he affirms.

"Learned to dance and loves to read. Who even are you, Captain Stone? What other secrets are you hiding?"

He avoids my question with one of his own. "How do you know I love to read?"

"Well, the bookcase in the living room is filled, and since I assume Gracie and Logan aren't reading *The Alchemist* or *Atomic Habits*, I have to guess they're yours. Hardbacks, too. That means you're a reader for real, not just a vacation kind."

He nods but again offers nothing.

"Don't think I didn't notice all the Shakespeare," I add.

"Would that all women had thy wit and understanding."

What I wouldn't give to crawl into this man's brain for a little while. To see what makes him tick.

What I wouldn't give to crawl into his heart for a long while. To see if maybe I could stay.

"Which one is that quote from?"

"*Much Ado About Nothing.* My mom taught high school English. She loved to read. I love to read." His hands slip from their hold and link at my back, pulling me closer to him, forcing me to reach up, hands clinging to the back of his neck.

This is infinitely more intimate, especially when I can feel his torso expand and fall with each breath. The sunset has painted the sky pink and purple, and with the twinkly lights above us swaying in the slight breeze, it feels like something out of a book. Like someone wrote this moment for us. Like the hundreds of love songs that describe this moment. When a man looks at a woman with sincerity and whispers something to her he would never tell anyone else.

"My mom would send me her favorite Shakespeare with lines or passages highlighted. It kept me connected to her, whether I was in Virginia or on the other side of the world. Or, I guess, in another existence now."

"That's beautiful." I scratch my fingernails over the nape of his neck, the hair there too short for me to toy with, but he seems to like it, lowering his head.

"You're beautiful," he rasps, and I duck my chin, over-whelmed by his unremitting honesty and the harsh voice in the back of my mind, reminding me that I'm not good enough. That I never will be.

"Andi." He tips my face up to his with his fingers under my jaw. "Why are you crying?"

I blink a few times. "Because you're sweet, and I'm not sure... It's hard to hear sometimes, is all."

"It's hard to hear you're beautiful?" When I nod, he frowns. "It's not what you look like. It's what you are. Your heart. It's beautiful."

If I didn't love him before, I sure do now, and I lean my temple against his shoulder. His grip on me tightens, and we sway in contented silence until I spot Elsa. I temper my voice as I tilt my head back to meet Griffin's eyes. "Why would you date someone who didn't like your kids?"

He jerks back. "What?"

"Elsa," I say quietly. "Your ex-girlfriend."

He frowns. "I...I'm not sure what you mean."

On another slow turn, I see her again and sigh. "The kids told me that she wasn't very nice to them."

His brows shoot up toward his hairline. "I had no idea."

"Overheard her saying she would send them to boarding school when she married you. Were you going to marry her?"

His fingers adjust their grip on my waist, as if making sure I can't go anywhere, and he takes a deep breath before explaining, "We were together for about a year. She was the one serious relationship I had, and, yes, we had talked about marriage, but I never once told her I'd propose. It was a planning sort of conversation, you know?"

I snort. Yeah, I know. Griffin Stone and his schedules.

"If I'd known she ever said that, I would have ended it immediately."

I nod, peeking over his shoulder to see Elsa is no longer watching us—good—and when I glance back at Griffin, he's gazing at me with a curious twist to his lips. Not quite a frown, but not quite a smile either.

"You're really upset about that?" he asks, and I nod.

"I couldn't believe that you would ever be with someone who wouldn't treat your kids right."

He shakes his head, wincing. "I wouldn't. I only wish they would have told me."

"If it makes you feel better, I think they would tell you now."

"It does make me feel better," he says, gliding one of his hands up my back, so he's holding me more like a hug, tugging me right up against him. "Also makes me like you even more for defending Logan and Gracie."

"I will always defend them," I promise, and he bends like he wants to seal it with a kiss, but stops himself, close enough that his warm breath wafts over my mouth. I am immensely disappointed, but I can't blame him. One of us has to keep our head.

He doesn't say anything for long seconds, but by the time he finally does, the song is over, and his fingers release their grip on me. "Thanks for the dance, Andi."

"Thanks for bringing me to the party, Griff."

His smile is fleeting, but the gift of witnessing it is enough for now.

Chapter 14
Griffin

In the three days after Ian's party, Logan and Gracie both came down with a stomach bug that had apparently taken out nearly the whole of the fifth grade, class by class. Grace was the first to succumb, looking a little green around the gills when she got off the bus. By the time I got dinner on the table, she was running to the bathroom. Logan hit the deck the next day. It lasted about twenty-four hours, and I was home to take care of them, but it was Andi who really stepped up. With both kids sick, it was difficult for me to clean the house and do their laundry while also chasing them around with puke buckets, crackers, and Gatorade. She didn't need to help since these were technically her days off, but she did. She wiped their foreheads with cool cloths and sat with them when they couldn't sleep. At one point, I stood in shadows outside Grace's doorway as Andi stroked my daughter's head, singing softly to her. It was the most maternalistic care my children had ever received, which both broke my heart and mended it back together.

So it shouldn't surprise me when I find her lying on the

couch after I arrive home from work, but it makes my own stomach turn all the same to see her looking so ill. "Andi, you okay?" I rush over and sink to my haunches, setting my palm on her forehead. Her skin is hot and damp. "How long have you been like this?"

She swats at me, though there's no energy behind it, her hand missing me completely. "I'm fine. I just need a rest."

"You're sick."

"I am not," she insists, rolling from her side to her back with a groan.

"Have you eaten today?"

"Um..."

"How about liquids? Did you drink any water?"

"This morning, yeah." She angles her head back, her eyes heavy with exhaustion, and I already know what she's going to say. "I couldn't keep it down."

"We have to get something into you," I say, and that earns a soft giggle from her.

"I see what you did there."

I loop my arm around her, hauling her up to a sitting position, taking nearly all her weight against me. "Did what?"

"Get something into me," she mutters, resting her head on my shoulder. "You can get into me."

I cluck my tongue. "I think you're delirious."

"A little bit," she says, and I press my fingers against her pulse point, making sure it's normal before placing a pillow behind her head.

"I'm going to get you some ginger ale and toast. Don't move."

"Yes, sir, Captain Stone, sir." She salutes me but accidentally smacks herself in the head. She's a mess. A bewitching little mess.

I barely brown the piece of bread before putting it on a

plate, offering it to her along with the warm soda. "Here, sweetheart. Take little sips."

I hold the can up for her so she can wrap her dry lips around the straw. I encourage her as she drinks and then manages a few nibbles of the dry toast. Even if she chews like it's the worst thing in the world. "It tastes like sand."

"You're cute like this, all loopy and out of it."

She wrinkles her nose and spits out the mangled piece of bread from her mouth onto the plate.

"What's wrong? You—"

That's when she gags and slaps her hand over her mouth, stumbling to stand. She trips over me as she races to the bathroom in the hall, where I hear her retching before I get there.

I sit down beside her, holding her hair back as her body rids itself of the little food and drink it had. After she's done, she holds the sides of the toilet and whimpers. "I hate puking."

"Yeah. It sucks."

"Everything hurts."

I reach for the hand towel, hanging from the loop on the wall, and nudge her to sit up so I can wipe her face. Her skin's pale, and her eyes are bloodshot when they meet mine. She frowns. "Bet you don't think I'm cute now."

"I think you're cute all the time."

"Liar," she mumbles, scooting away from me to lean against the wall and close her eyes. We sit for a while, neither of us speaking. I assume she doesn't feel up to standing yet, so I don't force her to. Plus, she might not be done.

I'm proven right when she throws herself back at the toilet, her hands slapping on the tile floor, her back bowing as she vomits. I instantly reach for her hair, but I don't scoop it all up in time, and the poor girl gets some puke on a few strands of hair. I wipe it off as best I can with the towel, but she notices and lets out a pitiful moan. "I'm disgusting."

"You're sick."

"And disgusting. I'm all sweaty," she says, curling up into a ball on the floor.

"Do you want to shower?"

She waves me off. "Just leave me here to die."

"Can't do that, sweetheart." I scoop her up, and she squeaks out a protest.

"No, don't. I'm gross. Put me down."

"You're not staying on the bathroom floor." When I cradle her against me, the fight leaves her pretty easily, and she relaxes. I think about that first day she stood in the basement, holding Cat, how jealous I was of him. Now I've got this woman in my arms, holding her the same way, her arm even flopped out to the side.

I can't help the twitch of my lips, and Andi notices. "Are you laughing at me?"

"I would never."

"Then what are you smiling at?"

"I was remembering something funny. Do you want me to help you get cleaned up?"

"I can do it," she says, even as she tucks her head against my shoulder. I carry her downstairs and set her on her bed. She immediately falls to her side in the fetal position.

"Are you sure you don't want my help?"

She stares at me for a long time, her tongue gliding over her cracked and dry lips. "You can't shower with me."

I bite back a chuckle. "That sounds like a question."

She blinks sleepily, her fingers lifting toward me. "You can't shower with me, but you can turn it on for me."

I find the toothpaste so she can brush and then turn on the shower, making sure she has a fresh towel and clothes before closing the door to the small bathroom. As soon as it snicks shut, I curse myself for not making it bigger. For not bringing her up to my bedroom and putting her in my more spacious bathroom. We could both fit in the shower, and I would gladly stand under the water fully clothed if she needed me to hold her up.

Behind the door, I hear her moving around, groaning every once in a while. The shower shuts off after a few minutes, and I turn around to wait until she opens the door. When she does, she's in the shorts and T-shirt I found.

"Feel better?" I ask, and she nods, accepting my hand when I extend it. I usher her to the bed, where I hold the covers up so she can get in, but she doesn't. Instead, she goes to the small nightstand, where she picks up an elastic band.

"Here. Let me." I take it from her then snag the brush I spotted in a basket on the dresser and point to the bed for her to sit. When she does, I get to work, combing the long strands of wet hair, the light golds and dark ambers blending together to create my new favorite color. After I have all the tangles out, I separate her hair into three lengths and braid them together, tying it off at the bottom. It's been a few years since Grace wanted me to braid her hair, so my skills are a little rusty, but it'll do.

Andi runs her hand over her hair. "You braided it."

"I know."

"You know how to braid hair."

"I do," I say, even though it wasn't a question.

"Is there anything you don't know how to do?"

I lift the covers up again, and after she crawls under them, I tuck them around her before sitting back down, stretching my legs out, my back against the headboard. "I don't know how to crochet."

She closes her eyes, snuggling into my side, and I drape my arm around her, skating my fingertips over her forehead and temple. She hums. "That feels nice. Please don't stop."

I'd never. Not even if a hurricane swept through here.

"I miss it," she says quietly.

"Miss what?"

"Being touched."

I stop for a stunned moment. "What do you mean?"

"Physical touch is my love language. I need cuddles and hugs and holding hands."

I blow out a breath, my mind having run away with all the possibilities she could have meant. I will give Andi whatever she needs, anything she wants to feel comfortable. But the thought of her missing a sexual touch has my skin on fire. Even now, after a minute, my heart rate still hasn't settled into its normal rhythm.

"Bet the ice queen would be so mad if she saw us now," Andi mumbles, and I skim my index finger down her nose.

"The ice queen?"

"Elsa. Your Elsa," she says, like that explains everything. It does not.

"She's not my Elsa. You know that."

Andi slants her head so she can look up at me, and I sweep my fingers across her jaw and down to her throat, where I find her pulse. I lay my fingers over it as she admits, "I was jealous of her talking to you at Ian's party. She's beautiful and had all your attention."

"That's not true."

"It felt true. But then you came over to dance with me, and Elsa looked like she wanted to freeze me."

I huff a laugh, and she offers me a stilted smile. "I like when you laugh. You should do it more."

"I'm laughing because you assume I actually care about what she thinks. I don't." I trail my fingers up to Andi's temple, trace the shell of her ear, and smooth my palm along her neck before sliding my fingers over the hair at the top of her head.

"There's nothing there anymore. Especially after what you told me. I don't want anything to do with her."

"But she wants something to do with you," she points out, and I shrug.

"I don't even remember what she and I talked about. All I could think about was the way you looked in that purple sundress and your cowboy boots. How it felt dancing with you. Like nothing else mattered."

I'm not sure if this conversation is happening because it's been a long time coming or because confessing my feelings to her in this state is like talking to a drunk person. I'm not sure how much of this she'll remember.

But she hasn't even been here a month, and already, I feel like she's changed my entire world. It's true what Ian said. She's turned me inside out and upside down. There is no way I can pretend she hasn't picked the lockbox I keep my emotions stored in. She blew that motherfucker right open.

And for all of my bluster, my nothing-can-hurt-me, grumpy-as-fuck exterior, I'm not sure I ever want that box closed again. Not if it means I might lose the best thing to ever happen to me.

Because that's what she is. This woman who took me by storm. Who has earned every crack in my armor with each of her smiles. Busted down all my walls with her joy and patience and love for my children. This woman who is much too beautiful and young to be with a fortysomething son of a bitch like me has wound her fist so tight around my heart, I don't think it would ever work right again if she left.

So, I guess, there is only one thing to do.

Ring the bell. Bow out. And admit I am no match for Andrea Halton.

She's won.

Chapter 15
Andi

The stomach flu flattened me for nearly two days, and I could barely lift my head, let alone do my job. Griffin hired me to take care of the kids, but he ended up taking care of me. In my foggy memories of those forty-eight hours, I know he carried me downstairs, helped get me changed, even braided my hair. Then he cuddled me and talked to me for a long time, all but confessing his feelings for me.

I figured he'd get sick too, after being my nursemaid, sitting next to me while I threw up repeatedly, and bringing me fluids and snacks every two hours like clockwork. The man was nothing if not always on time and efficient.

But of course, Griffin remained healthy. I doubt anything short of a nuclear war could take him out. Which is all the better because his firehouse is hosting their annual fundraiser, and as the captain, he's expected to be there.

The two blocks leading up to the firehouse are lined with cars, and I truly didn't expect it to be this big. I assumed it was a small picnic, but there are people everywhere. Peppy music pumps from towers on either side of the building, and I have to lean into Logan and Grace to hear them when they ask if they can go play in the bounce house.

"Be careful," I shout as they take off. "You're big kids, so watch out for the little ones!"

Logan waves at me that he heard, and Griffin gazes down at me with soft eyes.

"What?" I ask, lifting my chin.

He lifts one shoulder, curling his hand around my hip. "I like hearing you, seeing you, with them. They listen to you. Respect you."

"I hope so." I laugh nervously, not sure if he's surprised or happy about that. "You raised them to be respectful."

"But you and I both know what they were like before. With the others."

I'm not sure what to make of the fact that he won't say the word "nanny" in this context. It feels like he doesn't want to say there were others. Or maybe that's only my interpretation. My silly little jealous notion. That not only do I not want him to have girlfriends, but I don't want there to be other nannies either.

Still, I try to downplay it. "I think they needed someone to get on their level. To show they're understood."

His eyes make a circuit of my face, settling on my mouth. "And to put me in my place."

"That, too." I smile, and his gaze lifts to mine, humor crinkling his eyes.

"Come on, troublemaker." He guides me through the crowd with a hand pressed against my lower back. We pass a fire truck parked out front where people are taking pictures in and around it. There are tables set up with pamphlets about fire safety and free first aid kits. There's even somebody handing out plastic firefighter helmets. The guy offers me one, and I turn him down with a laugh.

Inside, Griffin points out the office and steps that lead upstairs to the sleeping quarters.

I gesture to the fire pole. "How much action does that see?"

"A lot less than TV shows would make you believe."

I pout. "You are a true dream killer, Captain Stone."

Again, his attention lands on my lips, heavy and unblinking. I skim the tip of my tongue over them, and he inhales deeply enough to raise his shoulders, his grip tightening on me. "Sorry, sweetheart."

Something comes over me. Demons, possibly. Delirium due to post-flu dehydration, more likely. But either way, I say, "Maybe you can show me sometime."

I feel each of his five fingers expand, covering as much space as possible, with his thumb on my hip bone and his pinkie slipping into my back pocket. "I think we can work something out."

My mouth goes dry as the implication settles over me. He wants me.

Griffin wants *me*.

And there's no hiding or running away from it.

But I can't even begin to accept or consider what it would mean to act on this because one of Griffin's coworkers greets us. I'm introduced to him, along with a handful of other firefighters, though their names slip my mind almost instantly, too distracted by Griffin's proprietary hand on my hip.

After we've done a lap around the firehouse, written our names down for a couple of items in the silent auction, and bought a handful of 50/50 tickets, we spot Ian and Taryn with her two kids. Maddie immediately runs off to play with Logan and Grace, while Jake plays on his cell phone as we wander over to the tables of food. One has six crockpots on it, all filled with chili for the tasting contest.

Griffin gestures for me to help myself, so I do. He watches as I consider each carefully, the corner of his mouth lifting as I put on a terrible French accent and critique the flavors of each. One's too spicy, another too bland. But I like the second to last and cast my ballot for it then ask, "Why chili?"

"We all take turns cooking, and all of our meals are basically anything that can be put in a slow cooker."

By the time we sit at one of the tables with Taryn and Ian, who's on his second bowl of chili, I realize how easily I've slotted into this life. Into Griffin's life.

Taryn includes me in the conversation about the renovations she wants to do at the B&B. She even asks my opinion on what I thought of my short stay there. Ian and Jake get into an intense discussion about sports, and I learn that Jake excels at soccer. He's a freshman in high school and has been playing in a club league for a long time, but after this year, he'll be moving up a level and is worried about making it. Ian and Griffin encourage him, both offering whatever they can do to help, money to buy new cleats or rides to and from practice. I notice Taryn's cheeks going a little pink, her eyes a bit glassy, and she turns her head away, sniffling quietly, hiding her emotion from her brothers and son.

I don't know what the situation is, but I surreptitiously slide a napkin across the table to her. When she notices, she offers me a ghost of a smile and uses it to dab at the corner of her eye and nose.

It's sweet how this family is so close, and I wouldn't mind becoming more integrated. I'm not sure what I would have to offer, but tissues are easy enough.

A little while later, a female firefighter named Marybeth uses a bullhorn to call everyone's attention. It's time for the ice bath competition. She points to a whiteboard and a list of a few firefighters written, including Griffin. She explains how each one will pair up with a civilian to see how long they can last in the ice bath. Winners will have their names added to the 2x4 affixed to the wall. From the cheers, I gather this is a long-standing tradition, with plenty of names on that piece of wood.

"An honor," I tease, shouldering Griffin's side, and he responds with a tug on my ponytail.

"Who are you paired up with?" Taryn asks, and Griffin tips his chin to his nephew.

Jake's eyes widen. "No way. I did it last year."

"And you can do it again. You afraid?"

"Yeah. Of my balls shriveling up."

We all crack up, even Griffin, and it's my new favorite song. The deep timbre sends goose bumps down my spine, and I lean into Griffin, who doesn't hesitate to drape his arm around my shoulders.

Ian notes it with his keen, dark gaze. "Why don't you do it, Andi?"

"No," Griffin says immediately, but his brother shakes his head, eyes never leaving mine.

"Call it initiation into the Stone family."

I consider him then Taryn and Jake, studying me with interest and a little humor, before turning to Griffin. I shrug. "I'm in."

"You don't have to."

"I want to. It'll be fun." I glance at the massive tub filled with ice water, shivering at the sight.

Jake snorts. "Fun isn't the word I'd use, but okay."

Griffin looks me over. "You can't do it in that."

That, meaning my cute flare denim with the star patch I sewed on myself to cover a hole because these jeans are my favorite, and I'll wear them out until they disintegrate off me. He takes my hand. "I have something you can wear."

He leads me to another room with lockers and opens the one with his last name on it to dig through a bag full of what I suppose are extra clothes, because he pulls out a T-shirt and shorts. Then he points me to a bathroom where I change out of my clothes and into his. I have to roll the elastic waistband so many times the shorts barely poke out from under the bottom hem of his shirt that hangs on me like a nightgown.

When I emerge, Griffin is waiting for me, stripped down to only a pair of shorts that leave little to the imagination. I swallow hard, trying not to stare at the expanse of tanned skin, the ripple of muscles, and curving tattoos. I've seen him without a shirt before, but still... I can't stop staring. At the breadth of his shoulders, the tiger inked on his pec so big it encompasses the whole thing, and I've never been especially drawn to men's nipples before, but I have the sudden urge to lick Griffin's, trace them with my tongue, and then become very acquainted with the tiger. Farther down, a thin line of dark hair disappears under the waistband of his shorts. He's all hard lines and raw power, and even has those indented muscles at his hips. I know he's athletic and has to train hard for his job, but my god.

It's not until he coughs that I blink back into reality. A flirtatious scowl slants his mouth, and my skin heats in some embarrassment but mostly desire. "Sorry."

His eyebrow ticks up. "Are you?"

"Not one bit."

He rakes his gaze in appraisal over me, like I did him, and even from where I stand a yard away, I can see how his pupils dilate. With a stiff shake of his head, he refocuses and places my clothes in his locker then takes my hand to lead me to the front of the garage, where we wait a minute for our turn. Marybeth writes the last team's time on the board, one minute and seven seconds, and Griffin mumbles his disapproval. "That's nothing."

I laugh, a little too loudly. "A minute is a long time in zero-degree water."

He pushes me closer to the tub so I can see the thermometer. "Fifty-three degrees."

"Oh." I laugh in absolute terror. "Fifty-three degrees." Fifty-three sounds fine...for a fall day with a cute knit hat and scarf. Not water with ice and barely any clothes.

"You can handle it," he tells me with a confidence I don't feel.

Marybeth calls us over and asks my name so she can introduce me and Griffin. Shouts and applause go up because Captain Stone is evidently very popular with his coworkers.

"You ready?" he asks with a low voice, and I shake my head but place my hand in his and step into the tub with him, gasping at the cold.

Marybeth counts down from three, and Griffin taps on his watch, starting a timer before sitting down in the water. I follow and inhale so fast and hard that my lungs burn.

"You're good," he says from behind me, wrapping his arms around my shoulders, pulling my back against his chest. He presses his cheek to my ear, his mouth by my temple. "You're good, Andi."

"Oh my god. Oh my god." I grip his forearms, my nails digging into them. I don't mean to, but my body is in fight mode, and I can't relax my fingers from their contracted position.

"Breathe. Come on, breathe." He inhales and exhales slowly, his chest rising and falling, his warm breath rushing past my mouth. "Try to relax into it."

"I can't."

"You can. Do it with me." He inhales and exhales purposefully, so I join him. "Good girl. Keep it up."

The crowd around us is a blur of noise and color, cheering and shouting about our time. But all I can concentrate on is Griffin's voice, how he envelops me with his arms. "Attagirl. You're doing so good."

"Griffin," I groan, and he tilts his face so his mouth is right against my ear.

"Yeah, baby?"

"I am never doing this again."

He laughs. Actually laughs!

I'm not sure how because my organs are shutting down, but he seems to be enjoying himself.

"I'm going to kill you," I threaten weakly, and I feel more than hear his hum.

"Yeah? Think you already did, seeing you in my shirt and shorts. Reminded me of the day we met."

I don't know how he's talking, yet I want him to keep going. It's the only thing keeping me alive at this point.

"You had on tiny little shorts and a white shirt. No bra. You were wet from the rain, and all I could see were your nipples, those hard little peaks. I dream of them at night. Touching them. Sucking on them."

I gasp my next breath, and next to us, Marybeth's voice rings out from the bullhorn. "One minute!"

"Are you thinking about that now?" Griffin asks, tightening his arms around me. "Me sucking on your tits. Making them red and shiny?"

"Oh shit," I mutter, and he huffs in my ear.

"I'll take that as a yes."

I nod. I'm delirious. From him. From the cold. From the blood loss in my brain.

"Can you do ten more seconds?" he asks, and I nod again.

I'd agree to anything he wanted at this point.

"You're so good," he praises. "So fucking perfect." He lifts his wrist to show me his military watch, counting down in my ear. "Nine... Eight..."

Each second is a battle, the cold biting into my skin, my teeth chattering uncontrollably. But there's a fire burning inside me, a heat that has nothing to do with the temperature and everything to do with the man holding me.

"Three... Two... One." When Griffin releases his arms from around me, I shoot up, wrapping myself around him like a koala as soon as he stands. The crowd laughs, but I can't bring myself to care, not when I'm shivering so hard, it feels like my teeth might shatter.

As Marybeth announces that our time is one minute and twenty-four seconds, Griffin steps out of the tub easily, as if I'm not clinging to him. Someone throws him a towel, and he wraps it around me, rubbing his hands up and down my back, creating friction and warmth. I bury my face in his neck, my lips brushing against his cool skin.

Eventually, my shivering subsides enough for me to release my death grip on him, and he wraps a towel around his own waist, then turns back to me, concern etched on his face. "You okay?"

I nod, managing a small smile. "Yeah, I think so."

"You did so good, sweetheart."

I melt faster than the loose pieces of ice on the floor and lean into his side. He wraps his arm around me just as the twins run up excitedly.

"Aunt Taryn said we can sleep over tonight," Grace tells us.

"And Jake said I could play GTA with him," Logan adds.

Griffin and I both swing our gazes to Taryn, who's standing with Jake and Maddie, smirking.

She knows. About Griffin and me.

Sophie Andrews

And she's gifting us a night alone. Without the kids.

Griffin clears his throat then turns back to the twins. "Okay. Be good." He touches each of their heads. "I love you."

"Love you too," they both chirp and then, to my utter delight, throw themselves at me for hugs.

I squeeze each of them. "See you tomorrow."

They run off back to Taryn, who waves at us. Ian takes his leave, too, with a knowing salute in our direction.

Then it's just Griffin and me and a whole night ahead of us.

"You ready to get out of here?" he asks, and I am breathless with anticipation, barely able to get the one syllable out.

"Yes."

Chapter 16
Griffin

My hands are on Andi as soon as I shut the back door at home. My lips on hers, my palms on her jaw, and her back against the wall. Our kisses are messy and desperate, all clashing teeth and tongues. Her hands tunnel into my hair, mine grasp her thighs and ass, pulling her closer, needing every inch of her against me. Our breaths are ragged, panting, like we've been running for miles, and fuck, maybe we have. We've been dancing around this for weeks, and now, it's exploding all around us. Uncontrollable, that's how I feel.

Wild, that's what we are.

She moans into my mouth, and I can't get close enough, so I lift her up, wrapping her legs around my waist. I can feel the heat of her pussy through the jeans she changed back into after our dunk in the water, and it's driving me out of my mind.

"I have to get you naked," I tell her, and she nods, searching for my lips again, her tongue gliding against mine. Holding her, I stagger my way through the kitchen and upstairs, our mouths still locked, my hands still gripping her ass cheeks. I'm not graceful or smooth, too fucking riled up to care about tripping over the steps. I have to get her to my bedroom. The sooner, the better.

When I do finally make it, I toss her on the bed, and she lands with a laugh, her hair splayed out around her, cheeks flushed, lips swollen. She's a goddamn vision. I crawl over her, capturing her mouth again, my hands roaming her body, over her perky little tits to her waist and down her thighs that she pulls me closer with.

"You don't know how many times I've thought of this," I confess, and she weaves her fingers into my hair, directing my mouth to her throat.

"Probably not as many times as I have."

I pause and set my palms on either side of her head so I can meet her gaze, her dark eyes alight with lust. I imagine mine are the same way. "Every time I jerked off, I thought of you."

She licks her lips, her voice a low rasp when she says, "Every time I used my vibrator, I thought of you."

I bury my face in her neck with a groan. "Fuck, Andi. Don't tell me that." I lower my weight on top of her, angling my hips to rub my cock over her pussy, up and back, and I know I've hit her clit when she exhales harshly. "You've been downstairs getting off with that big pink thing when I've been here with my hand on my cock. You could've had the real thing."

She claws at my T-shirt, ripping it over my head. "You told me we had to keep it professional."

"I'm an asshole. Why'd you listen?"

She cups her hands on either side of my face, stroking her thumbs over my cheeks. "I don't know if anyone's ever told you this before, but you can be kind of intimidating."

"You're the last person I want to intimidate," I tell her honestly, and I'm offered a smile in return.

"You're the last person I want to disappoint."

"You could never disappoint me."

At this, her good humor flees, tension taking over her features, and I sit back, giving her breathing room. I don't like the uncertainty in her gaze or the way she suddenly seems nervous. My skin pricks with annoyance. Not at her, but at whatever has made her feel this way.

"What's wrong?"

She nibbles on her lip, looking anywhere but at me.

"Andi."

She slants her eyes to me, her throat working on a swallow. Still, she remains quiet, and I know I'm going to hate whatever she is going to tell me. Because she will eventually.

I rub my hands over the sides of her thighs, trying again. "What is it?"

After a moment, she props herself up on her elbows and takes a deep breath. "I'm not very...experienced." She drops her focus to my fingers at her hips. "With sex. And I don't..."

I lean forward so she'll meet my gaze. I don't want her to be embarrassed about this, but I know she is. "It's okay. We don't have to do anything you're not comfortable with."

When she chews on her lip again, I tug it out from under her teeth and hold her chin in my hand so she has to look at me. I need to hear whatever it is she has to say.

It's a long time before she finally says, "I don't orgasm with other people. I never have."

I shake my head in confusion. "What do you mean, never?"

"I've only had sex with two people, and I've never..." She shrugs. "I don't want you to be, like, upset or something."

I smooth my hand up her face, burying my fingers into her hair. "You won't. I don't care that you're not experienced. It doesn't matter to me. I only care about you and how you're feeling."

She nods, but I can tell there's more. "I just... I want you to enjoy it. I want to make you feel good, and I don't want you to worry about me, okay?"

I'm stunned. I can't believe what I'm hearing. This beautiful, amazing woman has never had an orgasm with another person? And she's worried about me enjoying it?

"Andi." I make my voice as gentle as possible...which is to say, not very much. "Why?"

I know she needs contact. She needs physical assurance. So I can't understand why no one has given her an orgasm.

"It's complicated," she says eventually, and I don't like that answer.

"Uncomplicate it for me."

Her responding laugh is frustrated. "I can't. It's... I don't want to talk about it right now, but I'll tell you it's hard for me to relax and enjoy it, I guess. I..." She sighs and flops back down to the mattress. "I want to be with you. I want to do...sex with you, but I'm nervous, okay?"

I give in to a growing smile. "You want to do sex with me?"

"Don't tease me," she whines, though she's smiling.

I skate my hands down her body, from her collarbone to the inside of her thighs. "I want you to tell me the reason why later, but for right now, I'm going to work on making you comfortable. I want you to enjoy this as much as I'm going to."

I stand to remove my shirt, and her eyes track my movements as I strip off my socks and jeans, leaving me in only my boxer briefs. "I'm going to get condoms, but if we don't actually have sex, that's fine with me, okay?"

When she nods, I slip into the en suite to find the small unopened box in the closet. They're almost a year old because, even though I may have slept with more people than Andi, there have only been two since I had the kids. So, it's been few and far between. I place the box on the nightstand then sit on the bed next to Andi and bend to kiss her, taking my time now that I appreciate how special this is.

Andi is extraordinary, but being allowed to touch her like this, to be given the opportunity to give her pleasure that no one else has been able to, makes me feel like a giant. With great power comes great responsibility. So I make sure to be careful.

Shifting to kneel over her, I trail kisses along her jaw and throat, urging her to sit up so I can tug off her T-shirt. I cup her tits over her bra, sweeping my tongue across her bottom lip, the one she likes to bite on and take a nip myself. She inhales sharply, a sweet moan of pleasure, and I kiss down her neck and collarbone, pausing only briefly to unclasp her bra. Before I slide it off her shoulders, I remind her, "If I do something you don't like, tell me. And if I do something you really like, you have to tell me that, too."

She dips her chin, her breath hot on my shoulder when she whispers in my ear, "Yes, Captain."

"Fuck me, you're perfect." I whip off her plain tan bra to finally reveal these breasts I've been fantasizing about. They're small and round and sit up like cupcakes on her chest. Unable to wait a second longer, I mold my hands around them, brushing over her reddish-brown nipples, sucking on one until she squirms. "Yeah," I say around the stiff peak. "I'm gonna make sure you love this as much as I do, because I really fucking love this. Love hearing you whimper like that. Makes my dick so hard."

I move to the other side, licking and sucking while plucking at the nipple I've already made wet. Andi's hands scrabble for something to hold on to, knocking the pillows off the bed, eventually holding on to the end of the mattress. Which is perfect because it brings her tits up even higher in an offering. I go back to laving the first nipple, and she gasps. "I never knew I was so sensitive like this."

Figures. Whoever she was with before didn't take the time to find out what she liked and what worked for her. It pisses me off, but I recenter myself on the present, on making her feel good.

I worship her tits for a few more minutes, playing with them until they're red and shiny, like I've imagined, then sink lower, kissing down her flat stomach. I drag my fingertip over her piercing, gently toying with it before tugging at the button of her jeans. When I look up at her, she nods, so I undo it and then the zipper, and slide them off.

Which is when she tenses.

An automatic reaction.

I know she was enjoying herself before, so I start all over again. I hold myself above her, kissing only her mouth, and when she seems to relax a little, I lower myself to my elbows so she can feel how badly I want her. How much I'm turned on.

I nestle my cock between her thighs, and with only two thin pieces of cotton between us, I can feel how damp she is. It makes me even harder, but I focus on working the tension loose in her limbs. I urge her arms around my neck as I leave open-mouthed kisses from behind her ear to her shoulder. Eventually, she curls her fingers around the back of my head, and when I move lower, back to her breasts, she brings her thighs to my sides, rocking her hips up, searching for relief.

"I like that. Keep doing that," she tells me on an exhale when I scrape my teeth over her nipple, and nothing has ever felt like a bigger achievement than getting this girl to admit what she likes when it's difficult for her.

There is no more vulnerable position than this, and I'm so proud of her for being honest. Even more grateful she's allowing me to be the person she's being honest with.

I catch on to how she needs a slight bite of pain, a pinch here and there before soothing it with my tongue, and I wonder if I can get her over the edge like this. Especially because she's rocking her hips now, making it awfully difficult to concentrate on what I'm doing since I just want to fuck her already with how her body is begging for it.

I stretch out on my side, keeping my mouth at her chest while reaching my right hand between her legs, finding her underwear soaked. This woman will be the end of me. "I'm going to touch you now," I tell her. "You tell me what feels good, yeah?"

She nods, and I quickly pull the cotton down and off her legs. Of course, she closes her thighs to me, so I simply place my hand on her stomach and keep licking and nipping at her nipples until she loosens up once again. I glide my hand down slowly, over the trimmed hair on her mound to her pussy, but I don't do any more than palm her, letting her know I've got her. I'm not going anywhere. No matter what.

When she starts swaying her legs side to side, I wiggle my hand, pushing her thighs open wider until I can spread my fingers, my middle digit over the length of her slit. She's soft and wet, and I ease inside her.

"Still with me?" I murmur against the underside of her breast, and she nods. "I want to make you come. I want to feel you clench around my fingers. Feel how wet you get. Then I want to lick you clean."

She inhales deeply, her eyes focused on the ceiling, and while she's not tense like she was in the beginning, she's also not close to orgasm. I drag her slickness up to her clit, circling it, and her next inhale is sharp.

"How do you like it?" I ask. "Fast or slow?"

"I'm not sure."

"Yes, you are. When you get yourself off with your vibrator, how do you like it?"

"Um." She shakes her head and closes her eyes. "In between, I guess. Not too fast, not too slow."

I bite her shoulder. "Well, Goldilocks, we'll find what works for you. Just keep talking to me. Don't be quiet." When she doesn't reply, I nudge her nose with the tip of mine. "Andi."

She tilts her head to me, her mouth against mine when she says, "Please, a little faster."

"Atta-fucking-girl."

I dip two fingers inside her, coating them with wetness before giving her what she needs, a little faster on her clit while sucking on her nipple and plucking at the other with my free hand. It's a balancing act, to keep her in the moment and out of her head, listening to her breathing, feeling how she responds, and while she likes it, I know she's not there. So, with one last kiss to her nipples, I shift up to kneel.

"We're gonna try something, baby." I slide my fingers back inside her and use my left hand to take over her clit.

She immediately responds. "Ooh. Yes. Yes."

I crook my fingers, pressing them against her swollen wall, stroking it over and over, and she shoots her hands out, digging her fingernails into my forearm like she did earlier. I fucking love it.

Her skin turns blotchy as she closes her eyes, and I feel her tensing, fluttering, finally finding it. I don't even know if Andi realizes, but she's thrashing back and forth, hips moving with abandon. I don't change a goddamn thing. I merely keep praising her, working her over with my fingers, enjoying the thrill of being the one to get her there. To the place where she's about to fall over the edge. "That's it, sweetheart. Ride it out. You're doing so good. So fucking perfect."

"Please, Griffin," she whines, all sweet and breathy and pleading.

"Let go. I'll catch you. Just let go, baby."

She does. With a glorious cry, she comes on my fingers, and I've never felt more accomplished in my life than watching this girl blink her eyes open and smile at me like I'm her hero.

Chapter 17
Andi

I can't believe it.

I had an orgasm by someone else's hand.

Better, by the hand of the man I've come to care for very deeply. He was patient and sweet, never once making me feel uncomfortable or like something was wrong with me. It was more than I could have asked for.

In the afterglow, I breathe heavily, my skin hot and damp. Griffin gently eases his fingers out of me, brushing them up and down the length of my opening like he's testing to see how I feel. So I place my hand over his heart and tell him, "That was amazing."

He rumbles an agreement that I feel more than hear. "You want more?"

"Yes, please." I boldly skate my hand down his abdomen and slip under the waistband of his underwear to curl my fingers around his considerable length. He's hot and hard, and when I drag my thumb over the tip, finding a drop of moisture there, he hisses and buries his face in my neck.

"I won't last long," he says quietly, maybe a little embarrassed.

"That's okay."

"But I want to show you how good it can be."

I move my shoulder so he'll meet my gaze. I smile, one that comes from deep inside. "You already did show me. Even if that was the last orgasm I'll ever have, I can die happy."

He scowls at me. "Not the last. Not even close."

With renewed energy, he pushes off the bed to pull down his boxer briefs, releasing his cock. It stands away from him, curling up slightly, and I can't keep my eyes off it as he rips open the box of condoms, quickly dispatching the wrapper of one and rolling it down his shaft. When it's on, he fists the base as he kneels on the mattress once again.

"Are you nervous?" he asks, and I finally force my attention up to his face.

"A little," I admit. It's been years, and I sort of feel like a virgin all over again. I'm somehow both hot and cold, goose bumps racing over my arms, and I instantly draw my legs together, but he stops me with his hands on my thighs.

He kneels between them, rubbing his palms in circles. They're a little rough, callused in places, but I don't mind. Soft and hard, that's innately Griffin. I wouldn't want him any other way.

He slides a pillow under my lower back, propping my hips up, essentially putting all of me on display. It's...unnerving. But he licks his lips and murmurs, "I can't wait to taste you."

That idea makes me squirm, and I pull him down to me, hoping he doesn't notice my cringe. "Please, I need you."

He's careful not to put his full weight on me, his arms taut, abs clenching, and I don't waste the opportunity to explore his body, running my hands over his shoulders, down his back, and around to his stomach. As I explore, he watches me with tender eyes, an ever so slight uptick to his lips.

"I like this," he grates out as I drag my fingertips over his chest, scratching at his nipples. "You not being afraid."

"Because you make me feel safe." I lift my head to kiss him, sliding my tongue along his, and that's when he adjusts his position, widening my thighs with his so I pull my knees up. Then I feel the first push into me. He's broad, and I stiffen reflexively.

I hate that I do, yet I can't help it. But he simply waits for me, kisses me, tells me how I'm doing so well, that I'm perfect for him, in between licks on my throat and nibbles on my jaw. After a while, he dips his chin, staring between us, at where we're barely connected. "You ready?"

I bite my lip and nod, giving him permission to keep going. Little by little, he works himself inside me, taking his time, his breathing becoming audibly louder, his control slipping. I start to tell him it's okay, but I can't. I'm unable to talk when he thrusts again, deeper and so much fuller than I ever remember it being like. He grunts, retreats, and then drives into me again so fast and hard that air wrenches from my lungs. It takes me a moment to breathe again, and when Griffin notices, he lowers himself to his forearms, bringing us even closer, my nipples brushing against his chest. "I'm sorry, baby. I didn't mean to hurt you. I'm so sorry."

"It's okay," I whisper. "I just... It's never felt like this. So full and...deep."

He drops his head, the scruff on his chin scratching my temple. "You feel so goddamn good." He turns his hands to hold my head, forcing my eyes to his. "Jesus, sweetheart, I don't think I'll ever recover from this."

"You and me both," I say on a breathy laugh, and he kisses me once again, this one more teeth than tongue as he drives forward, hitting the spot that sends waves of pleasure coursing through me. I gasp, my nails digging into his back, urging him on. "Ooh, please, please, please."

His pace quickens, his breath coming in ragged pants. I can feel his heart hammering against my chest, echoing my own. He's close, I can tell, but so am I. So damn close.

"Fuck, fuck, fuck," he chants. "Andi, fuck, I'm coming."

He groans, a deep, guttural sound, and stills over me, his body trembling with release. I'm right there, on the edge but not quite over, and when he realizes, he dips his head to place a quick, soft kiss on the hollow of my throat. "I'll make it up to you. Give me a second."

He pulls out of me and turns away to deal with the condom, giving me his back, sleek and muscular with two little divots above his ass cheeks and red tracks on either side of his spine. He returns to the bed seconds later and throws himself between my legs. This time, I'm not quick enough to stop him, his mouth open and wet against me.

I hiss and shove at him with my hands and feet. "No, you don't need to do that."

When he tips his head up, his features are pulled down in a frown. "But you didn't come. I'm not going to be the only one who finishes."

"I already did," I say, trying to scoot away from him, but he clamps his hands around my hips.

"I want to make you feel good, Andi. I want you to come," he says, almost like he's mad about it.

"It's fine." I scramble back, pulling the sheet up to cover myself, and he scowls as he sits up.

"What's going on?"

"It's not that big of a deal."

He wipes his hand over his face, gazing at me for a long time, assessing me. Whatever he sees has him nodding once before picking up the pillow from the floor and righting the covers. He joins me under them and tucks me against his side with his arm around me, my head on his chest.

We cuddle like that for a while, him toying with my hair and me tracing the tiger tattoo on his chest. I suspect he's waiting for me to explain, so I close my eyes and tell him a story. One only very few people know. Three, to be exact.

"I had a boyfriend in high school. Robbie Davis."

"Please don't tell me this is going where I think it's going and he...hurt you."

"No." I move so I'm reclining against the pillows. Even though I can look at Griffin like this, I don't really want to. What happened has already shaped me so much as a person, I don't necessarily want to see how it might change how he thinks of me. Like I'm being overly emotional.

Because that's what I'd been told. That I'd been dramatic over the episode. That if I wanted to be an adult, I had to act like it.

Griffin places his hand on top of mine to stop me from picking at my nails and links his fingers with mine. With the tip of my index finger of my other hand, I follow the veins of his forearm and his knuckles, rubbing the few scars and tapping on his short, square nails that seem too nice for his work-rough hands.

"What did happen?" he asks, and I lift a careless shoulder, still avoiding his gaze.

"I loved him. Or, at least, as much as I could back then. He made me laugh a lot and was really sweet. We were together for a long time."

When I stop, Griffin prods me along. "How long is a long time?"

"He asked me to be his girlfriend at the homecoming dance of sophomore year. He was my first real kiss. And as we got older, we started...fooling around."

144

"Having sex?" Griffin guesses, and I nod.

"It was toward the end of senior year, and the first time lasted, like, three seconds. It was bumbling and awkward, and Robbie felt so bad. He promised it would get better." I laugh at the memory, out of fondness for the boy who was only ever sweet to me. A great first boyfriend. If it had turned out differently, Robbie and I might be happily married now.

But I live in this timeline and grew up with my parents.

"My dad is not great. He has this old-school mentality when it comes to men and women and work and home, and... I don't know what my mom saw in him when they got together. I suspect it was stability since she was raised by a single mom. That's probably why she didn't like that Mimi and I were so close. She thought I was too much like her mother, who she didn't like. Didn't respect, to a certain degree."

When I pause for a breath, Griffin lifts our linked hands to kiss the back of mine, and I finally slant my gaze his way. I've written songs about love, but now I know what it actually feels like. It's not pretty words on paper. It's safety and comfort, silent promises to always be there, and not-so-silent ones about taking care of each other.

I continue with my eyes on his, that unblinking stare holding me steady. "We were kids, barely eighteen. We loved each other the best way we knew how, and I didn't think we were doing anything wrong. I mean, I knew it was wrong. My pastor said so. My youth group leader was this granola crunchy dude who said it was cool to wait until marriage, even though he was probably having a lot of sex when he went home at night."

Griffin agrees with a grunt.

"It was the third time we had sex. We were up in my room because we were let out of school early, and I assumed my parents were out working, but they walked in on us. I'd never been so embarrassed in my life," I say, my skin heating at the memory, like it did that day when my father screamed at us to get up, but both of us were naked. Robbie tumbled out of bed, covering himself with his hands, and ran out of my room, snatching up his clothes on the way out. I wrapped my blanket around me as my father yelled in my face, called me names I never expected to hear from him.

"My dad lost it." I swallow thickly, the harsh words echoing in my mind. "He called me a whore. Told me he didn't raise me to be a slut, and that no man would want a used-up piece of trash like me."

"*What?*" I feel Griffin's muscles coil beneath me, and his jaw works so hard, I fear for his teeth. "Your father... No one should ever say that, let alone a father to a daughter." He tugs me to him, wrapping his arms around me, cupping one hand at the back of my head, the other smoothing up and down my back. "That's really fucked up, and I'm so sorry, sweetheart."

My eyes burn with tears. I know what my father said about me wasn't true, but that didn't stop it from hurting. From making me afraid to be with anyone else.

Still.

It still hurts. It still makes me afraid. Whoever said sticks and stones can break bones but words can never hurt was wrong. Words can do more than hurt. They can build up religions, tear down governments, speak truth to power, and break a young girl's heart.

"The worst part was my mom just stood there. She didn't try to stop him or say anything to defend me. After he left my room, I was crying on the floor, and my mom came over. She hugged me, and I asked why he would say those things to me, and she said..." I sniffle, chin wobbling, and I bite the inside of my cheek in an attempt to stop it. "She said, in her sweet

Southern accent, that he might have used the wrong words, but he was right."

I wipe a tear but another falls in its place, and Griffin kisses my head, telling me it's okay to cry. So I do, my words broken on a sob. "He called me a whore and a slut, and she said he was right."

"No. No, he wasn't right. She wasn't right either. You are none of those things. But even if you were fucking the whole football team, no one has any right to demean you."

I rest my cheek against his bare chest as I catch my breath, and he continues to soothe me with his warm hands stroking me. "I'm not sure what I would do if I ever walked in on Logan or Grace having sex, but I know it wouldn't be that. You didn't deserve that."

After a few moments, I wipe my face and raise my chin, tired of being so ashamed about something that happened ten years ago. I needed to hear from someone else that it wasn't right. That it wasn't true. And, no, my parents should not have treated me that way. My father shouldn't have called me those names. My mother shouldn't have defended him and later told me to stop being so dramatic about it.

"If you want to be an adult, you have to live with the consequences," she'd said over breakfast a few days later when I still didn't feel like talking to either one of them. As if my being hurt over my parents calling me trash was the problem.

"It was difficult growing up in that house," I tell Griffin, and he holds my cheeks in his hands, frowning at my words. "But that day felt like something ripped away. Like I lost something I knew I wouldn't be able to get back."

"You still talk to them?"

"Occasionally. I left as soon as I graduated. Mimi gave me some money she'd saved, and I packed up my car to drive to LA. So, on top of being a slut, I was also a disappointment because I didn't stay to work on the ranch. I wasn't doing anything to keep the family business going."

"But you were doing what made you happy," Griffin says, as if all men are as logical and even-keeled as he is.

"My parents never cared about my happiness."

"Apparently not." He places a soft kiss on my lips, barely backing away when he says, "That's why you're uncomfortable with sex."

I nod. "It's been difficult for me to be open. I've always made excuses with boyfriends to avoid it, and they've always broken up with me because of it. The one who I actually felt good enough to go to bed with told me it was my fault I couldn't come. I was the one bad at sex. So I basically gave up on it altogether, which was easy to do when I worked for Ryder."

Griffin moves his fingers to my hair, gripping it to keep me in place as he leans back, putting a few inches between us. I can feel the tension in his body, the controlled anger. When he finally speaks, his voice is low, steady, his words firm, unyielding. "You are a strong, intelligent woman who deserves to be treated with respect and kindness."

"I know." A smile tugs at the corners of my mouth. "I know that now."

"Good." He pulls me to him. "Give me these lips."

I speak my reply against his mouth. "Yes, Captain."

Chapter 18
Griffin

When I wake, my bedroom is mostly still dark as usual because of my curtains. What is unusual is the petite woman next to me. She's nestled against my chest, her breath warm on my skin. My arm under her neck is half asleep, but I'm not going anywhere. I'd lose all feeling in my extremities before I moved.

Andi's revelation last night about her parents plays on a loop in my mind. The thought of anyone hurting her, especially those who should have protected her, stirs a fierce protectiveness within me. I want to shield her from the world, from anything that might cause her pain, and I reflexively hold her tighter. After pressing a kiss to the top of her head, I stroke my fingertips over her temple, sliding a few loose pieces of hair behind her ear.

She rouses, first with a flutter of her lashes and then a slight tightening of her muscles before she stretches and yawns. She tilts her head back to look at me, eyes all soft and hazy and utterly fucking adorable.

"Morning," she mumbles, and I trace her lips with my thumb.

"Morning."

"What time is it?"

I briefly pull away from her to grab my watch from the nightstand and buckle it around my wrist. "Quarter to eight."

"But since the kids aren't here, we don't have to get up, right?"

Her smile is hopeful, and while I'm not usually one to laze around in bed all day, I couldn't be paid to get up right now. Instead, I roll to my side and curl my arms around her. She snuggles back against me, her ass against my thighs, and while my cock likes it, I don't intend to make any moves for anything beyond this.

At some point late last night—after we talked more about Andi's parents and her grandmother, her childhood in Texas, and she finally divulged how my devil children tried to torment her—she slipped one of my T-shirts over her head, and I put my underwear back on to go to sleep. She said she's just not comfortable sleeping naked.

Which is perfectly acceptable.

Especially when what she does want is to be held like this. To have me roll locks of her hair between my fingers. To trace the contours of her body with my fingertips until she giggles. Her favorite thing, though, is a hand massage. I started doing it mindlessly, pressing my thumb and index finger into different spots on her hand while we talked, but as soon as I stopped, she simply held up her other hand and pouted.

I couldn't say no.

Obviously.

My girl gets what she wants.

So, I massaged her other hand too, this time with more effort. And the moan she let out was what led to me putting on another condom and telling her to get on top. It took a while for her to let go and figure out what she liked, but she eventually got there, riding me like a fucking champ.

It was a long night. A long and perfect night. So, I shut out thoughts of what this all means for us and my kids. I don't think about the future or how she may or may not feel about me. Instead, I dust kisses on her ear and neck and shoulder before laying my head on the pillow behind her, closing my eyes to sleep for a little while longer.

We get about twenty minutes before Cat leaps up onto the bed, meowing and stepping all over Andi. She laughs, nuzzling him. "Yeah, I know. I'm in the wrong bed. Were you looking for me?"

He paws at her, almost like he's answering in the affirmative, and she strokes his back.

"Sorry, I'll make you breakfast. No need to get sassy with me."

"Let him starve," I grumble as she rises, walking away from me. She shoots me a baleful look over her shoulder, but it quickly melts into a smile. One that's solidly in my top five. The playful one that she always tries to stop from growing by biting into her lower lip. It never works.

Much to my satisfaction.

"Come on," she says with a wave to me. "I'll make you breakfast too."

When I get up, I smack her ass. "No. I'll make you breakfast."

As Andi slips into the en suite, I head to the kitchen to give Cat his breakfast before jogging back upstairs. Leaning against the doorframe, I watch Andi rummage through my bathroom cabinet, helping herself to my toothpaste. She squeezes a dollop onto my toothbrush, tosses the tube back onto the shelf, and starts brushing her teeth as if she's done it a thousand times before. Strangely, I'm not grossed out. In fact, I find it oddly endearing, the way she's making herself at home in my space.

She catches my eye in the mirror, foam gathering at the corners of her mouth. "What?"

"Nothing."

She rolls her eyes but loses the battle with her smile. After she finishes, she hands me the brush for my turn while she splashes water on her face, the little baby hair around her temples wet. Once we're both finished, she tugs on my T-shirt that she wears, her legs bare. "Can I borrow another one of your sweatshirts?"

"You don't have to ask." I wave my hand toward my closet, and she helps herself, finding a hoodie to pull over her head. It hangs almost to her knees, and I reach out to tug on the strings. "My clothes look better on you anyway."

She blushes a pretty pink, and I don't hesitate to take hold of her face, my hands on either side of her cheeks, my tongue sweeping into her mouth. My new favorite way to wake up in the morning. Next to Andi, brushing our teeth together, kissing lazily. It's only when I smooth my hand up her thigh to her bare ass that she backs away from me. "You said you'd make me breakfast."

Her pussy is so much more appetizing, and I grunt unhappily. "I did, didn't I?"

Almost as if she can hear my inner thoughts, she laughs. "You don't have to make it."

"No." I cup the back of her head to kiss her once more. "You're getting fancy French toast."

"Ooh la la."

"We'll circle back to this later," I say, letting my fingers caress the curve of her ass and down to where she's bare beneath my T-shirt and sweatshirt.

In the kitchen, I plug in the portable griddle and add

cinnamon to the egg and milk mixture as Andi watches from the seat I insisted she take.

"I'm not sure any man has ever cooked for me before," she says quietly, like she didn't mean to admit it out loud.

I glance over my shoulder. "Is it wrong to say that makes me glad?"

She crosses her legs and sets her chin in her hand. "No. But why do you feel glad?"

I shrug, turning back to the task at hand. "Just do."

"That's not an answer."

As the French toast sizzles, I work on cutting up strawberries and a banana. "I hate that you've had the bad experiences you've had, but I'm not really sorry that means you sort of avoided men altogether. Because men are shit."

Behind me, she giggles. I don't think I'm particularly funny, but it makes me feel brand-new whenever I earn a smile or laugh. Although, I shouldn't be so impressed with myself since she laughs easily. Smiles even more.

"I don't need to go on dates or have sex to know that," she says. "But if men are shit, does that include you?"

I don't answer until after I've divided the fruit onto two plates and flipped the French toast. Then I face her, leaning against the counter. She's staring up with wide eyes, and I'd sooner break my own heart than break hers. "I've done shit things in the past."

"Like what?"

I fold my arms over my chest. "I don't know. The usual bullshit things guys do. Not returned calls and texts."

"You were a ghoster?"

I nod, not one ounce of guilt. "Got her name on a Saturday, never spoke it again after Sunday morning."

"Savage, Captain."

"I don't trust people," I say before I even really comprehend the words, and Andi tilts her head, studying me. She hums curiously.

I swing around to remove the French toast from the griddle and add them to our plates before retrieving the maple syrup and can of whipped cream from the fridge. I don't usually have it, but the shopping lists have been subtly changing since Andi has moved in, and now I have things like Reddi-Wip, Nutella, and salt-and-vinegar chips in my kitchen.

I spray a dollop of whipped cream on my fruit and a whole heap on hers. When I finally bring our breakfast over to the table, she lights up. "Very fancy. Thank you, Griff."

I like when she calls me that. That she feels comfortable enough with me to shorten my name.

We dig in, but she doesn't let the conversation drop. "You trust me, though?"

My mouth is full, so I can't talk, but even if I could, I don't know if I would. Too honest already. That I do trust her. Implicitly with my kids, and nearly wholeheartedly with me. I don't trust people not to leave or give up. But I do trust Andi not to, and it grows stronger with every passing day. Instead of saying all that, I merely nod, and she grins, spearing a piece of strawberry and French toast. "For the record, I think you're the best man I've ever known."

Before she can take her bite, I intercept her mouth, kissing my appreciation for her into it. I don't stop until her fork clatters to her plate, spraying whipped cream on her so that she shrieks. I chuckle and lick a few drops off her neck. "Delicious."

She swats at me, playfully ordering me to stay on the other side of the table until she's done eating. After we both finish our breakfasts and clean up, I receive a text from Taryn informing me she'll drop the kids off at noon, and I show the message to Andi.

She twirls her hair, a terrible actress, as she makes her

twang thicker. "So many hours to kill. Whatever will we do to fill the time?"

I know she's talking about sex, and, yes, but also... "Actually, I was hoping you could play something for me."

She drops her hands to her sides. "Really?"

"Yeah. I want to hear one of your songs."

"Okay," she says with a big smile. "I'll be right back."

Five minutes later, we're in the living room. Her on one end of the couch, guitar in hand, and me relaxed on the other end, facing her with one knee up on the cushions as she plucks a few chords.

She clears her throat. "I wrote this one a while back. It's... Well, you'll understand."

When she starts to play, I watch her fingers dancing over the strings, her voice filling the room. She sings of heartache and leaving home, leaving a piece of herself on the floor of her bedroom and in the reflection of the mirror. It might be interpreted to be about a breakup, but I know it's really about her parents. It's melancholy yet catchy, and the way she closes her eyes, body swaying slightly, is spellbinding. The way her voice cracks and goes off on different notes makes me smile. She strums certain chords, and it sends chills down my spine.

The song is beautiful, and when she finishes, I have to clear my throat, chest tight with emotion. "That was incredible," I say eventually. "You're incredible."

She stares down at her guitar, blushing as if she doesn't know. "Thanks."

"No, really. That was really good. I don't understand why you'd leave LA. I mean, you're obviously talented enough to make it big."

She snorts a laugh as she sets the guitar down. "Not really."

"What do you mean?" I lean forward. "You're amazing."

I'd heard the term fangirl before. Gracie says she's a Swiftie and a fangirl. Well, that's me. Fangirl. Whatever the Swiftie version for Andi is.

She redoes her hair, unraveling her messy bun only to redo it so it looks exactly the same, and I suspect it's to waste time. So I sit and wait. With a huff, she gives in. "It's all about who you know. Who you can get your foot in the door with. When I moved to LA, I didn't know anybody or what to do. I was so green, I was literally still putting my songs on CDs and dropping them off with the people at the front desks of record labels."

I frown. "What's wrong with that?"

"They get thrown in the trash, and no one uses CDs anymore."

I rub at my forehead, suddenly feeling one hundred years old. "It's not like you were using cassette tapes."

Andi's brows pinch. "What?"

I drop my head. "Oh my fucking god. Remind me what year you were born?"

She bursts out with a laugh and slaps my leg. "I'm kidding! I know what cassette tapes are. I'm not that young."

I sigh and meet her gaze. "Well, I feel that old."

She crawls into my lap, scratching at my stubble. "You're mature."

She's not making me feel particularly better, especially when she appears so young without makeup on. She's got freckles. *Fucking freckles.* They're dotted across her nose and cheekbones, faint but there, nonetheless. And those brown eyes of hers are so innocent. Makes me feel like a goddamn pervert when I focus on her lips and every thought I have is depraved.

"I'm a different generation," I grate out, and she shrugs. "So?"

She doesn't understand. Wouldn't get it. How it feels to inhabit the stereotype of a man going through a midlife crisis.

To do the math—multiple times—about how the age gap between her and me is close to what it is between her and my kids. Not to mention how Logan and Grace might feel if they ever found out.

Blinking a few times to clear my head, I meet her gaze and refocus the conversation. "What happened in LA?"

She takes a deep breath and starts talking. She tells me about how she met Dahlia and they started writing music together. How they'd do gigs, Andi playing guitar and Dahlia singing. Then she explains how she eventually got a job with the Ryder guy, some big-time producer who needs to be knocked around for how much of an asshole he is. How he belittled her, made her feel small, and eventually fired her at a party in front of important people, agents and other producers.

Who wouldn't be embarrassed by that? But I also hate the idea of Andi giving up on what she loves.

"You know, you're doing a great job with Grace, teaching her how to play."

Andi smiles proudly. "She's doing really well with it."

"What if you did that more? Teaching guitar to other people. You play the piano too, right?" When she nods, I keep going. I hadn't thought of it before, but now that it's out there, it makes sense. "There're music schools around here. Or you could do private lessons or something. Even songwriting. Is that a thing? Teaching someone how to write songs? Probably like writing poetry. You can either do it or you can't."

She laughs at my bumbling. "Yeah. There are classes about songwriting."

I raise my brows in a challenge. Right there is her answer. She can still make music. She can still make money from it. Might not be her original plan, but it's not nothing.

She considers me for a minute. "Yeah, okay. I'll look into it."

I palm her thighs, pushing her to straddle my lap, as I kiss her. Looking into it is not a promise of forever, but it could be the start of something. The start of Andi staying here, living here...with me. With the kids.

It could be the start of an *us*.

I kiss her again, deeper this time, my hands roaming her body. She's soft and warm, her skin smooth beneath my touch, and when I trail my mouth down her throat, I can feel her heart racing, matching the pounding in my own chest. I want to go slow, to savor every moment, but my body has other plans. I'm already hard, my cock straining under my shorts, eager to sink into its favorite place.

When I slide my hands up the T-shirt and sweatshirt of mine she's wearing to cup her breasts, plucking at her nipples, she arches into me. I love her tits. They're the perfect handful, and I push the cotton up so I can lavish them properly, licking, sucking, nipping until she's writhing beneath me, her hips grinding against mine.

Since she's not wearing underwear, I can feel her wet heat against my shorts, and since I spent so many hours learning what she likes last night, I have a hard time not skipping ahead. But even as she's becoming more and more comfortable with sex, I need to remind myself to go slow.

With the window right behind the couch, morning light streams in, highlighting all the things I love best about Andi, her swollen lips, her glittering eyes, and peaked little nipples, and I don't want anyone else seeing. I lift her up in my arms, snap the curtains shut, and carefully lay her down on the carpet.

"This is better," I murmur against her lips.

"Rug burn," she says with a smile in her voice as I kiss her throat.

"Don't worry. I'll be gentle." I'm completely serious even though she was joking.

"I know you will be."

I settle on my elbow and lift her shirt up a few inches so I can trace my fingertips over her lower belly and down between her legs. She inhales audibly, bending her knees to give me more room when I sink my index finger inside her, soaking it before circling her clit. She moans and tangles her fingers in my hair, pulling me down to her for a kiss, taking what she wants.

"Let's get you good and ready," I rasp into her mouth, and she relaxes even more, so I push my finger back into her, crooking it to find the spot that makes her cry out. I add my middle finger, stretching her, preparing her for me, telling her how perfect she is, how pretty she looks, how I am so hard for her, I'm not sure I can wait much longer.

Of course I would, though. I will always give her whatever she needs.

Fortunately, I don't have to be patient for long.

Her orgasm hits her hard, her body convulsing, her pussy clamping down on my fingers. I ride it out with her, my mouth never leaving hers, fingers stroking her through the tremors as she comes down.

Once she settles, I reach into the pocket of my shorts, happy I decided to toss a condom in there just in case and rip it open with my teeth.

Beneath me, Andi sucks air through her teeth. "I don't know why I find that so hot."

"Yeah?"

"Reminds me of a caveman or something, ripping apart meat with your teeth."

I press my mouth into a flat line, concentrating on pushing my shorts down to roll the condom on, pointedly not laughing.

"You think you could kill a mammoth for me?" she asks, and I notch myself against her pussy, feeling the intense pressure to slide home in one thrust, but I hold off. Barely.

"I could definitely kill a mammoth for you."

"With your bare hands?"

"Goddamn right."

She bites into her bottom lip, feminine satisfaction crossing her features, and that's it. That's all I can take. I push inside slowly, giving her time to adjust to my size. She's tight, her pussy gripping me like a vise, and I grit my teeth, fighting the constant urge to thrust, to claim, to *take*.

Once I'm finally fully seated inside her, I dip down to kiss her, my tongue mimicking the slow, steady pace I set as my cock slides in and out of her in long, languid strokes. She's wet and warm, and I groan into the crook of her neck. "Sweetheart, you make me feel like I can do anything."

"You can." Her teeth scrape my ear as she wraps her legs around me, her heels digging into my ass, urging me on. I speed up, my thrusts becoming more urgent. Still, I'm careful she doesn't get rug burn, which is hard when all I want to do is rut.

Be the caveman she wants me to be.

Fuck her hard and fast. One day, I will.

But today is not that day.

I sit back on my heels, staying inside her while I reach between us to strum her clit. I think the sudden loss of motion throws her for a loop, and she whines. "Griffin."

"Yeah, baby?"

"I'm so close."

"I know, so give it to me." She pants as I circle and rub and push her right up to the edge. "Come on. Be my perfect good girl."

That's when she loses it, her eyes flutter closed, inner muscles clamping on me, and I level myself back over her, thrusting once again, drawing out her pleasure, both of us riding out our orgasms until we collapse completely on the floor, a tangle of limbs.

Once I catch my breath, I snatch a tissue from a box on the coffee table and take care of the condom before holding myself above her, tugging her shirt and sweatshirt back into place. A soft smile plays on her lips. "No rug burns."

"Told you," I say with a nip to her lower lip. I spend a few moments taking her in, the blush on her skin, the mess of her hair, and I wish I had more time to revel in her warm glow, but I don't. "We should get dressed." I press a kiss to her forehead. "The kids will be home soon."

Andi groans, but she sits up, and I can't resist one last kiss, a sweep of my tongue along hers, before standing. I adjust the elastic of my shorts as I pick up my cell phone, a notification on the screen for a new email. Unlike Andi, who lets her emails pile up so much that my eyes nearly bugged out of my head when I saw she had over 3,000 in her inbox, I categorize each message as it comes in.

This one is a reminder from the school about the safety drill they're running tomorrow. I tense reflexively, a familiar anger bubbling up inside me. Andi apparently notices because she smooths her hand up and down my back. "What's wrong?"

I sigh, running a hand through my hair. "There's a safety drill at the school tomorrow. I just... I hate that they have to go through that."

"Safety... Like a shooter drill?"

I nod, and she winces. "Yeah, those suck."

"Gracie always gets so nervous, it takes a few days for her to calm down about it after, and you know Logan. He's so sensitive. I hate..." I grit my teeth and growl out my frustration. "I just fucking hate it."

I step away from her, my contempt for this particular blight on our society making me pace as I spit out my words. "I spent years—*years*—flushing out terrorists, making sure this country was safe. But then I had to come back to *this* country to find out it terrorizes our own kids because a few people like to wave the constitution around for gun rights and a well-regulated militia, pretending they'd have the balls to do what I did in the *real* militia."

Andi's eyes soften, and she steps closer, stopping me in my path. I draw up short, breathing through my nose to try to calm down as she molds her palms to my jaw. "You have every right to be mad about it."

Her touch drains the fight from me. "Why did I do all that? Why did my brothers and I go through all that? Some of them never made it back, and for what? Freedom?" I lift my arm out at my side. "Freedom to sacrifice students? Force them to hide in closets, scared for their lives?"

She wraps her arms around me, her head resting on my chest until my heart rate is back to normal. After seeing and doing the things I did during my service, I find it difficult to send my children out into the wide world to begin with. Add this ridiculous and easily solvable problem to the mix, and I resent it. It's not often I feel this way about my military career, but it's impossible not to see how this very American problem is the most un-American thing about our country. *Home of the free. Land of the brave.*

I could personally attest to that not being true.

Andi tilts her head back, her chin against my chest. "You are a good man, Griffin. The best man. And I hope you know you can talk to me about your time in the service whenever you want."

"I don't talk about it much," I say, soothing myself by dragging my hands up and down her back.

"I know, but if you ever want to. Talk to me." She rubs her fingers over my collarbone. "You take care of everyone around you. I hope you allow me to take care of you every once in a while."

Her words land like a punch in my solar plexus, and I nearly buckle under the force. My perfect, sweet girl. "You take care of me, sweetheart." I sweep my fingertip over the slope of her nose and then across her lips and down to her pulse at the base of her throat. "More than you know."

She smiles, and I capture her mouth in a soft, slow kiss, tender and full of promise. One that ends far too soon because we really do need to get dressed before the kids get home. "Better get moving." She tosses me a saucy wink as she struts out of the living room. "Can't get off schedule."

And for once, I wish we could.

Chapter 19
Andi

In the last week since Griffin and I spent the night together in his bed, I've slept in my bed downstairs every night, but on the days he was home from work, we spent a few hours together kissing and laughing and getting naked. At least until we had to pretend we didn't when it was time to pick up the kids from the bus stop.

I'd officially been their nanny and living in the Stone house for over a month. It's been amazing—after that slightly bumpy start, of course. I've slotted so easily into life here, and while I never thought I'd enjoy childcare, Logan and Grace are awesome kids. They're smart and funny and reveal things about myself that I didn't know. Like my hatred of folding any laundry that isn't my own and my reticence to relearn math skills but love of history. And how I'm more cut out for being a parental figure than I assumed.

It's the twins' birthday, and Logan has been begging his dad for a cell phone. Griffin has been resolute that they will not have cell phones until they're fourteen. Grace doesn't seem to mind since she has one best friend and that's about it, but

Logan is Mr. Popular. I know all his friends have cell phones because he's told me. Multiple times.

After dinner and cake, when the twins received their gifts—from me, sunglasses for Logan and a Taylor Swift shirt for Grace, from Griffin, fifty-dollar gift certificates to their favorite food places—Logan brings it up again, pointing out, "Aunt Taryn got Maddie a phone in fourth grade."

I thought the gift certificates were more than enough. While it wasn't the most personal gift, they're useful and perfectly Griffin, but Logan's still upset, unable to understand his father's side.

After a quiet moment, Griffin says, "Your cousin needed a cell phone. You're not in the same situation as her."

Logan throws his arms out to his sides. "But I can't Snap with Valentina!"

I can see Griffin holding his temper in check, ever careful not to raise his voice to his kids, even if they shout at him. "I don't know who Valentina is, but I swear to God, if you bring up the damn cell phones one more time, you won't see one until you're out of this house."

Grace tosses me a nervous look and scurries out of the kitchen just as Logan opens his mouth to argue again. Griffin lifts his hand, which silences his son immediately. "You wanna talk shit?" Griffins says quietly. Too quietly. Like the calm before a storm. "You'll go clean shit."

I don't know what that means, but I guess Logan does from the way he shakes his head.

"Go do your homework and chores," Griffin orders, and Logan stomps off, mumbling curse words I know Griffin pretends not to hear because there's no way he didn't.

Once we're alone in the kitchen, I move closer to him. "You wanna talk shit, you'll go clean shit?"

He answers without looking at me. "Scrubbing the toilet with a toothbrush. The consequence of talking back."

Tough but effective, and clearly a takeaway from his past life in the military. I would also assume the kids hate it and that it might make them resent him a little.

After a minute, Griffin's jaw slackens. "Was I too hard on him?"

I consider the question, wagging my head side to side. "I imagine it's not easy to be a kid in school without the thing everyone else has. I remember how that feels."

He grunts and spins around, glaring out of the window over the sink. I don't let him fume long, rubbing my palm over his back. "I also imagine it's hard to be a single parent and have to carry the weight of every decision alone, bear the brunt of the kids' emotions alone. Especially for someone who doesn't like feelings."

At that, he turns to me, his frustration melting, face softening. "Have to call me out like that, huh?"

"You were the one who said it first. That day you came home from work all cut up. We were in the bathroom, and you said you don't do feelings."

He squints. "I did, didn't I?"

"Not so true anymore?" I guess, and he bends, rolling his forehead against mine.

"Not true anymore."

I bunch his T-shirt in my fists and close my eyes. "It'll be hard for you and for them to figure out how to navigate this time. I don't think it'll get any easier. Logan wants to push boundaries and flirt and go out with friends. I predict Gracie will cry a lot, feel insecure and left out. You'll have to learn to be more open with them." I lean back to meet his gaze. "Like you are with me."

He blows out a long breath. Agrees with a scowl. "You're right."

I curl my lips over my teeth so I don't let my laugh escape, and he shakes his head like I'm naughty. When I do give in to a grin, he traces my lips before blinking as if a thought just occurred to him. "What the fuck is a Snap? And who the hell is Valentina?" I pat his shoulder patronizingly, and he grumbles. "Don't you fucking start with me too."

I pivot to put away the leftover cake, pushing my butt out. "Or what?"

When I glance over my shoulder, he's staring. "Or we'll see how much you like my hand making your ass red."

I bite my lip at the idea because I think I might like that. He raises his brows, reading my mind, and pulls me to him when I've got everything put away. "Tell me."

"Snap meaning Snapchat. It's social media. Kinda like texting."

He's legit angry about this. "Then why don't they just text?"

"Because...it's more fun," I say, but it sounds more like a question. How do you explain Snapchat to someone who doesn't use it? "You can send pictures and videos."

"Like you can with a text."

I roll my eyes. "I don't know, Griff. It's fun, okay? And a lot of people, especially kids, use it to talk to each other."

"Do you use it?"

I show him the app on my phone. "Yeah, but not a whole lot. See?"

I let him skim through it, but he's not impressed and places it back into my hand. "What about Valentina? Who's that?"

"A girl Logan likes. And if she's on Snapchat and he's not..."

Griffin sighs. "He's going to hate me."

"No, but you can talk to him about it. Explain your reasons for not giving them cell phones, for not wanting them on social media." With his focus somewhere over my shoulder, I make a suggestion. "How about we go to an amusement park tomorrow?"

He quirks his eyebrow, slowly bringing his attention back to me. "A what?"

"An amusement park," I repeat slowly, as if he's never heard the words before. "You can go on rides and play games. Usually there is ice cream and cotton candy. People go there for fun. Fun is a feeling people can have when they do activities they like."

He slaps my ass, and I gasp. "Griffin!"

"I warned you."

I fold my arms over my chest, but I'm no match for him. He hauls me up onto the counter, stepping between my knees, his hands gliding up and down my bare legs, fingers dipping under the hem of my cotton shorts.

"We're not really an amusement park family," he says, and I poke him in the chest.

"Well, you are now, because we're going. My treat."

"You're not treating."

"It's my idea. And you don't even like amusement parks."

"I never said that. I said we weren't an amusement park family."

I wave my hands between us. "Either way, you're getting me off topic. I think it would be really fun for all of us to go, and it would make really great core memories for the kids. You can go talk to Logan about the cell phone and tell him." When Griffin doesn't move, I nudge him. "Now, I mean. Go now."

He huffs with a squeeze to my calves. "You're awfully bossy when you want to be."

I sit up tall, my hands on my hips. "I am the nanny after all."

He shoots me a look of pure lust before backing away, waiting until the last moment to turn around and head to Logan's room, and I don't see anyone for the rest of the night because Griffin spends the next few hours alone with his kids. Which is pretty amazing, considering it's a Friday night and the newly anointed eleven-year-olds might want to hang out with their friends.

But at about ten o'clock, I receive a text from Griffin. One single word: **Thanks**.

The next morning, I'm woken up bright and early by Logan and Grace stampeding down the steps to the basement, shouting about how we're going to Hershey Park. According to their excited tail wags, it's going to take about an hour and a half to get there, and I have to hurry up and get dressed so we can be there when it opens.

"Dad already made a plan how to hit all the roller coasters!" Grace practically screeches.

Logan picks up Cat so I don't step on him. "My friends have gone and said it's so fun! There's a waterpark, too!"

"All right. All right. Let me get ready, and I'll meet you upstairs in twenty minutes."

They rush back up, both of them still going on and on about all the things they want to do and see, and I smile as I step into the shower, and I continue to as I brush my teeth and plait my hair into two braids.

When I make it upstairs in sneakers, denim shorts, a tank top, and a purse looped across my body, Griffin freezes midstride. His gaze roves over me, multiple times, and while I'm not wearing anything super revealing—maybe the shorts are a little short, but my Janis Joplin tank top isn't, especially with my sports bra under it—he can't seem to take his eyes off me.

"Something wrong?" I ask after a while, and he shakes his head as he rinses out his coffee cup. I would guess he's the only homo sapiens male to always put his dishes in the dishwasher instead of near it.

"You're hot," he tells me like it's a problem.

"I...thank you?"

"I'm old."

I swat at him. "We've been over this already. I don't care."

"Well, I do," he snaps then quiets because he obviously didn't mean to. "I... You could have anybody. Somebody closer to your age. I'm..." He's slow to meet my eyes, dragging them over the length of me like it pains him. "I'm going to be forty-three at the end of the year. I have two kids. You..." He starts to gesture toward the door but drops his hand. "Never mind."

"No." I leap at him, forcing him to keep going, linking my fingers with his. "Tell me. I want to know."

"I want you to stay. I want to be with you, but you shouldn't. You should go figure out what you want."

I have a hard time fighting my smile and press his hands to my heart. "I don't know what my future looks like, but I know I want you. I like that you're a dad, that you're going to be forty-three. I like that you take care of me and that you are a secure and thoughtful man. I know you think I should go out and have more experiences, but I don't need them to know how I feel about you."

He's hopeful. His eyes are bright and wide open, almost like he's allowing me to see everything he hides in himself. All his trepidation and worry. But I don't want him to fear what he feels for me, and I definitely don't want him to doubt what I feel about him.

He sucks in a breath, and when I think he's going to speak, he doesn't. Though, he does give me something just as good. Maybe better. Because he grins.

"I—"

Grace and Logan run into the kitchen, stopping me from telling him that I think I might be falling in love with him, and if they notice how close Griffin and I are standing or how we're holding hands, they don't mention it. All they do is yell about how they'll be in the truck.

I laugh and tug him toward the garage. "Come on!"

He grabs his keys and wallet, and we head out the door.

The conversation on the ride is lively, the tension between Griffin and Logan evidently squashed, which makes me really happy. Even happier when Grace picks me as the person she wants to sit with on the first ride. Logan calls me for the second. Griffin tips his head to me then and deadpans, "Third."

I giggle uncontrollably, my heart too full to contain it.

Hershey Park is bigger than I expected, with costumed candy people wandering around for pictures. The kids and I head right over to Kiss for a photo, which Griffin dutifully takes. For an uptight SEAL and fire captain, the guy can let loose when he wants to. He, of course, keeps us on a tight schedule, making sure we fit in as many rides as possible, constantly checking his watch and how far away the next attraction is, but he laughs and screams like the rest of us when we crest the top of every coaster. We don't go to the water park, but we do ride the log flume then stand on the bridge to get soaked by the even bigger boat ride. We dry off at a table in the sun while eating a lunch that consists of chicken fingers, fries, pizza, popcorn, and blue cotton candy, at my request.

After, Logan challenges his dad to a basketball shootout that Griffin lets him win, and then we all lose a water gun race. But it's a huge panda bear Griffin wins when he tosses a ball into a milk jug. He hands it right to Grace, who jumps up and down, barely able to hold on to the thing.

Without thinking, I curl my arm around Griffin's waist,

happiness flooding my veins, and lean my head against his chest. In response, he slings his arm around my shoulders in full view of the kids, who stare at us with matching head tilts.

"Is this okay?" Griffin asks, and Logan merely shrugs. Grace squints behind her glasses, making the same face her father does when he is seriously debating something. After a few moments, she nods and tries to hug me, but the panda gets in the way.

"Yeah. I'm okay with it."

I kiss the top of her head. Griffin kisses the top of mine.

And it's the best feeling I've ever had. Like being on top of the world.

Which I might as well be when we sit on the Ferris wheel at sunset, admiring the park below us, the neon lights shining around us. Next to me, Grace points out a direction she wants to go in to ride something else. Logan demands to go in the other direction. Across from me, Griffin watches his children bicker with a smile, looking like he has not a care in the entire universe.

Then he faces me, the breeze ruffling his hair, the corners of his mouth kicked up. He lifts his sunglasses off and tucks them in the collar of his shirt before leaning forward to kiss me. Since we have the kids' blessing, I don't feel bad about dragging my fingers over the scruff of his jaw and snaking my hand around the back of his neck, although we do keep it PG.

Once we part, he tugs on the end of one of my braids. "Thanks for making us do this."

"Thanks for letting me tag along."

"You're not tagging along. You're one of us now."

And almost as if the kids heard it and agree, they both shift over, Gracie leaning into my side, and Logan absently sticking his feet out to bracket mine. It reminds me of something a child might do with their mother, mindlessly wanting to touch her.

That could be my own desire talking, but it's the first time since leaving Dahlia that I've felt part of a family. One I think I might want to stay in forever.

Chapter 20
Griffin

By the time we get home, it's almost midnight, and the kids are passed out in the back of the truck. They're zombies, walking upstairs to their rooms, and I follow them up only to make sure they make it to their beds. With them both flopped on their mattresses in their respective bedrooms, I tell them I love them even if they can't hear me and stroke their heads. They're eleven now, but wasn't it only yesterday I was figuring out how to feed them both at the same time? Now Logan has a girl he likes and big plans for middle school next year. Grace has posters of female scientists and Taylor Swift all over her walls, along with a scattering of schoolbooks and printouts of music on the floor.

Time flies.

I make my way downstairs, double-checking the locks and that all the lights are turned off, thinking about the day we had. How much fun it was. How I should have been having days like this all along with my kids.

Guess I needed Andi to kick my ass into gear.

It's silent in the house, save for the quiet hum of the refrigerator, and I pause outside of the door to the basement, leaning my ear against it to hear if there is any sound.

It's slight, but I can tell she's moving around down there, and my heart pounds in my chest, remembering her admission to me this morning. I know I'll have to speak to the kids about it more, but I'm glad Andi and I don't need to hide what we have. We can figure out what we can be together and do it in the open. As a family.

I pad down the steps to the basement, where she's in the middle of pulling her shirt off, her back to me, hair out of braids and all crimped, falling below her shoulders, her back bare. She's so pretty. Too pretty. Like a delicate vase of flowers. Better to be admired than touched, but I can't help it.

I reach for her waist, and she startles, spinning around with her tank top covering her chest. "Oh Jesus."

"Not Jesus," I say, kissing the slope of her neck. "Griff."

She breathes a laugh and angles her head, allowing me more room to skate my lips up and down the column of her throat. "Mmm. Griff."

I gently suck on a spot she likes then nip at her earlobe, my teeth catching on her piercings. She sucks in a breath, and I pivot to walk her back toward her bed.

She releases her shirt and winds her arms around my neck as I lay her down, following after, holding myself up so I can mark all my favorite places, leaving red spots on her throat, the swells of her breasts, her stomach. She squirms underneath me, breathing heavy, and I hold her gaze as I pop the button on her denim shorts, quickly ridding her of them so she's only in a thong.

I exhale harshly, more like a growl, and her answering smile is pure sex. A temptress, she lifts her arms above her head, putting her body on display. As if I need any more of an invitation.

I place my hands on her thighs, admiring her, paying my tithes, offering my appreciation with every slow drag of my fingertips over her soft skin. Her nipples are peaked and begging for my mouth, so I bend, spending a long time praying there too. I don't stop until she's mewling and wriggling so much I have to stop to take hold of her hips.

"Settle, sweetheart."

"I can't," she whines, and I can't stop the smile crawling across my face. The one that makes her pout like *I* am the one torturing *her*.

But she's got it wrong. She's got it all wrong.

She is everything good and right in the world. Everything that turns me on. From the way she speaks, how her plump lips form words, to the way her voice lowers an octave and turns raspy when she says my name underneath me.

"Griffin."

I lower myself over her, my legs between hers, my forearms on either side of her head. I kiss her like I can pour every ounce of gratitude into her. Like she can taste it, feel it, know it in her bones. Her mouth is soft, pliant, opening to me as I trace the seam of her lips with my tongue. She sighs, combing her fingers into my hair, scraping her nails over my neck.

It sends goose bumps over my spine, tightens my skin, not to mention my balls. My cock is steel and aching, but I can't worry about myself now. Too busy memorizing her curves and valleys with my tongue, counting the freckles that dot her shoulders with my lips.

But I want more. Need more.

To taste her. Make her come undone.

"Andi," I whisper against her ear, trailing my hand over her shoulder to the side of her breast and down, spanning her stomach. My fingertips barely graze the shape of her under the cotton of her thong. "Let me put my mouth on you."

I feel her swallow when I kiss her throat, tension radiating through every inch of her. "I know you're nervous, but we'll go slow."

She molds her hands to each side of my face, forcing my head up so I meet her gaze. "What if you don't like it? What if—"

"There is nothing I want more. I've been dreaming about it. Your flavor and the way I know you'll sound when you come. There is no what-if. I'm going to love it, and I'll make sure you do too." I scrape my teeth over her collarbone, lowering myself down her body, brushing my thumbs back and forth over her nipples, sucking on the skin between them. "Please, baby. I need to."

I flatten myself to the bed, set my chin on her stomach, watching as she nibbles on her lower lip. I understand her unspoken words. No one's ever gone down on her. No one's ever made her come like that. The thought makes me want to hunt down every selfish asshole she's been with. But more than that, it makes me want to show her how good it can be. How good I can make her feel.

When she eventually agrees with a hesitant nod, I sit up. "Get your vibrator out." Her brows narrow in question, and I stand, staying close to the edge of the mattress and removing my T-shirt. "I told you. We'll go slow. So, before I put my mouth on you, I want to watch. I want to see what you do when you're on your own down here and I'm upstairs."

Her eyes widen as pink blooms on her cheeks, lips pressed together like she's nervous, even as she shifts to her hands and knees, pushing her ass out to me, glancing over her shoulder. Little minx.

She reaches over to her bedside table and pulls out the toy I saw the day we met, the same one that I accidentally powered on while I carried her bag. It's bright pink but transparent enough that I spot where the battery goes. It's thick and long and remarkably close to a real-life cock. Except for the small attachment clearly meant to stimulate her clit.

And I'm going to see her use it.

Lucky bastard.

Blood rushes south, and I remind myself to breathe, force my muscles to relax as she rolls back to the center of the bed and slips off her thong, flicking it at me. I shake my head at her, but my stern mask melts at her playful grin. As always, she pulls my own mouth into a semblance of a smile. I can't help it.

When she's happy, I'm happy.

But I try again and jut my chin out with an order. "Show me."

Naked and laid out like every one of my fantasies come to life, Andi turns on the vibrator, the soft buzz filling the room. She tentatively touches the head to her clit, then lower, rubbing the length of it along her slit, coating it in her wetness. She's still not as confident as I know she can be, still timid with her free hand close to her side, eyes closed.

That won't do.

"Open your eyes."

She does, and I nod, making sure my voice is even when I say, "I love watching you. See?" I swiftly drop my shorts and boxer briefs, wrapping my fist around my erection. "See what you do to me."

She watches as I pull on the length, echoing the movement with her own, swiping the vibrator along the seam of her pussy.

"That's it," I murmur. "Getting good and wet. So pretty."

She sucks in a breath I feel in my own chest as she pushes the tip inside her, and it would take my heart giving out for me to force my gaze from the image of her pussy swallowing the pink dildo. I lick my lips, transfixed, unknowingly moving closer to her until my knees hit the bed.

"Oh fuck, Andi. Fuck me, this is... This is the hottest thing I've ever seen in my life. You are perfect."

Her eyelids flutter, tits rising and falling rapidly, that arm that was previously at her side is stretched out, fingers aimlessly pulling at the bedsheet. She's getting worked up, starting to forget about her nerves, and that's exactly what I want.

I want her to let go, ignore me and what I may or may not be feeling and thinking, and concentrate on herself. On how she feels. On what she wants. On how close she is to reaching the peak.

I stay quiet, even as it's hard not to praise her for being brave and beautiful and better than anything I could have dreamed. But I don't want to pull her out of the daze she's in as she fucks herself with the vibrator, the little attachment hitting her clit. She must find the place she needs because her back arches, skin flushing red, and she slaps her left hand to her breast, pinching and tugging at her nipple.

Her brow pulls down, head thrown back, quiet, short moans coming from her open mouth, pursed in an O. I stroke myself in time with her movements, matching her rhythm. The faster her breath comes, the faster mine does as well. Her whimpers grow louder, my hand works quicker. We're both racing toward orgasm, and I try as hard as I can to hold back, keep my eyes open to watch Andi crest the wave first.

Her body tenses as she cries out, her release crashing over her. I follow her over the edge, my cock pulsing in my hand as I come, her name on my lips, and I slump over, catching my breath, finally allowing my eyes to close, my heart rate slowing.

It takes a minute to recover, and I stand upright again to see the vibrator tossed aside, her body limp and mine for the taking. I wipe my hand on my discarded T-shirt then dive between her legs, wrapping my arms under her thighs, keeping her in place.

I can smell her arousal, delicious. See it glisten on her skin, mouthwatering.

"Hands on my head," I say, lips brushing the thin line of hair, damp with her desire. "Direct me. You're in charge."

Andi's throat bobs on a swallow, her fingers tentatively combing into my hair. Holding her gaze, I trace the outline of her pussy with my tongue. She gasps, her hips jerking reflexively before easing again when I tighten my grip. Then she fists her fingers in my hair, and I reward her with the flat of my tongue over her clit.

She sighs, more pliable tonight than last week, and I hope that means she's trusting herself more, realizing she can have whatever she wants, if only she allows herself to. She should know by now, I will give her whatever she needs and wants—my fingers, my mouth, my cock.

My whole goddamn heart.

It beats wildly in my chest when her belly tenses, head lifting off the pillow, as she rasps, "I need... I need..."

"What?"

"Your hand."

"Attagirl." I slide my middle and index fingers inside her as I suck on her clit, making her thighs quiver and her inner muscles clench. Stroking in and out, I focus on the swollen spot that makes her cry out.

Her own hands squeeze, holding me to her, hips writhing, showing me the rhythm and strength she needs. I'm so proud of her for asking for what she wants, and when she hisses out a low *yes*, I hum my approval.

She comes again, body convulsing, hands gripping my hair tightly. I ride out her orgasm with her, my tongue softening, my touch gentling as she settles down, and when she finally stills, I press a soft kiss to her clit, then move up her body, gathering her in my arms.

She groans, eyes heavy, limbs loose, but she smiles when she turns to me, swiping her palm over my mouth. "You have…"

"You all over me?" I guess, then kiss her, permitting her no time to be embarrassed. "Did you enjoy yourself?"

"I think you know I did."

I tuck her head beneath my chin. "You're right. Just want to hear you say it."

"I loved it."

Warmth spreads from my chest outward, thickening the blood in my veins, and I have to clamp my jaw shut to keep the words from escaping my mouth. *I love you.*

"Sleep now," I say, pulling the comforter over us. "I got you."

Andi yawns and settles against me, soft and sleepy, one hand curled under her chin, the other on my chest.

She falls asleep easily.

I don't. I stay awake, learning what it's like to live with my heart split three ways. For Grace, Logan, and now Andi.

I used to believe life is too precious to fuck it up with something as capricious as feelings. Now I know life is too precious not to feel it all. Because this time with Andi is worth any possible heartache. Today, with my family, their smiling faces are the reward for the difficult things I've been through in my life. I can't have the good without the bad, but I know there is so much more good, if only I allow myself to accept it.

Chapter 21
Andi

I wake up cold, blindly reaching for the covers, pulling them up over my naked shoulder, intent on going back to sleep, but my nose itches and I have to pee. Cracking my eyelids open, I remember last night, Griffin watching me bring myself to orgasm before he did with his mouth. I recall falling asleep, wrapped up in his arms, and the feel of his skin on mine making it so easy to drift off.

But he's gone. I sit up, my sunshine lamp cloaking my little basement apartment in hazy, fake morning light. Griffin is nowhere in sight, and I check the time. It's after eight o'clock, and he's probably been up for two hours already. His unfailing daily schedule is a reassurance as much as it's a disappointment. Because I'd rather him be here with me in bed.

Even though he was with me all night.

A melody circles my brain, and I hum as I use the bathroom. Try out a few words as I brush my teeth and wash my face. Start to put it together as I toss on shorts and one of Griffin's hoodies. I've pilfered three of them now, not including the zip-up he gave me on the day we met.

Soon, my whole closet will just be his clothes.

I like that line and open up a notebook, jotting down lyrics about refusing to give back his sweatshirt like I refuse to give back his heart. As I strum a few chords, it comes together, a song about making a home with a man. The words flow easily once I get going, and before I know it, three hours have passed, and I only stop at the sound of footsteps on the staircase.

I look up to see Griffin, dressed in navy-blue work pants and polo shirt with the fire station's emblem on the chest. His eyes soften, a small smile playing on his lips, his voice a low rumble. "Morning."

"Morning." I smile back, and he leans down, pressing a soft kiss to my lips. It lingers, and I can feel the promise of more in it, but he pulls away too soon.

"Your song sounds good."

"Yeah?"

He nods, pride shining in his eyes. "I wish I could stay and listen, but I've got to head out. Logan's in the living room. Grace is in the kitchen."

I set my guitar down then and stand to circle my arms around his torso, my cheek against his chest, his heartbeat steady under my ear. He kisses the top of my head as he smooths his hands up and down my back. Both of us are quiet for a long time, and I don't think either one of us wants him to go, but he has to, eventually stepping away from me with his hands around my biceps.

"What are your plans today?" he asks, and I shrug.

"I was thinking about taking the kids downtown to hang out for a bit. I need to pick up a few things."

He kisses my cheek and then my mouth. "Be safe. Have fun. Text me tonight to check in."

"Yes, Captain," I say against his mouth, and he growls with a light slap to my butt before pivoting to head upstairs. I follow him, standing at the door, watching him leave like some 1950s housewife before making myself a smoothie with the chocolate protein powder he specifically bought for me since he thinks I don't eat enough.

I find the kids, and they agree to do some shopping with me, so we all pile into my Jeep an hour later. I'd taken it upon myself to liven up Griffin's house. Little by little, I've made changes, small as they are. Like adding fun magnetic tiles to the fridge to make words, buying decorative hand towels for the powder room and a cute gnome doormat for the front door. Today, I'm on the hunt for picture frames to place around the house. I accidentally found some old family photos buried in a closet, and I thought it would be nice to have them displayed.

At the request of the kids, our first stop is Sweet Cheeks Bakery, where we munch on the most delicious cinnamon buns I've ever had then pop right next door to Stone Ink. Ian greets us and shows me around his tattoo shop, trying to talk me into some ink. I tell him another time and leave with a hug to Griffin's brother, a testament to how I've been accepted by not only Griffin and the kids, but by their extended family as well.

Next, we head over to Chapter and Verse, where the kids separate. Grace goes to the nonfiction section, while Logan doesn't seem all that interested in books and sits in the corner to pet the store cat, leaving me to browse through the poetry and music books. I pick out Cher's memoir and a small collection of poetry by a Palestinian woman and set them on the check-out counter as I hear familiar voices calling my name.

I turn to see Marianne and Clara and hug both of them. "How are y'all doing?"

"We're good," Marianne says, waving to the woman behind the counter, who begins to ring me up. "How've you been?"

"Great," I answer honestly.

Clara beams and motions to the kids. "Everything working out well with the job?"

"Yeah."

"And our favorite fire captain?" My cheeks heat at Clara's question, and she teasingly knocks my arm. "Ooh, I knew it! I knew you two would be good together." She puts her hand on the side of her mouth, stage-whispering in booming surround sound, "In more ways than one."

Marianne puts her arm around her wife, quieting her. "What she means to say is we're happy you're happy."

I am *so* happy. Because of Griffin, the kids, and the kindness of the local community, it's all more than I could have ever hoped for.

"What about you?" Clara asks the woman who hands me a paper bag with my books. "How's that husband of yours?"

I step to the side so Marianne can pay for her book as the woman turns red. "Oh, you know..."

Clara leans in, suspicious. "Haven't seen him around in a long time."

"He's really busy."

Clara nods sarcastically, but I don't think the woman notices, her eyes cast down as she punches a few buttons on her computer keyboard.

"Well, you know if you ever feel like treating yourself, maybe giving your husband a little something to...motivate him, you can stop over to Lux any time. Friends and family discount," Clara tells her and then winks at me. "Same goes for you."

I laugh and thank the woman, following Marianne and Clara out of the door, Logan and Grace trailing a few steps behind, and now that I'm one of them, I need the tea.

"What's the story there?" I ask Clara, and she lowers her voice, slipping her hand around my elbow.

"That's Nicole Kelly, so great. So lovely. Has a bit of a grown-up Rory Gilmore vibe."

I nod. "Yup. Got that."

"And her husband has a bit of a grown-up Logan vibe."

I jerk my head back. "Why do you say that like it's a bad thing? Logan was the best boyfriend."

Clara pulls her hand away from me like I'm covered in slime. "We can't be friends anymore."

I laugh. "So, what? He's rich and hot?"

"Definitely not rich. He's good-looking in a beige sort of way. He's a professor at the college and treats Nicole like..."

"Like she's disposable," Marianne fills in, and I shake my head.

"That's too bad." Especially because I know what it feels like to be put first. And not for the first time today, I smile simply because I'm thinking of Griffin.

"We were going to get some sushi for lunch," Marianne says. "Do you want to join us?"

I turn to the kids, who wandered off to the corner. "Hey, you want sushi for lunch?"

Clara holds out her hand to Logan, and he immediately walks to her so she can wrap her arm around his shoulder, and I have a feeling he's got a bit of a crush on her from the way his cheeks turn ruddy. "Yeah, I could eat sushi."

Grace shrugs and takes my hand when I offer it as we all walk down the street, spending an hour yapping and laughing.

Later that night, with Logan and Grace in their rooms, I'm spread out on the living room floor, surrounded by photos and frames, when my phone rings. I answer the FaceTime call, propping the phone against a pile of books on the coffee table, and Dahlia's face fills the screen, her smile wide and eyes sparkling.

"Hey, I—"

"I got a record deal!" my best friend screams without preamble, and I scream too, jumping to my feet.

The kids race down from their rooms, Logan with a hairbrush and Gracie wielding a textbook. I laugh when I spot them, ready to protect me with their weapons of choice. With tears in my eyes and emotion swirling in my chest, I pull them to me.

"Are you okay?" Logan asks, squirming away from my hold, checking me over in a pretty good impression of his father. "You're not hurt?"

"No, I'm not. Just excited." I turn my cell phone so they can see the screen. "This is my best friend, Dahlia. She called to give me some really exciting news. She signed with a record company. Dahl, these are my kids, Logan and Grace."

"Hi." Logan is unimpressed, his shoulders dropping now that he doesn't have to go to war with anyone.

Gracie exhales heavily and waves to Dahlia. "Congratulations."

"Thank you, honey. I'm so happy to meet you." She's grinning so wide I fear her face may never go back to normal. She has a huge extended family, super comfortable with kids, but with her floating off on cloud nine, I'm surprised she's even having this conversation. "Andi's told me so much about you."

Grace clings to my side when I sit on the couch, and I motion for Logan to join us. With the kids on either side of me, I set the phone back up and tell her to give us the rundown.

She informs us of all the shows she's been playing the last few weeks, the growth of her social media after one of her songs went viral, and finally, how she's been talking to an executive at Blue Note.

"She came to see me at the gig last night and then asked for a meeting today," Dahlia explains, and I press my hands to my cheeks.

"I can't believe it. It's finally happening."

"Finally!" she agrees with a laugh.

"What's Blue Note?" Logan asks, and I loop my arm around his shoulders.

"This record company with a really great track record for signing amazing artists. They'll produce Dahlia's album and then hopefully put her on tour."

Gracie leans forward, pushing her hair behind her ears and fixing her glasses. "What kinds of songs do you sing?"

"A little of this, a little of that," Dahlia says, and I butt in.

"Folk-rock with a bit of a Mexican influence."

Grace has no idea what I'm talking about.

"I'll play you some later," I promise, and she nods.

Dahlia goes on. "They want to start recording next month."

"Next month?" I echo, surprised. "That's so soon."

"I know, right?" Dahlia laughs. "But they've got a whole plan mapped out, and I'm not about to slow them down."

I can't help but feel a pang of envy. She's made it. She's found the yellow brick road. Meanwhile, I'm nowhere close. Even if I love the life I've found here in West Chester, I still wonder what it would be like if my time in Los Angeles had been different for me. It feels like a punch in the gut to miss out on what could have been.

And I hate myself for it.

I try pushing all those bothersome feelings aside. "This is incredible, Dahl. I'm so proud of you."

"I couldn't have done it without you. Without you, there would never be me."

I don't know what to say, so I stay quiet as the kids ask questions about the music industry and what it's like to perform onstage. Dahlia answers them patiently, her passion for music shining through, as hopelessness takes root in my stomach. Hard as I try to rip out the weeds, they immediately grow back, so fast that I can't keep up with the conversation, my mind too busy imagining Dahlia's success and my dreams dead. Flattened in the middle of the road. Crushed by the foot of an ogre. Smashed under hooves at a ranch.

Soon, Dahlia is saying she needs to go because Vic is taking her out to celebrate, and I think I promise to talk later, but I can't be sure. I press the red button to end the call before looking to Grace and Logan, who both watch me with matching questions in their eyes, eyebrows pinched.

"Are you mad?" Logan guesses, and I shake my head.

"Happy?" Grace guesses, and I nod.

"But you look a little sad," Logan adds, and I shrug.

Then, moving together, they both hug me.

Grace lays her head on my shoulder. "It's okay to be sad. That's what you told me the other day when I was crying."

I rub my hand on her back, blinking at my tears. "You're right."

Logan loosens his grip around my waist to back away, meeting my gaze. "Last year, my friend got to be point guard even though I really wanted to be that position. But I got really good playing forward, and this year, we won almost every game."

I sniffle. "Yeah, sometimes our friends will be better than us at things we love. We just have to realize that doesn't make us any worse, or let it get in the way of our friendship, right?"

They both nod and hug me again before I send them back off with kisses to their heads. I follow them to the bottom of the staircase. "Sleep good."

They turn over their shoulders, and I swear with how they act now, I never would have guessed they're supervillains because they both smile at me, saying together, "We love you."

I press my hand to my chest, right over where it cracked open. "I love you too."

Once they're upstairs with their doors closed, I bend over, letting the tears flow. Love and heartbreak. Guilt and pride. Gratitude and anger.

It all comes pouring out of me, and it's not until a long time later that it stops.

Chapter 22
Andi

I'm curled up in the living room, staring at the screen saver of Beyoncé in her Cowboy Carter glory on my laptop, when the back door opens. Shoes thump on the floor, keys land in the bowl, bag is placed on the counter, and then Griffin is behind me, wrapping his hands around my face, tipping my jaw so he can kiss me upside down.

"It's so quiet in here." He lets go of me to round the couch and sit next to me. "It's never this quiet."

I turn to face him, and he frowns.

"What's wrong?"

I feel so foolish to still be sulking all these hours later, but I can't seem to make sense of any of my emotions. I've pretty much been sitting here since I dropped the kids off this morning.

"What happened?" he asks. "When you texted last night, I figured everything was fine. You were sorting photos or something."

Wordlessly, I stand to retrieve the gift bag and handful of frames and pictures I put together and hand them to him. Then

I slump right next to him, leaning against his side with my feet under my butt. He lifts his arm so I can snuggle even closer as he sets the photos down on his lap, lifting each one up at a time.

The first is a picture of Griffin with Logan and Grace as toddlers, both of them holding on to each of his pinkies, all of them walking toward whoever was taking the picture. It's adorable.

The next one is Griffin and his siblings at some kind of picnic when they were younger. I point to the little boy. "That's Roman, I assume."

He grunts an affirmative and moves to the next one, him in a cap and gown, an unsmiling high school graduate. So serious even then.

He sets down the photos then opens the gift bag, pulling out the four frames of a photo I reprinted. It took a bit of research to find a place that would restore the picture and blow it up from a 4x6 to the 10x12s I got made for Griffin and his siblings. I thought it was too beautiful for them not to have.

Griffin releases a gruff sound from the back of his throat when he sees his mother, a bright smile on her face. She must have been in her twenties, leaning her chin in her hand, a book open in front of her, and almost out of frame with the window directly behind her, the sunshine backlighting her.

And the only reason I knew it was his mother is because of what her children look like when they smile. Though a rarity, they have the same exact smile as Violet Stone.

"I hope it's okay that I framed this. I thought you'd like it. You and your brothers and sister. I made one for each of you. I don't know how much they have of your mom, but..." It seems silly now, maybe even stepping over the boundary. Assuming. "I'm sorry."

"No." He sniffs and clears his throat. "It's perfect. Thank

you." He slants his watery gaze to me. "Where did you even find it?"

"They were all thrown together in a box in the hall closet upstairs. You probably forgot you even had them since they were behind a bucket of cleaning supplies."

"Definitely forgot," he says, and I drag my fingertip over his mother's smile. From the snippets of his family I've gleaned, I know his father is not in his or his siblings' lives and that their mother passed away from a stroke a long time ago...fifteen years or so. I also know Griffin well enough to recognize that these stuffed-away photos represent how he stuffs away his feelings. He doesn't want to face what he feels. What he lost.

His beloved mother.

"She was beautiful."

"She was." He inhales audibly and raises his chin toward the ceiling, his voice like gravel when he quotes, "'Doubt thou the stars are fire; Doubt that the sun doth move; Doubt truth to be a liar; But never doubt I love.'"

"Shakespeare?"

"Hamlet." He lowers his gaze to mine, his eyes rimmed red. "That line was her favorite. When she'd write letters to me, she'd sign them, never doubt I love."

I gasp, making the connection of the ink I've noticed on his ribs, a long line in delicate cursive, almost like someone wrote it on his skin. "That's your tattoo."

He nods. "In her handwriting."

Below it are the kids' initials with their birthdate, and I shift away to lift his T-shirt, finding the quote, tracing the letters with my fingertips, my eyes burning with his shared lingering grief. I swallow the lump in my throat. I don't know what it feels like to lose a parent, but I know what it feels like to mourn the loss of what could have been. I also know how I've come to feel about Logan and Grace in such a short amount of time, and if it is one-third of what Violet felt about her children, I can understand the sentiment. There is nothing more true. No doubt about my love.

"We all have them," he tells me quietly. "Me, Taryn, Roman, and Ian. We all have tattoos for her. It was one of the few things we did all together after."

I don't know what else to say besides, "She loved you so much. Still does." Then I cup the back of his head and kiss him, comforting him as best I can. He sets down the photos next to him and hauls me into his lap, skating his hands under my T-shirt, warming my skin. I mold my hands to his jaw, licking into his mouth. His tongue tastes faintly of coffee, reminding me that I haven't had anything to eat yet today. My stomach growls, and so does Griffin. "You didn't eat today?"

I shrug. "Forgot."

"Let's get some protein in you." He stands with me in his arms—I'll never not love that—and sets my feet on the floor, tugging me to the kitchen, where he gets busy building chicken and hummus wraps, setting them on plates with my favorite salt-and-vinegar chips and some mixed berries. I accept the plate he offers me and settle across the island from him. We stand, eating in silence, watching each other, and it should probably be awkward, his dark gaze on me while I stuff my face, but it's not. I don't mind.

Especially because it seems to make him happy I finish everything. Once we're both done, he asks, "What's got you so upset you forgot to eat?"

I pick at the edge of the plate, trying to gather my thoughts. "Dahlia called me yesterday."

Griffin furrows his brow. "Okay?"

"She got a record deal." I say it quietly, trying to keep the bitterness out of my voice. I am happy for her, truly, but it's hard not to feel a pang of envy.

"And you're upset about it."

I force a smile as my eyes sting with tears. "I'm happy for her. So happy."

"But...?"

"But I feel like I missed my shot, you know? I went to LA for a purpose. To be a songwriter. To have a career with Grammys and money, and now..." I stare down at the striations in the marble top, unable to meet his gaze. "I never did it. I'm not going to do it. I'm just a nanny."

"Come here." He pulls on my hand, towing me around the island and into his body. I go willingly, burying my face in his chest, wrapping my arms around him. His heart beats steadily against my ear, a comforting rhythm. "You're not just a nanny. You're so much more than that. To me, to the kids."

"I know. And that's what makes it so confusing. I'm devastated about my career, but at the same time, I love being here and taking care of the kids. I love living in this town, and I can see myself being here long-term." I lean my chin on his breastbone, looking up at him. "Last night, the kids told me they love me, and I..." I bite my lip as my eyes sting. "It felt better than anything else in life."

He blinks slowly, though he doesn't seem as surprised that his kids told me they loved me. The worried crease between his eyebrows eases, and he sweeps his hands up to my face, holding my cheeks between his palms, burying his fingertips in my hair. Then he simply stares at me. For a long time.

His eyes drift between mine then down to my lips, where he glides his thumbs over my mouth. He studies me like one might study a painting, perhaps looking for imperfections or elements that make it unique. But he is the one with enigmatic features, near impossible to understand how he's feeling.

His mysterious smile flattens when I place my hands on his

wrists, nudging his hands away from me. "Tell me about their mom."

Griffin's eyes widen slightly, but he nods and takes a step back, busying himself with cleaning up our plates as he starts. "Her name was Beth. We met at a bar while I was on leave and in a really dark place." He shuts the dishwasher then pivots to lean against it, his arms crossed, gaze cast down. "My team had been on a mission, and one of my best friends died."

I don't dare reach for him, even though I want to. I don't want him to stop talking to me, explaining his past. It's good for him and for us.

"I got caught up and wanted to forget, I guess." He stops to clear his throat. "We found out she was pregnant right before I was deployed again, and we decided to get married before I left. We weren't even together four months, but I wanted to do right by her. I promised myself I wasn't going to be like my dad. I wouldn't leave or let her or my children down. I couldn't do that to her or them."

He clears his throat again, this proud man visibly uncomfortable at whatever he perceives he did wrong, and I hate that for him, but I wait for him to finish his story. "She went into labor while I was away. By the time I got there, she was already gone. Complications of eclampsia." He swipes his hand over his mouth. "I had two babies and no idea what to do. So, I left the service and came home."

After a minute, I move to him, placing my hands on his shoulders, squeezing until he loosens his crossed arms to hold on to my waist. "I'm sorry for your losses—for your mom and Beth. It's a lot to carry."

I stand up on my toes to place a chaste kiss on his mouth, but he doesn't let me back away. He keeps me close, one hand twisting the fabric of my T-shirt at my waist and the other around my neck. His exhale is shuddering, and I know he must feel wrung out, how much it takes for him to open up like that. It's not natural for him, and I couldn't love him more for offering it up to me. Letting me inside his heart to all the shadowy places.

"I could use a shower," I say, with a nod toward the staircase. "And I'd like to see just how big yours is."

I take his hand, leading the way upstairs to his bedroom and through to the en suite, where I start the shower then strip off my T-shirt and shorts. Griffin's gaze is hot on my skin, blazing a trail over my shoulders, breasts, and stomach before settling between my thighs. I squeeze my legs together, impatient for him to take off his clothes, although he's in no rush as the steam begins to swirl around us.

So, I do it for him.

Griffin fights a smile, his mouth pressing into a line that reluctantly twists up when I push his arms toward the ceiling, only to struggle lifting his T-shirt up his long torso and over his head. He's over a full foot taller than I am, and I have to shove him down to get it off, earning a quiet snicker. When he stands up straight again, he pulls his shoulders back like a soldier, allowing me to fully take in the planes of his muscles and the tattoos decorating them. I trace the lines on his left arm, up to his bicep with a pyramid and other Egyptian symbols—because he apparently used to be obsessed with ancient Egypt as a kid, a self-proclaimed nerd when he was younger—then over to the tiger—"I thought I was a tough guy and wanted people to know it" on his pec—where I flick my thumbnail over his nipple. In response, he grips my hip hard but otherwise stays still, his liquid gaze on me as I explore the thick ropes of his arms and the lines of his abdomen.

Hooking my fingers around the elastic of his athletic shorts, I pull them down and sink to the bath mat, kneeling between his feet. From this position, I tilt my head up, finding him breathing hard. Every exhale sounds pained, but I keep going, peeling his boxer briefs down his thick legs and tossing them to the side before curling my hands around the backs of his thighs.

His cock is hard and heavy, leaning out toward me, and while Griffin has never made me feel like I owed him anything, I do want to show him how I can make him feel as good as he makes me feel. I want to taste him, see him come undone because of me.

"Andi," he rasps, and I slide my hands up to his butt, squeezing lightly as I shuffle forward on my knees, close enough that the tip of his length touches my mouth, and his jaw goes tight, his words barely audible. "You don't have to."

"I want to." I tentatively wrap my hand around him, the soft skin over hard steel, and look up at him. His eyes are so dark they appear black, and he's watching me with an intensity that makes me shiver. I experimentally drag my fist up and down, from root to tip, thinking about the last time I tried to do this, and it took so long, the guy actually sighed, like he was bored. Not great for my self-esteem.

"You're gonna have to tell me what to do," I say and press a kiss to the head, right over the slit, then lick my lips, sampling the salt pearling there again already. I flatten my tongue and lick that up as well before growing a bit bolder to take more of him in my mouth.

Above me, Griffin groans, his fingers digging into my hair. "Keep your eyes on me, sweetheart."

I do, shifting so I can stare up at him even as my eyes water when I take him a little too deep. He's gentle when he curves his palm over my jaw and throat, even as he tells me, "Do that again."

I inhale through my nose and draw him to the back of my throat, more prepared this time, but it's not like it helps. I haven't been with a lot of guys, and Griffin's big, long and thick, and I have trouble being as ladylike as I want to be. When spit slips out of the side of my mouth, he nods, color rising high in his cheeks.

He likes it.

He likes me being messy.

And the idea is as freeing as it is empowering.

I think merely having my mouth on him would make him happy, but me letting go is what makes him feral. The gagging sounds and slippery mess are what makes him breathe faster and harder. It makes his grip tighten on me. It makes him thrust his hips ever so slightly, like he just can't not move.

"I dreamed about this," he grits out, muscles tense. "I imagined your puffy lips around my cock, exactly like this, and fuck, baby, it feels so goddamn good."

I preen under his praise, goose bumps racing along my skin in the humid air as desire pools in my core. Keeping one hand around him, I slip the other between my legs, dragging my fingertips over my aching clit, and Griffin tosses his head back to the ceiling, "Fuck yes. Touch yourself. Come with me."

I didn't realize how wet I was, how turned on, and it doesn't take me long to get there, tipping over the edge with fast circles of my fingers. I groan around his cock, bringing his eyes back to mine. "You gonna let me come in your mouth?" When I nod my answer, he clenches his jaw. "Atta-fucking-girl."

He orgasms, hot spurts coating the back of my throat and tongue, and I have to close my eyes, reminding myself to breathe as I gag again, but when he finishes and I open my eyes to him, swallowing his orgasm, he wastes no time hauling me up off the floor. Brushing his thumbs over my cheeks to wipe away the wetness, he laughs, genuinely. "Jesus, Andi, you need to come with a warning label. Fucking break my heart and my dick."

I laugh too, a little dazed as he unclasps my bra and pushes down my underwear before scooping me up to take me into the shower. While his shower is bigger than my little stand-in downstairs, it's not as big as the one in my fantasies. But Griffin is even better.

We take turns soaping each other up, and he's careful not to get my hair wet when I tell him it's not my hair-wash day, which I then have to explain. His eyes crinkle with amusement as he shakes his head in exasperation.

"You'll have to get used to it," I say, meaning he'll have a teenage girl living in the house soon, but he doesn't take it that way.

Instead, he wraps his arms around my waist, lifting my feet up off the tub's floor to kiss his understanding into my mouth. "I'm ready when you are."

Like he's only waiting for me to say the words.

I love you.

Chapter 23
Griffin

When the timer on my watch goes off, I carefully lift Andi's feet off my lap and stroke my fingertips down her cheek. She fell asleep in the middle of reading a book she picked up from Chapter and Verse, some collection of Middle Eastern poetry that she's slowly making her way through, highlighting certain lines and dog-earring other pages. In the last two days, we'd taken to reading together in the afternoons, and I hope we'll continue to.

Since I came home from work Wednesday, and she sucked my soul out of my dick, I've been attached to the girl like a barnacle. Probably because she owns me now. Got my heart in her back pocket.

She's joked about how I've been following her around. Even the kids noticed, making comments this morning about me needing to stop pretending I'm not creeping back up to my bed in the morning, when I assume they're asleep and can't hear me.

I suppose my stealth skills aren't what they used to be if I can wake my tween children at six in the morning. Then again, maybe it's a subconscious thing. Maybe I'd like my kids to figure it out, notice I've been sleeping in Andi's bed and be okay with it.

Because what I really want is for Andi to sleep in my bed. To move all her things upstairs. Have her hair ties on my nightstand and her sweet-smelling shampoos and soap in my shower. Her cowboy boots next to my work boots. Her cute little slip-on sneakers next to my HOKAs. Like I told her, I'm ready.

Her eyes flutter open, finding mine after a few seconds, and she leans into my touch. "I fell asleep."

"You did." I smile, another crack in my chest. It's been happening more and more. Every smile I let free tears down another brick from my wall. Pretty soon, there won't be any protections left, and all Andi will have to do is walk right in. Take the castle. Plant a flag on me.

"It's time to go pick up the kids," I tell her, and she nudges Cat off her lap then sets her book aside with a yawn. She's so cute like this, hair flopped over in something that's half ponytail, half bun, her brown eyes all sleepy, lips begging to be kissed. I give myself what I desire and plant my mouth on hers. "I'll get your shoes."

She yawns again and slowly stands, stretching her arms above her head, as I grab our shoes from the back door, stepping into my sneakers without untying the laces before carrying hers over. I kneel down to hold them out for her, putting them on one at a time. She balances with her hands on my shoulders. "You really are my Prince Charming, huh?"

I straighten with a tap to the side of her thigh. "Only if you're my Cinderella."

She laces her fingers with mine, leaning into me as we head toward the back door, exiting out of the garage. "I guess the broke-down car does count as the pumpkin, but I'm missing a fairy godmother."

"You could have two in Marianne and Clara."

She tosses her head back when she laughs. "You're right. They're absolutely my fairy godmothers."

We stroll down the sidewalk to the bus stop at the end of the development, the warm May sun shining on us while Andi goes on about an idea she has for a song, and my life has never felt more right than this moment. These last few weeks, I feel like I finally have a family. One that my kids deserve. One that I deserve.

I have a woman who cares about me and loves my children.

I have a house that is a home, with laughter and movie nights and decorative bullshit that doesn't make any sense to me except that Andi loves it, and I love anything she loves.

In hindsight, I know I never loved Beth the way a husband should love his wife. I cared for her, sure, but it was more out of obligation than genuine affection. She was carrying my children, and I wanted to do the right thing. But with Andi, it's different. I love her in a way that consumes me, that makes me want to be a better man, a better father. I love her in a way that makes me dream of a future I never thought I'd have.

When I imagine the years ahead, I picture Andi by my side. I see her cheering on the kids at their graduations, her eyes shiny with pride. I see us becoming empty nesters, filling our days with spontaneous adventures and quiet moments together. I see myself growing older, my hair turning more and more gray, and Andi stroking it, a playful smile on her lips as she tells me, "I like mature men."

What I can't do is imagine my life without her. More, I don't want to.

The rumble of the school bus pulls me from my thoughts. Logan is the first one off, which is unusual. He's normally the last, taking his sweet time to gather his things and say goodbye to his friends. But today, he skates right past Andi and me, his eyes fixed on the ground.

"Okay, buddy?" I call after him, but he doesn't acknowledge me. I turn to Andi, who shrugs, waving to Grace when she hops off the bus. She slings her backpack over her shoulder and tightens her ponytail before I drop my arm around her shoulders. "What's up with your brother?"

Grace squints at me behind her glasses then tosses a questioning glance to Andi, as if asking permission.

"Fail the science test?" she guesses, and Grace shakes her head.

"He got a B. I got an A."

Andi pumps her fist in the air. "Of course you did, you genius girl. So, what's wrong with Logan?"

"Valentina likes another boy," she says quietly, maybe feeling like she's breaking twin code or something by telling us, but I'm glad she did. This was the girl that he caught an attitude with me over.

He really liked her.

Poor kid.

And the brow Andi raises in my direction is a silent conversation. I'm gonna have to take this one. Talk to my son about his first heartbreak. I nod toward her, and she smiles at me before telling Grace, "Snack, homework, and then Girl Scouts tonight. I sewed your new patch on."

"Thanks."

"I was thinking we could go shopping this weekend to find an outfit for the talent show."

"Yeah?"

"Yes, my treat for your big debut."

Grace leaps out from under my arm and hugs Andi, bouncing on her toes, babbling excitedly about where they can go and shoes she wants to get. Andi matches her enthusiasm, and it's a physical ache watching them together.

The way they are with each other is how I always envisioned a mother and daughter might be. There is an ease that I could never begin to have with my daughter. An understanding. A whole other language.

The talent show is in two weeks, and Grace has been practicing every day for it. From what I've heard, she sounds good, and I'm happy she's stepping out of her shell to try something different.

Of course, I have Andi to thank.

Again.

Back at the house, after homework and chores are done, and Andi has left with Grace for Scouts, I find Logan in his room, lying on his bed and staring at the ceiling. His door is halfway open, but I knock on the frame anyway before opening it all the way. Logan doesn't move.

"Want to shoot around for a bit?"

My son lifts up on his elbows. "Not really."

I step into his room and backhand the bottom of his foot. "Afraid I'll beat you again."

He waves me off with a cocky, "Psh."

I grab his ankle, yanking him down the mattress. "Outside in five."

"Dad! I just want to lie down."

"And do what? Think about the girl? That won't help. We're playing basketball. Let's go." I clap a few times as I turn back to the hall, calling out, "Don't make me come and get you."

I'm dribbling around when Logan shuffles out, all slumped over. If he's like this in fifth grade, I don't even want to think about when he's older and somebody breaks his heart for real.

"First to ten, loser has to take out the garbage," I say, and he huffs.

"I have to take out the garbage anyway."

"Beat me, and you won't have to."

He rolls his eyes, so I try again.

"Winner gets ten bucks."

"No one uses cash anymore," he says like I'm a fucking dumbass, and I am really not looking forward to the next six or seven years of this.

"Jesus, kid, what do you want?"

He thinks on it. "Sleepover at Sebastian's house."

Sebastian is his best friend, and Logan's slept at his house before because I've met his dad and trust him, a fellow single father until recently who owns a candy store downtown. "Is his dad going to be home?"

"Yeah."

"I need evidence."

"Fine, whatever," he mumbles and takes the ball from my hands to stand at the other end of the drive, opposite the hoop.

He passes it to me, and I toss it back before squatting down to defend him. My son is a good athlete. I've never pushed my kids into any activities—hell, if they'd do less, it would be better for me—but basketball is what Logan is best at, and I hope he continues to play. He's fast, with good control and body awareness.

Even though I usually beat him one-on-one, he always scores a few points. Today, I let him score more. The game's even at nine-nine when he fakes a shot before dribbling around me to hit a lay-up. The ball circles the rim but ultimately doesn't go in. I snatch the rebound and take it back to the top of the key before sinking a jump shot, beating him.

He sighs but claps my hand when I extend mine, allowing

me to pull him into a hug. "You can sleep at Seb's house, but I will be speaking to his dad first."

Logan unfurls a smile, the first I've seen all day, as we plop down on the grass. I bend my legs up, setting my arms on my knees. Logan shadows me.

"So," I start, "you wanna talk about it?"

"There's nothing really to talk about."

Silence settles between us for a while, and even though it's almost eight, the sky is still light, the sun slowing its progression to the horizon the closer we get to summer, and I think about the possibilities. Things I've thought about doing with my kids but never felt ready or confident or competent enough to follow through with.

I always had this dream of renting an RV for a summer and driving to different states to camp. Go see the biggest ball of yarn or whatever dumb shit they have at weird highway rest stops. But I'd never brought it up because I assumed the twins wouldn't want to or I wouldn't be able to handle them on my own for that length of time. Maybe now, they'd want to. I've certainly accrued enough vacation time. Maybe I'd bring it up later, after talking to Andi. The kids have camps, but I'm sure we could work it out.

I lean over, bumping Logan's shoulder. "It sucks when you like someone and they don't like you back."

He dips his chin. "Yeah."

"But you know what that means?" I wait until he looks over at me. "She's not your person. And that's okay. Because one day, you're gonna meet someone who is your person. And she's gonna like you back just as much as you like her."

He considers this for a moment, his brow furrowed in thought. "How will I know she's my person?"

"Well..." I rub at the back of my neck. "You sort of...feel it, I guess. Plus, when you tell her how you feel, she'll feel the same way."

Logan stares out ahead of him, at the houses. A minute passes until he finally says, "I really liked her, and I thought I felt it."

"I think you'll feel a lot of things in the next few years, but it's different when you meet the one. I don't know very many people who meet their person in fifth grade."

He pulls on a few blades of grass, letting them float back to the ground in the breeze. Does it another two times before turning to me. "Is Andi your person?"

The question catches me off guard, but I don't hesitate. "Yes, she is."

He nods a few times, eyes out across the street again. "I like her."

"Me too." Understatement of the century.

I don't confess that I know he loves her and, instead, stay silent as the sky grows darker, the sun fading until lights in houses up and down the street blink on. And as Logan begins to tell me about how there are two Charlies on his baseball team and Coach Matthews has taken to calling them One and Two because he can never remember their last names if they aren't wearing their jerseys, Andi pulls into the driveway with Grace.

Andi shuts her door, smiling at us. "How's it going here?"

"Good," Logan replies as we both stand, and then the strangest fucking thing happens. Nobody even says a word. But suddenly, we're all hugging. All Andi has to do is hold her arms open. Logan takes up the offer first. Then Grace. I round it out, wrapping my arms around the lot. These three people are my whole world. My two kids and my person.

I only have to tell her so.

But for now, this hug is good, too.

Chapter 24
Andi

With Logan at Sebastian's house, I take Grace shopping and out to lunch before she asks if she can sleep at Taryn's house with Maddie. I text Griff to make sure it's all right then drop her off just as he messages me back, informing me he forgot to bring his new phone charger to work and asking if I can drop it off.

So, I double back, pick up the charger from the corner of the kitchen counter and head over to the firehouse. He's outside when I pull up to the curb, and he greets me with a kiss.

"I feel like this was a ploy to get me here," I say with a laugh.

"I wish. I'd rather hang with you than do this training."

Usually, he's off at noon, but he won't be home until after eight tonight, working an extra couple of hours. Tough job, saving the world and all.

I've watched videos of firefighters doing timed drills, running up ladders and staircases, carrying heavy bags. I'd pay money to see Griffin do that. "What's it for? Practicing saving people and stuff?"

He shakes his head. "New procedures, OSHA require-ments, system updates. All the boring bullshit stuff."

I wrinkle my nose. "So, it's just a few hours sitting at a desk?"

"No, I have to run it."

"Big boss man." I whack his arm, earning a stiff eyebrow raise that sets my panties ablaze.

And I am in sudden need of a rescue.

"What are you going to do all day by yourself?" he asks, and I try on my most flirtatious grin.

"I'm sure I could find something."

He grunts a rough sound like he'd rather be home with me —kid-free—than here. Especially when he winds a hand around my waist, squeezing possessively. He keeps me against his side as he leads me inside the firehouse. He introduces me to everyone we pass, some of them familiar-looking since I met them at the fundraiser weeks ago, but I'm not able to talk to them, too busy foaming at the mouth over how good Griffin looks in his fitted work pants and shirt with a radio strapped to his shoulder. So official.

He gives me a short tour of the house, including the kitchen and bunk room before we end up in his office with a closed door. I lean against it while he plugs in the phone charger.

"So, what do you do all day around here? Besides, like, look hot."

He raises his brows. "Excuse me?"

I wave my hand up and down the length of him. "You have basically the most attractive career on the planet. You're the stuff women fantasize about. I mean... Look at you!"

He shakes his head, mouth twitching, so I push him further.

"You're the stuff movies are made of."

He keeps his gaze on me as he sinks into his leather chair,

rolling it backward, creating space between him and the desk. An obvious invitation.

"What happens in these movies?" he asks, and I'm bolder than I've ever been when I slink over to him, standing between his open legs, my hands on his shoulders.

I pitch my voice higher yet keep it a whisper like Marilyn Monroe, "Oh no, Mr. Big Firefighter Man, my cat is stuck in a tree. You have to help me."

He slips his hands around my waist and tugs me to his lap, adjusting the arms of the chair so they aren't in my way anymore, allowing me to settle my thighs on either side of his hips.

He licks his lips and plays along. "Miss, you should go inside your house and put something on. You shouldn't be outside in only a bra and underwear."

I glance over my shoulder at the closed door. We didn't lock it, and there are no windows so no one can see anything, but I'm still not comfortable taking off my shirt, like I'm sure he wants me to. With that bra and underwear prompt.

When I face Griffin again, he's grinning, and the sight of his rare smile never ceases to amaze me. His straight white teeth and crinkles at the corners of his eyes. Brackets form deep grooves on either side of his mouth, and I trace them with my fingertips, cupping his stubbly jaw with my palms before leaning in to kiss him.

He grips my waist tighter, his tongue meeting mine with a moan like it's been a year, as opposed to only a day. But that's what it feels like. There is never enough time. There will never be enough time.

I've known the man for less than two months, but it might as well have been two decades for how I can translate his soft puffs of annoyed breath when something doesn't go exactly how he's planned or how he always inclines his head with a furrowed brow, like he's trying so hard to understand his kids when they talk about their friends. I adore the strained lines across his forehead when he doesn't grasp the nuance of fifth-grade social hierarchy and he glances at me to help him.

I love everything about him, the way he always smells vaguely of smoke but more prominently of his soap, and how he likes everything just so. How he never fails to take a moment when he finds something new I've added to his house—like the woven rug with a Southwestern vibe and small decorative basket I added to the entryway in front of the door—staring at it like it's the ugliest thing he's ever seen, before finding me with a nod and soft smile. Since he has yet to say a word about it, I keep decorating.

Because I think he secretly likes it.

Me in his house. Taking over his house.

Making it more like our house.

Now, I feel his erection growing beneath me, hardening so I can grind against him, rolling my hips with abandon. I've always been shy.

No, afraid.

I've been afraid to let go with anyone, but Griffin has silenced the voice in the back of my head. He's made me come alive in a way I never knew I could.

His hands roam my back and sides, pressing and squeezing, like he can. Like I belong to him. And I do. Completely. He doesn't need to pull on my neck to change the angle of the kiss. I go willingly, following where he leads us, further into this spiral of delicious heat.

My phone buzzes in my purse, a distant annoyance that I choose to ignore as Griffin drags his hands along the underside of my butt, his fingertips delving beneath the fringed hem of my denim shorts.

"I love when you wear these," he says against my throat. "Such a fucking tease in them."

To illustrate his point, he pulls me harder against him as he thrusts up, rubbing against my clit. Even through the layers of clothes, I can feel him. Like I'm sure he can feel me.

I'm putty in his hands. A desperate, panting mess, ready to take my clothes off in his office.

What have I become?

I don't recognize myself, this wanton woman, no longer embarrassed to ask for what she wants.

"Think you can come like this?" Griffin asks, voice low and urgent, skimming his hands up under my shirt, and I nod, my heart racing, pulse throbbing in my wrists and between my legs. When I angle my hips, my zipper hits at the right spot, and I hiss a breath.

"I feel like I'm sixteen," I whisper against Griffin's lips, "doing something I'm not supposed to be doing."

"Yeah, well, I am at work, but I can't wait till I get home." He wiggles his fingers under the cups of my bra, brushing his thumbs back and forth over my hard nipples. "And I only have a few minutes left on my break. So get there, sweet thing."

I grip his shoulders and rock against him, rubbing, working myself up into a lather, the temperature of the room rising.

"Yeah, yeah," he grunts almost inaudibly. "Show me you're not afraid."

I'm not sure if it's the illicitness of what we're doing that's making this so hot, but I'm already so close, and we're both still clothed. He's barely touching me. And yet this...dry humping is getting me off.

I drop my head down, biting into my lower lip as Griffin nips at my earlobe, whispering words like *use me* and *faster, baby* and *you know what you do to me?*

No, but I can guess. That I tear him to pieces only to put

him back together, because that's what he does to me. Uses his fingers and mouth to dissect me, finding every wound and cut, then bandages them carefully and sews me together with his love. I am stronger, not because of him but because he's allowed me to see how those hurts and sore places have made me who I am.

And who I am is a girl who can ride her man to orgasm in the middle of his office without taking off a stitch of clothing.

"Oh my god," I moan into his neck.

He grunts too, and I don't want to think about the mess he made in his pants. Not when his big hands are stroking down my back and butt, and when he cups the back of my head, kissing my mouth and chin and forehead.

As we catch our breath, my phone buzzes again. And again. The persistent sound cuts through the haze, a rude interruption that neither of us can avoid any longer. Griffin pulls back slightly, and I clear my throat, feeling overheated and damp in places I cannot easily ignore. "I should get that."

He nods and carefully helps me stand before turning his chair around, grabbing a few tissues while I retrieve my purse. I loop it across my body before looking at my cell phone screen, finding two missed calls from Dahlia and a text in all caps. **CALL ME.**

"Everything okay?" Griffin asks, in front of me once again.

"Yeah. It's Dahlia. I gotta call her."

He tucks a few strands of my hair behind my ear then opens his office door and takes my hand to walk me back to my car. "I'll try to be home as soon as I can."

"You better," I say, hitting the button on the key fob to unlock it. "I'll be waiting."

He watches me open the car door and lifts his hand with an almost accidental, "Love you."

He stops, and so I do. His eyes widen, mirroring my own

surprise. But neither of us says anything. We merely stand there, frozen. Staring at each other.

"I mean..." He finally drops his hand to his side. "See you later."

"Yeah, totally. See you later," I stammer and start up my car as quickly as possible, driving away from the curb with Griffin's stiff form in my rearview mirror.

I'm positive he didn't mean to say it. From his reaction, I'm not even sure he meant it.

But...

I sort of hope he did. *Does.*

Because I love him. I love Griffin Stone.

I dial Dahlia, putting the call on speaker, and she picks up after one ring. "There you are!"

"Dahl, oh my god, I was just at the firehouse with—"

"You have to come to LA."

I pause my giddy blathering. "What?"

"I need you to come back to LA. They want me to record our songs."

I blink, taken aback. "What? Who?"

"The record label," she says. "They love our songs. I was in a meeting with them this morning and played them our songs, and they love them. I told them you're my partner, that I want you to be on my album, and they agreed."

"Oh shit," I mumble, my mind stumbling over what this all means. I'm stunned to the point of being unable to do anything, and I pull over, parking on the side of the road. Almost in the exact same spot where I met Griffin.

"Tell me again," I say, my head on the steering wheel.

"It's always been you and me, And. We're a team. I need you to come to LA to help with the recording. Write some more songs with me."

This is it. The dream. What I've always wanted.

And yet...

I swallow, staring out through the windshield, seeing Griffin walking toward me that first time, and I have to close my eyes to it. To the memories.

Shaking his hand in the cab of his truck.

Him tugging on the strings of his zip-up.

"Can you believe it?" Dahlia says, yanking me back into reality. "We're getting what we always wanted. You'll have a writing credit on every song. Maybe we can even get you producing too. I'm so happy."

"So happy," I parrot, a whirlwind of thoughts circling too fast to latch on to any one besides, "But I'm...here."

"Yeah, but they know all about you. They know you're the brains behind our songs, and they think our dynamic is perfect. They want to capture it on the album. And they're willing to pay for your travel and accommodations. All I need is your okay, and I'll forward them your contact info, and they can explain it all to you. There is so much to go over, and we'll have to figure out contracts and stuff, but gah! It's fucking amazing, Andi! This is you and me, like we always wanted."

I nod. This is exactly what we always wanted, and I'm beyond grateful for the opportunity, especially when I thought I'd never have one again.

Yet I can't muster up the energy right this second to scream and dance around.

"You're in, right?" Dahlia prods. "I can't wait to see your face in person again."

"Yeah, me too."

"Okay, I'm gonna let them know you're in. It'll be Cynthia who emails you." She squeals and starts rambling in Spanish, something she does when she is really, really excited. I lift my face up to my rearview mirror, expecting to see bright eyes and a big grin in the reflection. Instead, it's red cheeks and a quarter of a smile.

"Okay," she says, back in English. "We'll talk later. Text me after you talk to Cynthia." She squeals one more time. "Te quiero. Te quiero. Te quiero."

"Love you too," I say, realizing I said the words to my best friend when I should have said them back to Griffin minutes ago when I had the chance.

Chapter 25
Griffin

I pull into the garage at a quarter to eight and practically fling the door open, anxious to see Andi and explain... What? I'm not sure.

I didn't mean to blurt out "Love you" like a fucking idiot, but it's not untrue. I do love her. I just wish I was a bit smoother about it. Tell her in a moment when she could really hear it, feel it.

I toss my things down, uncaring about where they land, and kick off my boots when I hear it, Andi's singing voice.

Following it from the kitchen to the living room, I find her laid out on her back on the floor, one leg draped over the other, her foot keeping time, wiggling back and forth. Her eyes are closed, headphones on as she sings about being young and reckless. Her voice is slightly off, but it doesn't surprise me because of the glass of red wine on the table, next to the open bottle.

I suspect she's a bit tipsy.

And I can't take my eyes off her.

I love watching her play guitar. Love hearing the words she

wrote, a window to her soul. I would guess she needs music to
live like she needs oxygen in her lungs and blood in her veins.
There is something about her connection to music, and even
when she's simply lounging around, getting drunk, and listening
to songs, she makes it come alive. Even to a casual observer.

Or not so casual.

I do love her after all.

Everything she does interests me. But watching her make
music, inhabit it, is like watching a sunrise. Magic. It's light and
color and beauty.

"Hey."

She doesn't rouse or hear me, so I sink down on the floor
next to her, drawing a line down the slope of her nose with the
tip of my index finger. She jerks away, eyelids flying open,
surprise quickly melting to my favorite smile of adoration.
"Griff."

"Hi, baby."

She tows me to her, all arms and legs like an octopus, and I
chuckle into her mouth. Her kiss is all over the place, scraping
teeth and uncoordinated lips and tongue, but I let her at it,
rolling so I'm on my back. I push her headphones off and
unplug them from her phone, and the music plays as she picks
up where we left off.

Soon, both of our shirts are off, and I'm pretty sure I'm
going to have a hickey on my chest. I hold on to her wrists when
she attempts to go for my belt. "How much have you had to
drink?"

She shrugs, though I can tell from the color of her lips and
her loose limbs that it's enough for me to press pause. At least,
for now.

Setting her aside so I can stand up, I tell her, "I'm going to
get you some water."

"I don't need any. I have this." She holds up her glass of wine in my direction then takes a healthy gulp.

"Maybe a snack too," I say and fill a cup with water before finding the bag of cheddar popcorn in the pantry.

In the living room, Andi's moved to the couch in only her bra and jean shorts, her stomach bare, belly button ring on display. I sit next to her, and she settles her legs on top of mine, smiling at me from where her head rests on a pillow.

She's adorable. And clearly drunk.

"You need to soak some of that up." I hold out the bag to her, and she takes a handful, but it's like she can't figure out what to do with her hands, both of them full with the wine and popcorn. She lets me take her glass so she can remember how her body works, and I can't help my laugh. "You're a mess."

"You like it."

I love it.

I run my hand up and down her shin. "I see you had fun by yourself today."

"Stopped for wine on the way home." Her smile fades, and she turns her head toward the blank screen of the television, eating pieces of popcorn one by one.

"You all right?" I ask and don't believe her when she offers me a quiet, "Mm-hmm."

But Andi is not one to keep secrets. I know she'll tell me eventually, so I give her space to process whatever it is she needs to. The song on her playlist changes to one I've never heard before. It's romantic yet melancholy. I point to her phone. "What's this?"

Her eyes find mine, and she sits up. "'Poison & Wine' by the Civil Wars. Good, right?" She continues right on, not waiting for my opinion as she helps herself to another fistful of popcorn and tosses some into her mouth. She's got terrible aim, and a few end up on the couch, so I eat those. "They broke up a few years ago. Tragic for me. They won a coupl'a Grammys and were at the height of their popularity, but one day, they up and quit."

There is something about the way she won't meet my gaze that I don't like, but I listen as she goes on and on about different songs, ordering me to listen closely to certain lyrics she plays for me. Before long, she's polished off almost the whole bag of popcorn and appears a tad more sober.

When she asks if I want to finish the rest of her wine, I put the cork back in the bottle. "I don't drink."

"You don't?" She tips her head, face pinching in thought, like her brain's been pickled in merlot. "Haven't I ever seen you drink a beer or something?"

I shake my head.

"Really?"

I shake my head again, and she shrugs.

"Huh. So much for my skills of observation." She picks up her glass of water and downs the whole thing before asking, "Why not?"

I sink back against the cushion, stretching my arm out to invite Andi closer. She cuddles into my side, her head resting on my chest, and I curl my hand around her bare shoulder. I should put her shirt back on her, cover her with a blanket, but I don't. Instead, I situate her on my lap, wrapping my arms around her, holding her close.

She tucks her face against the side of my throat, fingers gently scratching at the nape of my neck. It's a minute until she remembers. "So, why don't you drink?"

I trace random patterns on her thigh, hearts and stars and my initials. "My dad was an alcoholic."

She lifts her head. "You never talk about him."

"There's nothing really to tell."

She hits me with a glare full of attitude, but it doesn't have the same force when she's tipsy.

I like to pretend it hasn't affected me. That my dad's behavior didn't leave an indelible mark on my life, but his leaving was my first real heartbreak. Like all things, I don't think or talk about it because I don't want to remember.

Andi waits patiently until I eventually nudge her face back down to my shoulder and soothe myself with skating my hands up and down her spine. "When he was sober, he was fine, but that wasn't very often. Supposedly, he was an athlete in college when he met my mom, but he couldn't deal with never making it to the pros, and he never recovered. Blamed his shortcomings on my mother and all that bullshit. There was a period before I was born when he was gone for a few years. The story goes that my mom had kicked him out for drinking, and he went and found steady work and got sober and came back eventually, getting her pregnant with me. Then Taryn and Roman. My earliest memories of him are good."

I recall a night in winter and tell her, "There was this one Christmas, I must've been six or so, and he packed us all up in the van, took us to the drive-thru for donuts and hot chocolate, and we drove around to look at all the lights and decorations. I remember feeling like it was for hours, but now... I guess it was probably only thirty minutes, but it felt like forever. Listening to Christmas music on the radio, singing and laughing, the four of us kids and Mom and Dad. It was nice."

Andi makes a sad sound and kisses my pulse point once before settling again.

"But when he'd drink, he'd get mean. Unpredictable." I pause, remembering the tension that would fill the house when he'd stumble in late at night. "I saw what it did to him, to my mother, to our family. I never wanted to be like that." I exhale a loud breath, expelling the pent-up rage and resentment. "My mom taught full time, raised four kids, and still took extra work tutoring and teaching summer school for money because Dad spent it all. Then he'd scream and yell that we never had anything, when he was the one pouring it down his throat." I shake my head, jaw tight. "He left eventually. One morning, we woke up, and he wasn't there. Never came back."

"That's why you're afraid," Andi says so quietly I almost don't hear it. "You expect everyone to leave, either by choice or by nature."

Well, hell.

When she puts it like that...

Yeah.

That's exactly where my fear comes from.

She sits up and turns to straddle me, but there's nothing sexual about it. She hugs me, crossing both of her arms behind my neck, pressing us together. I squeeze my arms around her middle and keep the confessions coming. "It's why I get so frustrated with Roman. I've seen him spiral, seen him push everyone away." I pause to brush my lips over Andi's shoulder. It's so much easier to talk when I can comfort myself by touching her. "It's infuriating. He had everything, more than Ian, Taryn, or I ever had, and he threw it all away. Every opportunity and offer of help, he fucking wasted it."

"I can understand, but I think people can only accept help when they're ready."

"I fucking know that," I say, harsher than I mean to, and she unwraps herself from around me, and I'm instantly regretful.

"Did I make you mad when you came home and saw me drinking?"

"No. Not at all, and I'm sorry for snapping at you. I just get..."

"You love your brother," she fills in for me. "And it's hard to see someone you love mess up."

I nod.

She nods too, and smiles sleepily, moving to lay her head back on my shoulder, and I know I've got to put her to bed. "Let's get you upstairs."

"I have to clean up." She shifts as if to get off me, but I stop her.

"I'll do it tomorrow," I say, bringing her back in close to me, so I can lift her up, one arm under her back, the other under her knees, and she yawns, loud and long, then mumbles something I don't catch.

"What was that?" I ask, amused, and she relaxes into me when I start walking, completely at ease with me. Like she knows she doesn't need to worry about anything.

This time when she repeats her words, they're clearer, though she keeps her eyes closed, half asleep already. "You take such good care of me. That's why I love you."

My heart clangs inside my rib cage, and I hope she doesn't hear it or feel it.

Andi Halton loves me?

Andi Halton fucking *loves* me.

I look down at her, but she's already asleep, her lips slightly parted, her lashes dark against her cheeks.

She's perfect and beautiful and mine.

I carefully carry her upstairs to my bedroom. She doesn't stir when I lay her down but does wake up for a few seconds mumbling about taking her bra off. I silently laugh as I admire her, the golden color of her skin next to her soft pink bra and underwear, then carefully remove it for her so she's comfortable and get her into one of my T-shirts. She's a rag doll in my arms and seems to be in a deep sleep by the time I pull the comforter around her.

In the bathroom, I fumble with my toothbrush like a kid

getting ready for his first date, but Andi's drunken confession has made me feel that way.

She loves *me*.

She chose *me*.

And I can't move fast enough to finish up. I slip into bed in my boxer briefs and wind myself around her. She sighs and yawns and makes a cute smacking noise with her lips before settling again, and I place one last kiss on her shoulder.

"I love you too, Andi," I whisper, even though she can't hear me. I'll tell her again tomorrow when she's fully awake, and I drift off to sleep, knowing she won't be leaving me.

Chapter 26
Griffin

With Andi still sleeping in my bed, I fit a quick workout in then pop out to the store for a few items. It doesn't take me long, and when I get back and check on her, she's rolled over to her stomach, face mushed in the pillow, so I place a glass of water, Gatorade, and two aspirin on the night table for when she wakes up then head downstairs to fry up breakfast.

By the time I finish the hash browns, bacon, sunny-side-up eggs, and toast, she's made her way downstairs, still in my T-shirt, with a pale face and pillow crease across her cheek. I greet her with a kiss on her temple. "You look good."

"Yeah, feel great too." She folds her arms on the table and places her head down on them, moaning something about a headache.

"Did you take the pills I left out for you?" She answers with a hum that I assume means yes, and I set the plate of food in front of her, along with a fork and napkin. "Eat, Andi. You need some protein."

That gets her to sit up, a half-coy, half-still-waking-up smile aimed in my direction. "Yes, Captain."

"It would be more effective if you weren't hungover."

She aims a cute little growl at me then digs in, and I join her with my own plate. I wait until she's gotten through most of her breakfast to ask, "So, what happened yesterday?"

I've been over this a few times this morning while jumping rope, and I don't think she went and bought herself a bottle of wine because of my *love you* slip, especially when I know she feels the same for me, so I can only guess whatever is bothering her is something big. Maybe something with her family or her friend back in LA.

But with how she won't meet my eyes now, I think maybe I'm wrong.

She scratches the tines of her fork in the egg yolk smeared on her plate, and the longer it takes her to answer, the itchier my skin gets.

All these fucking *feelings*.

I've had so many since meeting Andi, but none like this...dread.

She's safe, whole, and unhurt in front of me, and yet there's a pit in my stomach. A whisper of foreboding, like right before my SEAL team walked into that operation in the mountains, the silence heavier than a loaded gun, filled with the weight of the unknown and the loss that could come from it.

That's what it feels like now, sitting across from her. Waiting for the axe to fall.

She puts me out of my misery when she takes a deep breath and pastes on a smile that isn't her real one. "Dahlia called me yesterday, and the record company wants me to come out to LA with her as soon as possible. They're willing to bring me on to her team to write the album."

This is it.

Her dream.

And the last thing I want to hear.

"Wow," I finally spit out. "Congratulations. That's...huge for you."

She nods, setting her fork down to use her hands while she talks, though her eyes stray around the room. "I spoke to the A&R rep yesterday, and she really believes that Dahlia needs me on the album with her. She said our songs have something special that she's not sure Dahl would have with someone else since I already understand who she is as an artist, you know?"

No, I don't know, but I nod anyway. "Yeah. Sure. Of course."

"After I got off the phone with Cynthia—that's the A&R person—then I talked to someone in HR about payment and contracts, and it's not a huge amount of money, but it's...a good amount. Plus, I'll have my name on the album and writing credits." Andi tucks her hair behind her ears, rambling now. "Dahlia said she would push for me to get producing credits, but I'm not sure about that. I mean, I've been in a recording studio before, but I don't have a ton of experience. Besides, like, working with her for all those years. So, I mean, I guess I am the person who could advocate for her or whatever, if she needs it, but when it comes to actually making the decisions with the songs, I'm not sure they'd let me. And that's a lot of pressure."

Her nervous energy is palpable, and I stop her by reaching over to catch her hand, holding it in mine, stroking my thumb over her knuckles. "Are you happy?"

This offer is her dream. I want her to be happy.

And yet, all I can think about is how much I want her to stay here with me, with us. I'm a selfish bastard, plain and simple.

She licks her lips and finally meets my gaze, her brown eyes the tiniest bit bloodshot and watery. "I don't think I should go."

"*What?*" I don't think I heard her right and shake my head. "You aren't going to go?"

Did I say all my inner thoughts out loud? Does she know my most selfish, awful hopes?

Oh my fucking god. I swallow past the giant rock stuck in my throat—the one threatening to bring up my breakfast—as she shakes her head.

"Andi, sweetheart." I take her hand in mine. "What are you talking about?"

She shrugs, face crumpling. "I don't know what to do."

"Come here. Come here." I drag her chair next to mine and wrap her up in my arms, letting her soak my T-shirt with her tears. It's a long time before she catches her breath and quiets enough for me to ask, "Talk to me. Tell me what's going through your head. I thought this is what you wanted."

She rakes her teeth over her lower lip. "This is what I've always wanted. But I also don't want to leave you."

I'm such a fucking asshole for the relief I feel.

Just the absolute worst kind of garbage person.

So I resolve to make sure she does not sense one ounce of hesitation from me. "No, no, you have to. This is your dream."

She gazes up at me with such tenderness, my heart breaks. "But what about you? What about the kids?"

"This isn't about us. It's about *you*."

"But I lo—I can't leave y'all."

That's not exactly what I wanted her to say, but I see the genuine worry in her eyes, and it tugs at something deep inside me. I don't want her to be concerned. At least, not about this. About us.

I know I have to be a fucking man about this and put her needs and desires ahead of my own, even though I really don't want to. It's easier to pout and growl and fucking stomp away. Hell, it's easier to never even get involved in the first place. To not feel anything to begin with, but the day I met Andi shot those plans to shit, and now I have to face this.

With a goddamn smile on my face.

Or...you know...not a glaring frown.

"If this is what you want, I'll figure something out," I say, making my voice as steady as possible. "But do you still want to be with me?"

She nods, and I press a quick kiss to her forehead. One of reassurance, though everything in my body fights me. I don't want her to go. Who wants the love of their goddamn life to go across the country?

I don't, but I know she'll regret this forever if she doesn't. *I'll* regret it forever if she doesn't.

With some quick thinking, I sputter out a few ideas for a plan. "School will be out soon, and maybe it's time I give the kids more responsibility. They can stay home by themselves for a few hours after school since they've been begging me to let them anyway. I can ask my brother or sister to take them overnight or something. Or maybe one of Ian's kids can sleep here on nights I'm not home. Clara or Marianne."

She wrinkles her nose as if she doesn't like the idea, but I don't know what else to do. I'm certainly not going to hire another nanny. That just feels wrong. As if Andi is replaceable. She is not.

"I will figure it out," I say again, more forcefully this time, and she inhales a shaky breath, her eyes going watery again, and I might throw up for real. "What is it, sweetheart?"

She sniffles and rubs the back of her hand across her cheek, catching a tear. "I was nervous to tell you. I was scared about what you might say."

"Is that what last night was about?"

When she nods, I expel a rough breath of my own and pull her to me, sitting her on my lap. Knowing about her past and how she's been on her own in terms of support, I hate that she might have thought I wouldn't encourage her. Or worse, hold her back.

Obviously, I want her to go. I only ever want her to be happy, but I am happy having her here with me in our home.

Though I don't tell her that.

I couldn't.

Instead, I comb her hair back, holding it into a ponytail at the nape of her neck before tugging the elastic off her wrist to tie it in place. Then I drag my knuckles over her wet cheeks and wipe my thumbs under her eyes, drying her off before holding her jaw.

"You're amazing at what you do, and the world will be better if you're able to use your talent. You deserve this chance." I kiss her, speaking my next words against her lips because she has to know the truth. "And I do love you, Andi. I love you and want you to be happy. I want you to follow your dreams."

That sets her off on another round of crying, and our kisses turn salty, her whimpers coming on so strong that she has to pull away to breathe properly. She slips off my lap to get a tissue, and I use the time to retrieve the photo I framed this morning. After all the pieces of herself she's left around the house these last few weeks, I suppose I should give it to her instead of hanging it up on the wall like I planned.

It's the four of us—Andi, Logan, Grace, and me—at Hershey, all smiles and laughter, and I'm actually glad to gift it to her since she'll be leaving.

I set the picture down on the counter in front of her and then, without a word, stagger out of the kitchen, needing space to process everything.

Upstairs, I turn on the shower and step under the hot spray. I let the water run over me, washing away the tension in my muscles, but it does nothing to ease the turmoil in my mind. I can't stop thinking about Andi, about her leaving, about how much I want her to stay. I turn our conversation over and over in my mind, trying to figure out how I can make this work without her. I don't even know how long she'll be gone and she hasn't left yet, but already, I feel myself battening down the hatches, returning to old habits.

Rebuilding my wall.

The idea of her not here sends pain straight through me, but I have to endure it for her. Or rather, lock it down so I can continue on. Do what I need to do for my family. For my kids. For her.

I finish my shower and roughly dry off before wrapping the towel around my waist. When I step into the bedroom, Andi's there waiting for me on the bed. She doesn't speak.

She doesn't need to.

Not with how her face gives everything away.

She's nervous and scared yet still hopeful, and I can't do anything besides give her what she wants.

She stands up and strips my shirt off herself. I barely have time to acknowledge what she's doing before she pulls off her underwear and closes the distance between us, loosening my towel until it falls to the floor. Then she clings to me, arms tight around my neck, her breasts to my torso, her cheek against my shoulder, like she wants to be as close as possible to me. Nothing between us.

I bend and her lips find mine, our tongues tangling in their usual dance. Everything is instinct with Andi, like I hadn't been fully turned on until she came around and flipped the switch, and now I live for her.

My hands are hers. They were useless before I was able to touch her. My arms, they were made to lift her up and carry her to the bed. My breath, it's for her, to exhale into her lungs and keep her alive.

Lying on top of Andi, our bodies flush, I feel her heart pounding against mine. I memorize this feeling, her skin pressed against mine, the way she sighs when I skim my hands down her side and back up to her breast. I take my time, exploring every inch of her, committing it all to memory. I tell her I love her, whispering it into her skin, hoping the words will seep into her pores, into her blood, into her heart.

I scrape my teeth over her nipple, and she arches, digging her fingernails into my shoulders, and I hope she does it again. Sinks deeper. Leaves a mark.

Like I do to her. I move down her body and latch on to the soft flesh of her inner thigh, sucking on it until she squirms away, groaning, hips roaming. I refuse to give in to her, even as she grabs at my head because I'm too busy pressing on the bruise I left, wishing it were permanent. Something to remember me by.

"Griffin," she whines, and that's all I need to kiss the needy spot between her legs. Her responding cry is one of relief, her legs wrapping around my head. When I focus on her clit, her sounds turn shameless, and I curl two fingers inside her, stroking where she needs it. Taking her higher and higher, and my girl isn't so shy anymore. There is no blushing or hesitation.

No.

My perfect girl tells me, "I'm coming. Griff, I'm coming."

"I know, baby."

She rides my face and fingers through it, and when she quiets, muscles relaxed once again, I hold myself above her. "I'm so proud of you. For everything. I'm so fucking proud."

Her smile is tremulous, and she coasts her hands up my chest, around to my neck, tugging me down to her. She doesn't care about the mess she left around my mouth and jaw, licking into me like she'll never have another chance. And that's what it feels like.

Like maybe this is all we'll ever have.

I hate it.

Because I love her.

I pause only long enough to get a condom from the nightstand drawer and put it on. Then I'm over her again, burying my face in her neck, inhaling her scent, tasting her skin. I tell her I love her again and again and again. I can't stop saying it. I can't stop feeling it.

She holds tight to me, her legs around my waist, arms around my back as I push into her slowly, withdrawing even slower, not wanting to lose any connection to her. I lower to my forearms, so there is absolutely no daylight between us, and sink all the way into her, every part of her body welcoming me in. I couldn't pull away from her even if I wanted to.

I find a rhythm that is good for both of us, massaging her clit with every shallow thrust of my hips, and there is no heaven like being between Andi's legs, feeling her wet heat bearing down on my cock, bleeding me dry as I try to burrow further and further into her.

The closer we fly to the edge, the sloppier our kisses get, more searching tongues and biting teeth. Andi trembles and gasps beneath me, her thighs squeezing me, nails scoring my back, and I can't hold it anymore.

I release with a shudder as she cries out, and I collapse fully onto her.

We stay like that, wrapped in each other, our bodies still joined, as our heartbeats slow and our breaths even out. I press a kiss to her shoulder, her neck, her cheek. Then I tell her I love her one more time as I turn us on our sides, the bedroom that I thought would be ours going quiet once more.

She is slipping away, even as she lies here in my arms. I can feel the distance growing between us, the inevitable goodbye looming over us.

I want to beg her to stay. I want to tell her I can't live without her. I want to promise her the world, the moon, the stars, anything to make her stay.

But I don't. I can't. I won't hold her back. I won't keep her from her dreams.

So I commit to memory what her slow, sleepy exhales feel like against my chest, the flutter of her eyelashes against my shoulder.

And then we sleep.

Chapter 27
Andi

To say the rest of the day was awkward after Griffin and I woke up from our nap would be an understatement. For the last twenty-four hours, he's been in planning mode. Because Captain Stone is always prepared. Though it makes our last moments together a lot less romantic than I would like.

I want to go to LA. I want to be with Dahlia and record with her.

But I've also found my family here, and it's difficult for me to see how I can have both of these things at the same time. He thinks we'll be able to make it work, and I hope we do, but how?

Griffin lives here in Pennsylvania, the kids aren't going anywhere anytime soon, but my work is in California.

My work.

If I can call it that.

Songwriting isn't work. It's love.

Like taking care of Logan and Grace. They aren't work. Loving them isn't work.

What is work is packing up my whole life again. This time

around, there is so much more, including a heavy heart and multiple stolen T-shirts and hoodies. I didn't ask Griffin if I could take them because I didn't want to hear him say no. I need a piece of him—as many pieces of him as I can get—back in California.

I'm not sure how long I'll be away for, however long it takes us to write and record, which will probably be through the summer, and I can't stand the thought of not seeing him or the kids in all those months.

Especially after Griffin and I broke the news to the kids last night. They took it on the chin, telling me they were happy for me, but I know Gracie was really upset I'd be missing her talent show, and Logan would barely look at me. I keep telling myself that I am being a good example for them. I'm showing them what it is like for a person to go after their goals, but it's hard not to feel like a phony because, inside, I'm shriveling up.

I'm scared and nervous and sad to leave them.

I never knew a person could feel like they're moving in ten different directions, but that's what it's felt like. I'm being pulled apart.

When it's time for me to get going, I knock on Logan's door and wait for him to tell me to come in before I open it. He's sprawled out in his bed, intently focused on the Switch in his hands.

I sit at the foot of the bed and place my hand on his ankle. "Hey."

It takes him a minute before he finally looks at me. Frowning, actually. A good impression of his father. "Hi."

"I'm going to head out."

He doesn't react, aside from a tic in his jaw. Exactly like his dad.

"I wanted to tell you that I loved being here with you. I loved spending time with you, and I hope—"

"Yeah, yeah," he mutters, shifting away so I'm not touching him anymore. I guess he let his emotions simmer overnight and anger boiled to the top.

"Logan, come on, I'm not leaving forever."

He huffs, skeptical.

"I'm not. I couldn't. I love you."

"So then, why are you leaving?"

"Because I can't pass up this opportunity. It's huge for me, and your father and I agreed I should go. I promise I'll come back."

He rolls his eyes. "Whatever. I don't need some big goodbye."

I'm legitimately shocked by his level of ire. I knew he was upset, but I didn't expect this angry dismissal. "Logan." When he doesn't respond, I try again. "Logan, come on."

He shakes his head and lowers his chin toward his chest.

My throat clogs with emotion, and I find it difficult to be a mature adult about it. The kid I've come to love ignoring me.

"I'm sorry," I say quietly. "It's my job."

He snorts a dubious sound, and the only bright spot in this conversation is that I know this kind of thing is a rite of passage for a parent. I'll have to learn to roll with the punches I guess.

"I love you, Logan." I chance a touch, running my hand over the back of his head. He doesn't move, so I do it one more time, sifting a few of the short brown strands through my fingers. "I hope we'll talk later."

He doesn't answer, and I don't push it, shutting the door behind me on my way out. I swipe my fingers under my eyes and take a deep breath, but it's no use.

As soon as I walk into Grace's room, she starts crying. I do too.

Pulling her into a hug, I attempt to calm her with

supportive words. "You can call me anytime, and I'll answer. I'm here for you, no matter what."

She looks up at me, her tears spilling over her cheeks, fogging up her glasses. "But you won't be *here*."

I shake my head, and she lets go of me to take off her glasses and dry her eyes. She straightens herself out, wiping the lenses and fixing her ponytail, before looking at me again. "I'm sad you won't be at my talent show."

I wipe my own tears away. "I know, honey, and I'm so sorry. But your dad promised to send me the video. I'll be cheering you on, even if I'm not there in person."

I open my arms to her again, and she meets me for another hug. "I'm going to miss you so much."

"I'm going to miss you too," I say, kissing her head and cheek. "I love you." Eventually, we pull apart, and I point my finger at her. "No more tricks."

"No more tricks," she promises, and when I eye her, she laughs. "I swear!"

We hold hands as we make our way downstairs and outside, to where Griffin is waiting by my car parked at the curb. As if she knows we need time, Grace lets go of my hand so I can speak to her father in private.

He stands with his hands in his pockets, shoulders hunched, and I recall how he stood in the same way when we met. But that day, he was curled over from the rain. Today, I know it's for wholly different reasons.

"So, you all ready?"

"Mm-hmm."

With his brows furrowed and eyes squinted, he studies me. As if to see if I'm lying.

"Logan's really mad at me," I tell him, and he shrugs.

"I'll talk to him."

"Please remind Gracie to call me anytime. I'm worried about her."

"She'll be okay."

I rest my hands on his chest, scrunching the material of his shirt in my fingers. "What about you?"

"I'll be okay too."

Really? Because I'm not sure I will be. I'm not feeling very confident at all, faced with the reality of returning to the place of the highest highs and lowest lows. LA was not particularly good to me, but I would not be the person I am without the lessons I learned about friendship, love, and my worth.

"You're going to be okay, Andi," Griffin says, like it's an order. Like I have no other choice. And it's sort of easier to think of it that way.

I'll be okay because I have to be.

"You have your cell phone?" he asks, and I take it out of my pocket to show him.

"Gas?"

"I'll be filling up before I hit the highway."

"You know where all your stops are?"

"Yes, I have all the reservations you made."

Because he would not be Captain Griffin Stone without controlling a trip that wasn't even his, emailing me the best route to take, along with confirmations of hotel reservations he made for me in Columbus, Kansas City, and Albuquerque.

"So you have everything you need," he says like he's pissed about it.

Maybe I am too.

Because I need him.

He braces his hands on my arms, fingers wrapping around my biceps, and draws me to him, mouth on mine. It's perfunctory, with lots of space between our bodies, practically miles, and before I can even part my lips, he forces me away.

I start to tell him it's not enough, but he shakes his head, reading my mind. "I can't, Andi. If I start, I won't be able to stop."

He's right. The longer I stay, the more difficult it will be to leave.

As much as I'm proud of myself and happy to go live my dream, it's not easy to leave the life I've built here, no matter that it's not forever. It feels like it, when there is still so much left unknown.

Griffin steps away from me and drops his arms to his sides, hands fisting and unfisting in that familiar movement I've come to know means he's agitated.

Because of me.

"I'm sorry," I tell him, and he shakes his head.

"You have nothing to apologize for. You're going to do what you were meant to."

My eyes sting, and I inhale deeply through my nose, biting my cheek to stanch the flow. If I start crying again, my big softy will have no choice but to hold me for a while, and we'll have to start all over again.

So before I can get off track, I wave to Grace, blowing her a kiss. I spare a glance up to the windows on the second floor and spy Logan standing at his, so I offer him a wave as well. He pivots away.

Then I smile at Griffin. *Never doubt I love.* "See you, Captain."

Never doubt I love. "See you, sweetheart."

Then I get in my car and drive away from home.

At the end of the block, I glance to the rearview mirror to see the three of them standing in the street watching me, Griffin with his arms around Logan and Grace. As I make the left turn out of the development, I beep a few times, waving out my window.

Sophie Andrews

Never doubt I love.
Then I blast some Janis Joplin and pretend I'm not crying.

Chapter 28
Griffin

This fucking sucks.

Chapter 29
Griffin

I scrub my hand over my face and readjust my baseball cap, shading my eyes from the sun as I trudge down Aster Street. I debated blowing off coffee, but I didn't want Ian and Taryn to get up in my shit about it. I never miss our meetups, so if I did, they'd know something was up.

I jut my chin in greeting to one of the owners of the Tabby Cat, walking his dog and kid, and swerve to avoid a college-aged kid texting and not watching where he's going. I roll my eyes, mumbling a curse, and offer my elbow to an elderly woman who appears to be struggling to carry her canvas shopping bags. I help her across the street and around the corner to where her car is parked, although she's so tiny, I'm not sure she could even see all that well over the steering wheel. I wait a minute until she's off then head back the way I came, only for the door at Lux & Lace to fling open.

Clara grabs my arm, dragging me into the lingerie store, her strength belied by her stature. *Though she be but little, she is fierce.*

My chest physically aches, but I don't even have the chance

to catch my breath because Clara slings her arms around me. "We heard about what happened! How are you doing?"

Of course. Gossip moved quick in this town. Or should I say, on this street. Because of the tiny but strong pixie refusing to let me go.

I sigh and pat her back. "Yeah. I'm fine."

Marianne comes to my rescue, urging her wife to let go of me, but she doesn't look any less concerned. I hold up my hand. "Really, I'm fine."

Clara pouts. "We really thought you and Andi were meant for each other."

I jerk back. We are meant for each other. So why would she suddenly believe otherwise?

Marianne tilts her head. "Didn't you two break up? That's why she moved to LA."

"No, we didn't break up."

"Oh, thank god," Clara heaves, hand to her chest.

"She's in LA for work."

"For how long?" Marianne asks, and I shrug.

That's the part that's killing me. There is no date I can put on the calendar. No schedule I can rely on. Every day is an exercise in patience, and it's not like I had a whole lot to begin with.

Clara lifts her cell phone, tapping on it. "You're a Sagittarius, right?"

"Come on, Clare, the guy doesn't want to hear his horoscope."

Marianne is right. I don't care about horoscopes and stars and crystals or whatever weird witchy girl shit Clara's into.

"Let's just see what is in the cards for you," Clara says, then reads, "You might find yourself feeling an intense urge to put an ongoing issue to rest once and for all. This could relate to something in your home life that hasn't been addressed for a while. You'll be determined to resolve it and won't let anything divert your attention. Today, this issue will be your main focus."

I huff. "Yeah. Thanks."

Clara smiles at me. "See? Everything will work out."

I try to be grateful for her friendship, but her eternal optimism is grating. Especially when I want to sulk in my petulance. "I gotta go. Meeting Ian and Taryn."

Clara hugs me once more before Marianne walks out to the sidewalk with me. "We're happy to watch the kids whenever you need."

"Thanks."

She squeezes my forearm, and just when I think she'll turn around, she doesn't. Instead, she tells me quietly, "You know I used to have a crush on you when I was younger?"

"Really?"

She laughs. "You're so surprised."

"You're gay," I tell her, as if she doesn't know.

"I'm actually bi. I've just only ever been with women." She waves her hand. "But it doesn't matter. The point is, if the choice was you or the bear, I'd choose you. I think every woman would."

I shake my head, not understanding.

"You're one of the good ones," she says. "Don't ever believe any different."

Then she gives my shoulder a squeeze and pivots back to her store. I watch through the display window as she brings Clara into her, arms wrapped around each other, their kiss moving out of the PG rating, and I slant my gaze away, heading toward Jo's.

I'm the first to arrive, so I order our usual and claim our booth, setting the gift bag on the table. The one I'd forgotten about in the whirlwind of everything that happened recently, but I figured I'd finally move it off the counter.

I hate clutter, and without Andi around anymore, every loose item is pointless. She might've brought more energy and life into my house, but now that she's gone, everything seems out of place.

Before I can get too into my feelings about it, my siblings arrive, Taryn sitting next to me and Ian across.

"You wanna talk about it?" Ian asks, getting right to the point.

"Nope." My siblings were always the first to know when I needed a new nanny because they helped out with the twins in the interim, but this time is different. Andi isn't simply a nanny. She is the closest that Logan and Grace have to a mom. She is also my...everything.

I'd prefer to avoid talking about her, like I'd prefer to avoid scratching open a scab, but I have to explain the gift bag as I hand it over. "Andi had these made two weeks ago."

With a curious lift of her brows, Taryn pulls out a frame and gasps.

"What?" Ian leans over for a peek at it. "What is it?"

"It's Mom." She hands it to him and then takes out another frame. "Where did she...?"

"She found a bunch of photos I didn't even know that I had and thought we might like this one. Made a copy for each of us."

Ian sets his photo on the table and scratches at his beard. "Yeah," he says gruffly. "This is..."

"Incredible," Taryn finishes.

What I don't tell them is that when Andi handed me the small box of photos, I had a flashback. At the time Mom passed, she was living in a small apartment, and she didn't have a whole lot of mementos for us to go through. Ian volunteered to keep the few bags and boxes at his place until we were all together to decide who would get what. Ian chose the few pieces of jewelry Mom had since Taryn was always sportier and never much for it anyway. She wanted the *I Love Lucy* knickknacks. It was Mom's favorite show, and she had quite a collection. Roman was still in college, twenty years old and beside himself. I remember how he picked up this old pillow that her graduating students had given her one year with their names all over it. She loved that pillow. So Roman took that, along with the tattered baby blanket we'd all supposedly been wrapped in. By the time it came for me to decide, I didn't care. I was pissed and sad and just wanted to be done with it. I grabbed the box without even knowing what was inside.

And since I completely forgot that I even had it until Andi found it, I have trouble not thinking that's what was supposed to happen.

I don't believe in kismet or fate or whatever bullshit people like to blame or credit for things happening in their lives that they feel are outside of their control. But...

Watching my brother and sister stare in wonder at Mom's picture. Feeling my skin prick like someone is watching me.

I can't help but wonder if Mom is with us now. If Andi was meant to find those photos. If she was meant to make me remember and somehow bring us this gift of our mother.

Both Taryn and Ian clear the air, taking sips of their coffee, but there is still one frame left. I flick the edge of the bag. "One for Roman too."

"Anyone talk to him recently?" Taryn asks around her coffee.

Ian leans back against the booth. "Last time was for my birthday. He sounded...off."

"Like he's using?" I ask, and my brother shakes his head.

"He said he really wanted to come to the party but couldn't and promised to be at the next one."

Taryn clucks her tongue. "Huh."

Roman never makes promises because he always inevitably breaks them.

"He seems to be doing okay, though," Ian says then gestures to my cell phone. "Text him. Tell him about the picture."

So I do. I snap a photo and send it to him along with a message.

> Is your address still the same? I'll mail this to you.

I start typing another message that it's a gift from Andi, but I hesitate over the screen, unsure what to call her—My girl-friend? The kids' nanny? My whole world?—and decide to delete it instead.

It's not until the three of us are almost finished with our coffees that Roman replies.

ROMAN
> Wow. That's incredible.

I choke on a surprised laugh, and when Taryn and Ian toss me weird looks, I show them the text. Because it's unusual he responded so quickly and said the exact same thing Taryn did. My sister snorts while Ian juts his chin, silently directing me to keep the conversation going.

> I'll get it in the mail this week.

ROMAN
> No, don't worry about it. Hold on to it for me.

Hold on to it for him? I would really rather not, but we've

been picking up after him for this long, why not hold a photo of our mother for him indefinitely.

I swipe my thumb, exiting out of the text, only to open the thread I have with Andi, instinctually typing.

> Let me know when you arrive.

Never doubt I love.

She was on the last leg of her drive, set to pull into LA around eight o'clock Pacific Daylight Time. Only a few more hours and she'd officially be a Californian again.

ANDI
> Yes, sir.

> Keep your eyes on the road, please.

Never doubt I love.

ANDI
> I stopped for gas. Having a snack.

She texts me a selfie holding up a cheese stick and a pack of almonds. Protein.

> Attagirl.

Never doubt I love.

Then I put my phone away to find my siblings staring at me like I've lost my mind. And they're right. I have.

"What?"

Ian shakes his head while Taryn snorts. "Why didn't you tell Andi to stay?"

"How'd you know I was talking to her?"

"You have two modes, on and off," Ian says. "But Andi put you in a different one."

I rub the heels of my hands against my eyes. "I didn't really need advice from you two, seeing as how neither one of you has anybody."

Ian rolls his eyes. "Don't be a fucking asshole because you're sad."

Taryn shrugs like the answer's so simple. "Coulda just asked her to stay."

"And give up on her dream? No. Absolutely not."

Taryn sets her elbow on the table, turning to fully face me, to really make sure her next words hit their target. "Stop being so goddamn selfless all the time. If there's one thing I've learned from being married and divorced, it's that you have to ask for what you want."

Ian taps his coffee against hers. "Amen."

I fold my arms over my chest, tucking myself into the corner of the booth. "*Anyway*."

That earns a laugh from them both.

"Anyway," Ian tags on, "we love you, kid."

Taryn pats my knee under the table. "Top three of my brothers, for sure."

I refuse to give in to a smile. "Thanks."

Then we move on to the topic of some woman who came into Ian's shop to get the name of her ex covered up a few years ago, only to return last week, asking for the name back on after reuniting. Ian has a firm personal stance on tattooing partner's names, but I don't agree. At least not when it comes to Andi and me. I'd put her name across my forehead so everyone knows who I belong to.

If only I could be so sure when she would be coming back to me.

Chapter 30
Andi

The trip from West Chester to Los Angeles took four days, three nights, and so many bossy text messages I lost count. But they were all basically the same. Captain Stone checking in three times a day, ordering me around even from multiple states away, like...

CAPTAIN
Are you there yet?

Almost.

CAPTAIN
Don't text and drive.

It's talk to text. And you're the one messaging me.

CAPTAIN
Text me when you get in.

> Safely arrived in Columbus, Ohio—known for Ohio State University, Scioto Mile Riverfront, and the Columbus Zoo and Aquarium, according to a pamphlet.

CAPTAIN

Make sure your door is locked. Dead bolt, if you have it. Put your suitcase in front of the door.

> Actually, I was planning on leaving my door open all night with a sign that all were welcome for a party.

CAPTAIN

Not funny.

> I'm going to bed. Goodnight, Captain.

CAPTAIN

Goodnight.

CAPTAIN

And text me when you're leaving tomorrow.

CAPTAIN

Or I will assume something happened to you, and I'll be heading directly for Holiday Inn-Columbus with backup from friends who have been awfully bored since SEALs retirement.

> Don't threaten me with a good time.

CAPTAIN

Don't try me, baby.

I drove right to Dahlia's house and all but collapsed into her arms when she opened the door, both happy and sad tears dampening her T-shirt. We stayed up talking for hours and fell asleep in her bed while Vic took the bed in my old room, only for us to wake up the next morning and immediately get to work.

Yet it's not *working*.

It's been over a week, but I haven't been able to come up with anything new or close to exciting. I know it takes time to get back into the creative space, but I was able to write while I was in Pennsylvania. I felt really inspired there. Here? Nada.

It's like my brain stopped functioning somewhere around the Arizona/California border when it occurred to me that I never actually told Griffin that I loved him.

That I love him.

I will always love him.

He is everything I want and more than I could possibly need.

All I can think about is the last song that played in the car, "Please Call Home" by the Allman Brothers, so every lyric I attempt to write is something along the lines of I'll beg to come home/let me come home/can I come home?

Not to mention that little ditty about call me baby one more time and I'll come running.

"Maybe we need to take a break," Dahlia says from her chair in the studio, where we've been writing with a man named Uther, hired by the label.

"Another one? We just got back from lunch."

I rub my hands over my face and flip through pages in my notebook. "Why don't we just go back to the one we were working with yesterday?"

"No." He flicks a pen in a circle. "Number one, it doesn't fit Dahlia's voice. Number two, it's not the vibe. It's too sad. Like a Sarah McLachlan dog commercial. I mean, what the fuck are we doing here?"

Needless to say, Uther thinks I'm shit.

Not, *the* shit.

But *shit*.

"That's rude," Dahlia says, defending me, but it's true. I'm leaning way more into the crying while staring out the window at rain vibes than sticky dance floors and hot summer nights, like we're going for with this album.

"You know what..." I stand. "I'm gonna...go for a walk."

I'm halfway through the door when Dahlia follows. "I'm coming with you."

I hear Uther groan in frustration, but I'm too over him to care.

Outside, there isn't much to look at. NoHo is an industrial neighborhood with almost no greenery. It's all gray and concrete and quiet sidewalks. Not much to get the creative juices flowing or releasing tension on a walk.

Dahlia stays quiet until we round the block, heading for a Starbucks, although I know caffeine won't kick-start anything. But I'm glad she's humoring me.

"So, what's up?" she finally asks.

I shrug. "I feel...clogged."

"My abuela has a great tea for that."

For the first time in what feels like years, I laugh and open the door to Starbucks. Getting in line, I explain, "I can't seem to find my groove here. It's like I've lost my creativity."

"You didn't lose it. You just need to let it loose again." She elbows my side hard enough that I have to rub it. "You wrote 'In Your Dreams' and 'Bootlicker,' the two songs that got me this deal. You are literally the only person I know who can write a catchy chorus about getting ahead of a bootlicker."

I snicker. Yeah, that was a good one. I wrote it after watching these two guys try to cozy up to Ryder, assuming he'd put them on a record he was working on, and, of course, fail. But it was fun for me to see how far they were willing to crawl up his ass for it.

I order a cold brew with a splash of cream while Dahlia sticks with hibiscus tea, and we take them to go, continuing our walk. Although Los Angeles can be spectacular with amazing scenery and views, having that twenty-four seven here requires a lot of money. Most of us poors deal with traffic and gray buildings all day long. Dahlia stops to take a picture of a colorful tag on the back of a stop sign—she's got a thing for taking photos of street art for inspiration—and says, "I know you said you want to be here with me, but do you really?"

"Yeah."

Dahlia snorts. "Real convincing." When I don't reply, she wraps her arm around me. "You really miss 'em, huh? Your firefighter and the kids?"

I do. I really, really do. "I know I'm supposed to be happy here, Dahl. This is what I've always wanted, and I don't want you to think this has anything to do with you—"

"Oh, I don't."

This time, I elbow her, and she laughs, stumbling away from me.

"Griffin was so gracious about it all. He told me that I deserved this, and that we could make it work with him being there and me being here, but there has to be another way for me to do this, doesn't there?" I think back over the too-few months I spent with Griffin and how I learned to ask for what I want, to stop feeling shame about my desires, no matter what they were.

Well, what would this new and improved Andi do?

Ask.

"There is nothing in my contract about me having to work here. Would you be upset if I didn't?"

Dahlia squints at the sun. "No, not mad, but I would miss you. I do miss you. It's been hard being away from you."

"I know. I missed you so much, and I love you to death. You know that, but I need to do something, because this..." I circle my finger in the air, encompassing LA. "It's not working for me, and it'll only affect you negatively in the end."

When Dahlia thinks, she sings. It's a reflexive action. Like humming or rocking or tapping a pencil. So as we ramble back to the studio, she sings "Levii's Jeans" by Beyoncé, slowly dragging me out of my head until I'm snapping along to the beat in our heads. At one point, she takes my hand to spin me so I can pretend to be a sexy little thing, even without showering and wearing sweats. The cropped tee and dry shampoo are doing a lot of heavy lifting today.

When we arrive back where we started, Dahlia figures out where I'm going with this line of thinking. "You want to go home?"

"I want to go home," I repeat with a nod.

"To Pennsylvania with your firefighter and kids."

"Yeah."

"So, let's go."

I wrench back. "What? You want to come?"

"I'd like to officially meet this little family of yours, and I've never been to the other side of the country."

"You want to meet Griffin and the twins?"

"Of course. You're my sister. Your family is my family. And hopefully, we can get your hamster back on the creativity wheel. Light a fire under its ass," she says with a ridiculous wink that has me laughing and hugging her.

But a reminder strikes me. "Oh my god! Gracie's talent show. It's on Friday. You think we can make this all happen in two days?"

"I don't see why not. Besides, I'm fucking tired of Uther. You think we can get rid of him?"

I shrug. "It's your record. I'm just the songwriter."

She slings her arm around me. "You're much more than

that. I'm gonna go call Cynthia. I don't want any men on this album, if I can help it."

"Name it *The Bear*."

She gasps. "Fucking brilliant!"

Already, the hamster is crawling its way back as an idea starts to crystallize. A kind of theme that's reminiscent of a Spice Girls kick-you-in-the-face-don't-mess-with-my-friends kind of thing. And I head inside with a smile.

Uther's gonna hate it.

Chapter 31
Griffin

The last two weeks without Andi have been miserable. My kids and I had been doing fine before she came into our lives.

We were fine.

Then she waltzed in with her sticker-covered guitar case and ceaseless goddamn sunshine, forcing the growth of flowers through all the cracks in our family. All the broken pieces I tried to glue together with sheer might, she gently pasted together with patience and a smile.

And now that we know what it's like with her in our lives, the other option is living in black-and-white again. Sure, it's my fault. I kept us there with my rules and schedules and order, but I'm man enough to admit I needed Andi to show me how much better it can be when I bend the rules, loosen the daily schedules, and let a little disorder into my life.

Hell, I bought a sparkly hanging disco ball planter yesterday just because.

I don't even own plants. Nor do I particularly enjoy disco

or shiny objects, but missing Andi Halton has fucked with my brain.

Logan has been pretending he doesn't care she's gone. Learning to compartmentalize from the master—me.

Problem is, I don't compartmentalize as well as I used to anymore, and I don't want my son to either. I want him to be able to talk and express himself. Life is better that way. Living out loud.

Last night, Andi called me so she could talk to Grace. Which I appreciated because my daughter needed a pep talk, and yet I could use one too. A little "Hey, how ya doing? I miss you." Or maybe, "I wrote this song for you." I'd even take "I saw a fire truck, and it reminded me of you."

Something.

Anything.

Because I'm fucking pathetic and need to know she's thinking of me as much as I'm thinking about her. That everything in her world reminds her of me. Because everything in my world reminds me of her.

From the songs on the radio to the photos she framed and hung on the walls of our house.

It's actually nice to be away from the constant reminders and trapped here instead. In this elementary school auditorium while kids hyped up on sugar and pride perform "talents" for this end-of-the-year show.

Logan squirms beside me, his baseball cap pulled low, mumbling complaints every few minutes. I can't blame him, sitting through this test of endurance, but we're here for Grace.

She's been a bundle of nerves all day, though god knows she practiced enough to do well tonight. Hours of practicing on the acoustic guitar I bought her after she proved to me she'd stick with it enough to have her own instead of borrowing

Andi's. Good thing, too. Otherwise, Grace would be going onstage tonight playing air guitar.

The thought makes me fidget, and I refold my arms across my chest after checking my watch again. Forty-five minutes in, and the group of girls onstage do some stupid dance to "Tootsee Roll," but they're barely moving. Nor do they look like they're having any fun, with straight faces and baggy sweats. Next to me, Logan groans, and I elbow him.

He shoots me a look. "That's Valentina."

I bend down. "Which one?"

"Long black hair."

I huff. She's the only one smiling.

I don't know what to say, so I merely grip his shoulder, giving it a squeeze. "Almost over."

"Is it?" he asks hopefully, and I don't know, but I nod anyway.

"Your sister said she's number eleven, and these girls are ten, so she's up next."

He sighs and sinks farther down in his chair, and I don't blame the guy.

A minute later, the blank-faced girls plus Logan's crush exit the stage, and the principal comes back on, clapping like we just watched a ballet. "Amazing, weren't they? Thank you so much, girls! Now, you're in for a real treat by Grace Stone, who is normally known for being on the honor roll every quarter. But tonight, she's going to be showing off another talent. Take it away, Grace!"

I smack Logan's thigh so he sits up, and I lean forward, suddenly nervous as my daughter appears from the left side of the stage, carrying her guitar. She's got on tall brown boots, a green lace skirt, and a worn-looking T-shirt emblazoned with a unicorn that reads *Don't Stop Believing*. Between the clothes and her hair pulled back into a loose braid like Andi so often wears, they could pass for being related, and I rub at a visceral pain in the center of my chest before pulling my cell phone out of my pocket.

I hit the record button as Grace takes her place in front of the microphone stand and adjusts the strap around her shoulder. She strums a chord, gazing out at the audience, and I see the moment it hits her. Fear.

Performing onstage is so out of character for her, I wish I could help her somehow, but I'm useless.

Gracie's face pales as she offers a shaky smile and clears her throat. "H-hi. I'm... My name is Grace Stone, and, and..."

"Oh my god," Logan mumbles into his hands. "She's gonna puke."

"She's not gonna puke," I say, hoping she doesn't puke.

"I'm, um, going to—" she clears her throat "—I'm going to sing."

But she doesn't. She doesn't do anything except stand there, and I cup one hand around my mouth, shouting, "You got it, Gracie!"

She squints behind her glasses in my direction, and I wave. She takes a visibly deep breath and strums another chord, but this one doesn't sound right.

People all around me whisper and shift, impatiently waiting, but I patiently waited through all their kids' goddamn bullshit talents. They can wait a little longer on mine.

Behind me, the door bangs open, causing a commotion, but I don't pay it any mind, keeping my attention on Grace.

Until a familiar voice rings out. "Love you, Gracie! You're amazing!"

Logan and I both whip our heads around to the woman hooting and hollering like she's at a concert.

I love her.

I fucking love her so goddamn much.

I burst out of my seat, followed by Logan, and hightail it to the back of the auditorium, where Andi's jumping up and down next to another woman, holding a sign with big block letters. *Gracie rocks like a Stone* with stickers and glitter all over.

Onstage, Grace grins and acknowledges Andi with a few nods then closes her eyes for a moment, obviously re-centering herself, before she holds up her arm like she's some kind of rock goddess and hits a chord on a downswing.

I grip Andi's elbow, pulling her to me. "What the hell are you doing here?"

She places one hand on my chest and the other to my lips. "Shh. Our girl's about to sing her heart out."

Our girl.

Grace is mine. And Andi's. *Ours.*

Beside me, Logan stares at Andi, who smiles shyly at him then mouths, "I'm sorry."

My son doesn't answer, but he also doesn't fight her when she steps toward him, looping her arm around his shoulders, positioning him in front of her as Grace starts playing "You Belong with Me" onstage.

It's suddenly hard for me to breathe.

I don't understand what's going on. With Andi here and hugging Logan. Some random woman cheering and singing along with Grace when she gets a little lost on the guitar.

I missed something, but the more I think about it, the more I miss in this moment. So, I stop trying to control it and clap along with Andi as she keeps the beat. Soon, others join in, and my daughter smiles, even though the song seems a little slow and her voice cracks every so often.

Grace finishes with a flourish, holding the last note, and damn if I don't get teary-eyed.

The audience applauds. Andi cheers raucously. The

woman with the sign lets out a high-pitched hoot that I think would do well to torture our enemies with on repeat.

Onstage, Grace waves, bows, and runs offstage. I take the opportunity to grip Andi's wrist, telling Logan, "Don't move."

Andi holds up her index finger to the woman with the sign, silently asking for a minute, before I drag her out of the auditorium to the small vestibule where two parents are selling concessions at a table. I tow Andi over to the corner, lowering my voice. "I ask again, what the hell are you doing here?'

"I had to see Grace perform."

I don't like beating around the bush. "Why aren't you in LA?"

"Because..." She lifts her arms out at her sides and lets them flop back down. "I..." She puffs up her cheeks and blows out all the air with a shake of her head, like she really has no answer for me.

"Andi. Why?"

I need to hear it. I don't normally give a shit about what anybody has to say. But in this case, I really, really need to hear it.

Her big brown eyes dart around behind me, but I pin her against the wall so she can't escape, my hands on either side of her shoulders. I dip my head, closing my eyes. "Please, Andi. You left, and I was okay with it." I swallow thickly. "I was trying to be okay with it. I will eventually be okay with it. So, I need to know why you're back already. I need to know how often my heart will break. Make no mistake, I'd rather break it a thousand times than never have you in my life, but I'd just like to know what I'm dealing with so I can prepare."

When I meet her gaze again, her eyes are watery. She moves her hands to my sides, fisting my T-shirt. "Always so prepared." She leans up on her toes, reaching to kiss me, but she can't quite reach without me bending. I don't, and her lips land on the underside of my jaw. "I came back because I needed to apologize for leaving without telling you that I love you. I love you, Griffin. I love you so much, and I want to be with you. I want to be with the kids. I want us to be a family."

She ducks down to pull the framed photo I gave her from her purse. The one of the kids and us. "I want to put this in the living room, on the table next to the big couch, and then take a lot more pictures so there's a different one in every room."

I feel like I should be mad at her, like I should hold some kind of grudge for being so flighty, coming and going on a whim, but I can't. I told her to go, and I'm too happy she's back.

I only want her to be with me. Forever.

"Maybe we should get a big one." I slide my hands around her waist, lifting her off the floor so she shrieks and throws her arms around my neck, legs around my waist. "One of those obnoxious blown-up photos."

"All of us in matching clothes," she says, grinning. "Get a professional to take it outside during the fall."

I always hated the idea of doing that, but we'll do it. And I'm going to get a bunch printed. Buy a wallet with little plastic inserts just so I can print tiny photos and carry them around with me like my grandfather used to.

"I love you. I missed you so much," I say, molding my hand to the back of her head, urging her to me for a kiss that's one part adoration and one part fear. I don't want to have to live without her, and maybe I can kiss my desperation into her, so she'll know. She'll realize that she's changed my whole world, and without her in it, gravity doesn't keep me tethered anymore.

"I love you. I love you. I love you," she says, punctuating each sentence with a kiss to the corner of my mouth, my cheek, and my jaw before she hugs me tightly, pressing her face into the side of my head, her fingers scratching over the nape of my neck.

Fuck, I've missed that.

A throat clears, and I turn with Andi in my arms to see a woman glaring at me with raised eyebrows. I glare right back, carrying Andi to the doors of the auditorium, where I finally set her feet on the floor. "Ready to go back in?"

She takes my hand, lacing our fingers together. "Absolutely."

Inside, there's a kid onstage performing magic tricks that are getting a few laughs, and Andi pulls me over to the woman she arrived with, whispering, "This is my best friend, Dahlia."

I shake her hand. "Nice to meet you."

Dahlia looks me up and down. "Very nice to meet you, Griffin. I hope you're worth it."

I curl my hand around Andi's neck. Now that she's here, I can't stop touching her. Not that I could before she left either. "Me too."

"More than worth it," Andi assures both of us, then gestures to Logan, who approaches her with a wary frown. Andi speaks so softly to him that I can't hear what she says over the clapping and laughing of the audience, but Logan responds with a short answer and they hug, so I assume it's positive.

While the last acts wrap up, Andi and Dahlia whisper things to each other, and I can see Logan melting with every second. I know he was really upset with Andi for leaving. He felt like she was choosing something else over him, which I understand, but it's not true. We have room in our hearts to love many things. I should know. I learned that lesson in real time.

But it's wild to watch my son falling back in love with the woman I know he thinks of as his mother in real time. Not that I ever thought he wouldn't. He adores her, just like his sister does.

Who eventually comes running out after the show is over, heading right to Andi, hitting her with a hug so big, it earns an audible "Oof" from Andi. Then a laugh. She kisses Grace's head a few times, whispering about how proud she is of her, before finally letting go so I can hug her as well.

But as soon as I do, she's back to Andi. She introduces Dahlia, who I learn has talked with my kids for a few minutes over FaceTime. "You were great," Dahlia says. "Very impressive for your first show."

Grace turns bright pink. "Thanks."

Andi tightens her grip on her shoulder, rubbing protectively. "Listen. I know we have a lot to talk about, but I was hoping we could do it over ice cream? My treat."

I defer to the twins. Gracie hops on her toes. "Yes!"

Logan shrugs, all cool. "Yeah, okay."

So, I wave my hand out in front of me for them to lead the way, when a thought occurs to me. One I didn't even think to ask. I grab Andi's arm. "Wait a sec. How did you get here?"

"Flew into Philly," she says as Dahlia rolls up her homemade poster.

"I rented a car. Hope it's okay, but Andi said I could stay in your house."

I toss a questioning glance to her, and she hits me with fluttering eyelashes and a big whopper of a smile, silently pleading. As if I'd say no.

"Dahlia's like a sister to me, and I want her to get to know my family."

I nod at Dahlia. "Of course. You can stay in Andi's old bedroom."

Andi bites into her bottom lip, always fighting the losing battle against her growing smile. I kiss her temple. "You ride with Dahlia. We'll meet you there."

"Actually..." Grace lifts her hand as if she's in a classroom. "Can I ride with you too?"

Dahlia throws her arm around Grace's shoulders. "Definitely."

Logan cuts his gaze to me, a silent question that I answer with a playful roll of my eyes. "Yeah, you too."

Logan lets himself be pulled into Andi's side, and I follow the foursome out of the school, taking Gracie's guitar in the truck with me. The ride to the ice cream shop isn't long, and I park next to Dahlia's rented Toyota, watching as Andi and Dahlia walk with linked arms as Logan talks with his hands, appearing as if to explain something about the dance that group of girls did, and it gets a round of snickers from everyone.

Inside, I pay for the ice cream even as Andi tries to fight me about it. But she goes real quiet when I slip my hand into the pocket of her jeans and squeeze her ass hard. Logan and Grace claim a big booth, and I slide in next to Andi, who's beside Grace and opposite Dahlia and Logan.

They all talk, zigzagging from Andi having trouble writing songs in LA to the basketball camp I signed Logan up for to the next song Grace wants to learn to play to how long it takes Dahlia to dry her waist-length hair.

I sit back, taking it all in with peace and gratitude. Well, not quite peace. Not when the twins eventually start fighting because Logan told Grace she could've sounded better and Grace told Logan Valentina kissed Jackson Cruz, and she overheard her telling her friends she loves him.

Andi holds her hands up between them, trying and failing to get them to apologize to each other, eventually settling for them agreeing to stop kicking each other under the table.

Dahlia gestures to all of us at the table, an amused smile on her face when she asks Andi, "This is what you missed?"

She eyes each of us, Logan, Grace, then me, and turns back to her best friend. "Absolutely."

Chapter 32
Andi

Griffin clamps his hand over my mouth, his lips against my ear when he tells me, "Everyone's awake. You need to be quiet."

Then he nips my earlobe at the same time he tweaks my nipple. Unfair.

My moan is muffled, and he catches me around the waist as I bend over, needing to hold on to something that isn't his forearm.

It's been a week and a half since I crashed Grace's talent show and had a long talk with Griffin. I explained how I need to go back to Los Angeles while Dahlia records her album, but West Chester is my home. I don't plan on ever leaving it or him and the kids for long periods of time without a plan. He didn't say much other than to put me on my back and go down on me for a very long time until I promised him that I'd sell my car while I was out in California. Because "that piece of shit is getting replaced ASAP."

He made a very convincing argument.

Though I didn't need three orgasms, it did prove exactly how much he really wanted me to get rid of my Jeep.

I've spent every night in our bed and every day relaxing with Dahlia, walking around downtown, introducing her to my friends, and writing songs. We even had an impromptu concert when Griffin invited his family over for a cookout. While he grilled up hot dogs and hamburgers, Dahlia and I performed our favorites, then closed with Grace and the new song she's been working on, "Hey Lover"—the first song I ever learned to play. The one Dahlia covers at the end of every show.

It's been exactly what I needed.

"Yeah, I got you. I know what you need," Griffin murmurs, setting me on all fours, pushing my knees apart with his own as he rolls on a condom. "Head down on the bed, baby. Stay quiet."

I lay down my cheek and extend my arms above me to hold on to the edge of the mattress. Behind me, Griffin groans as he runs his palm along my spine, tracing the curve of my butt, sinking down to press his fingers against my entrance. I'm wet from the two orgasms he provided this morning, waking me up with his mouth between my legs. He'd already worked out and had breakfast. Now, he smears my desire all over my pussy and inner thighs, molding his hand to me for a long moment.

I love when he does that. Claims me. Without words, he lets me know that I'm his.

But he takes too long, and I shimmy my hips, pushing back against him. His laugh is gruff. "So impatient." He feeds his cock into me, slowly working in one inch at a time until I'm full and panting. He bends his big body over me, sliding his left hand up my arm to lace our fingers together while he finds my clit with his right, his fingers circling with the exact right amount of pressure. I whimper, unable to move, simply taking it. His weight and heat, it's all so overwhelming. Too much, yet not enough. I think I might accidentally suffocate trying to get him closer, but he'd never allow that to happen.

Always careful. Even when he breathes heavily against my ear, his damp chest against my back, pinning me in place. "You always feel so fucking good, but I can't wait to take you bare."

His words send chills racing over my sweaty skin. For a man of few words, he knows exactly what to say when we're together. Especially when he wants to get me off. Nothing feels quite like the pride in his voice when he makes me come and praises me for it.

In one of our discussions this last week, we'd talked about how neither one of us wanted any more kids besides Logan and Grace. Since we're committed to each other, we don't have to use condoms, save for the birth control, and he'd happily agreed to get a vasectomy. Griffin being Griffin, he already called to make the consultation appointment.

He rolls his hips, setting off another wave of pleasure, and he reminds me to be quiet again as I orgasm one more time. I bite my lip, stifling my sounds, and I feel him nod, his stubbly jaw like sandpaper against my temple. "Attagirl." He shifts up, eases off my clit to hold my hips, both hands gripping me hard. "Atta-fucking-girl. Always so good. So sweet."

He takes off, snapping his hips in quick succession, and I have a difficult time getting air into my lungs, trapped under him, being wonderfully used. Because even when Griffin is rough with me, fucking me like he's a little out of his mind, I know he's doing it because he wants me out of my mind too. He wants me to stop thinking and feel all the things I'd always been afraid to feel during sex. He wants me to be dirty and playful and filthy and his perfect girl.

"That's my perfect girl." He sucks in air through his teeth, a sign he's close to coming, his pace faltering until he stutters to a stop and falls on top of me for a few seconds. He kisses my temple and pulls me to his chest.

His heart beats steadily beneath my ear, a comforting rhythm that matches my own. We lie like that for a while, his fingers combing my baby hairs, mine lightly scratching over his hard pectoral muscle. Honestly, the man is 80% protein shake. Water? Never heard of it, unless he's forcing me to drink it.

"You packed up?" he asks after a few seconds, and while I pretend to hate this game, it's actually my favorite. The one where he makes sure I have everything anytime I leave the house.

"Yep."

"All the information about your car saved on your computer?"

"Yes, Captain."

He tugs on a few strands of hair as a reprimand. "It'll make it easier for you when you go to sell it."

"I know. I know."

"Do you have your plane tickets printed out?"

That has me lifting my head. "No one does that anymore, Grandpa."

His hand lands a sharp smack on my ass, and I squeal in surprise. Rolling so he's on top of me, he kisses me hard. As if it's punishment.

I wiggle underneath him, fighting a bit, and he pretends he's not a former Navy SEAL, allowing me to thump his shoulder twice before he holds both of my wrists down on either side of my head, bracketing his knees around mine so I can't move.

I smile.

So does he.

Then he rubs the tip of his nose against mine and kisses me once, softly. "You've ruined me."

"Good."

He huffs a chuckle. It sounds like he smoked ten packs of cigarettes last night. "No remorse whatsoever for turning me into some kind of simp for you?"

I shake my head. "You love it."

He glares at me as if he doesn't love it, giving in after a few seconds. He kisses me again, this time sweeping his tongue into my mouth, teasing me with short strokes interspersed with longer ones and scrapes of his teeth. He eventually lies next to me, his head propped up on his hand. "I'm going to miss you."

I turn on my side, matching his position. "I'll miss you too, but I'm looking forward to all the fun we'll have."

He rolls his eyes. "Yeah. Waiting in line for three hours for a ride that'll take three minutes."

"Hey, you had fun at Hershey." When he refuses to answer, I poke him. "Admit it. You can't wait to buy matching Mickey ears and get your picture taken in front of the castle."

He sighs, grumbling. "I'm not wearing Mickey ears."

As soon as the kids are done with school, the three of them are hopping on a plane to come to LA so we can spend a week exploring Southern California, including a visit to the Happiest Place on Earth. And he's absolutely going to be sporting Mickey ears with me.

As big as he is, he's no match for me.

Although I am no match for his alarms. His watch beeps, and he taps it, telling me, "Time to get up."

"Noooooooooo."

"Yeeeeeeeees." He scoops me up from the bed and carries me into the bathroom, where he starts the shower. He remains all business even as I try to convince him to get under the spray with me, but he reminds me that I need to be at the gate three hours before boarding, and if I don't get moving, I'll be late.

That's when I tell him this would all go much faster if he came in here to wash me.

He doesn't fall for it, and I have to finish showering on my own to the tune of Griffin's delightful warnings.

"Twelve minutes!"

"Five minutes! Your breakfast is ready!"

"One minute. Get a move on, Andi!"

I throw my backpack over my shoulder and make my way downstairs to learn he filled the rental up with gas last night and loaded our bags already. Griffin hands me a to-go bowl of oatmeal with berries and a drizzle of maple syrup.

"Protein," I say at the same time he does, earning a stark eyebrow raise. I kiss a grin into his lips then tug on his hand, leading him outside, where Logan and Grace are chatting with Dahlia.

Over the last ten days, my best friend has come to learn why I love my family so much, and I've come to understand that I don't have to sacrifice one dream for another; they just might look different than I thought they would.

Dahlia offers hugs to everyone then ducks into the car to give me time. I start with Logan, kissing the top of his head. Before he can turn away, I catch his elbow, whispering, "I know you're staying up late playing video games. If your dad figures it out, I doubt you'll be able to beat him in a footrace to the garbage can. He'll throw out your Switch."

His face drains of color, and I let him stew for a moment before I wink, letting him know Griffin won't be finding out from me. "Be good. I love you."

"Yeah, okay," he says quietly then backs up. "Love you too."

And hearing the kids tell me they love me will never get old. Never.

I hug Grace, squeezing her tight. "I can't believe next time I see you, you'll be a middle schooler."

"Not officially," she says into my shoulder.

"Yeah, officially. You're done with elementary school in two weeks. As soon as you walk out of that building, you can say, 'I'm in sixth grade.'"

She shrugs in agreement, and I kiss her cheek. "Love you."

"I love you too."

For the first time, the word *Mom* floats through my mind. They've never had a woman in their life to call Mom, and even though I've only known them a few months, I don't plan on going anywhere. And...maybe, somebody, they wouldn't mind calling me Mom. I wouldn't mind.

In fact, I'd really love it.

I finally turn to Griffin, covering my eyes from the sunshine as I peer up at him. He pivots, so the sun is at my back, and this man...

Too good.

Too perfect.

And all mine.

I hook my hands into his T-shirt. "So, this is goodbye, huh?"

"For now," he says, palms bracketing my face.

"We should probably say something else instead of goodbye." I lift my shoulder in question. "How about so long?"

He exhales like I'm exhausting, though he can't help himself and joins in. He clucks his tongue with a thought. "Farewell?"

I gasp, throwing up my hands, saying in singsong, "*Auf wiedersehen, adieu!*"

He doesn't get it, so I sing the famous song from *Sound of Music*. Dahlia joins in, and I hold my hands at my chest like I'm in a choir.

He remains unamused and waits until I finish my musical theatre performance to plant his hands on my waist, lowering his forehead to mine. "I don't know what I did in my life to deserve you, but I swear I'm not gonna stop trying."

That I believe, and I wrap my fingers around his wrist. "I love you, Captain."

"I love you, sweetheart."

He kisses me tenderly then lifts his dark gaze to me, those eyes that stunned me on a rainy day in March. He rubs his thumb over my lower lip and lets a smile loose. "I'll see you soon."

I nod, and he steps back, watching as I open the passenger's side door, blowing kisses. The kids wave, but Griffin goddamn Stone catches one of my kisses, grins, and presses it to his heart.

I toss my head back to laugh.

Stones do crack.

And I never stood a chance against the good stuff hidden on the inside of mine. All the love and loyalty and *feelings*.

Epilogue
Griffin

Ian and I step into The Nest, the bed-and-breakfast empty of all furniture and decoration, ready for the renovation Taryn has been planning for a long time. The owners of the place, an older couple who owns a bunch of B&Bs in the tri-state area, are relatively hands-off, giving Taryn full run of the place. As long as she keeps the money rolling in, of course. Which she does.

If there is one thing my sister excels at, it's pinching pennies and stretching a dollar. So she's planned out this reno down to the second, and I appreciate that. My brother and I find her in what was the dining room, typing on her phone, and pass her a to-go cup of coffee since she couldn't meet us for our usual catch-up.

She glances up, and I notice the dark circles under her eyes. She's pushing herself too hard. God forbid anyone points that out, though.

"Thanks, brother," she says, accepting the cup from me and tipping her chin at Ian. "You guys didn't have to come up here."

"Yeah, we did," Ian says with a pointed glance around. "Wanted to get one last look at the old gal before her facelift."

My sister pats at her face. "Watch how you speak about me."

Ian and I both give in to amused eye rolls and chuckles.

I peer out the windows at the fall foliage, all gold and red and perfect for a postcard. I snap a picture.

It's been six months since Andi Halton broke down on the side of the road and stole my heart—and my head—and my world has never looked brighter. After she returned to LA, she finished writing a few songs to add to the ones she's already written with Dahlia. Then, as planned, she got rid of her car, and we spent a week vacationing, where she did somehow convince me not only to wear Mickey ears but to get my picture taken with the rat. It's been smooth sailing ever since. Well, sort of. Now in middle school, Grace is in all honors classes and has a lot of anxiety about keeping her grades up, and Logan has another crush. God help us all. Dahlia's album is set to come out in the new year, but Andi has already made some inroads with people who want to work with her. She is considering each offer carefully while juggling a few lessons at a music center downtown.

And me? I'm happier than I've ever been. Even if Cat now sleeps in our bed every night, and I've had to download an app to make sure I'm watering all eight of our plants on schedule, because as much as Andi loves having green "babies" in our house, she's terrible at keeping them alive.

I check my cell phone when it buzzes with a text message from the woman herself, asking me to grab her a box of tampons on my way home, and I shoot a thumbs-up emoji back before turning to my sister. "So, you're all set for the renovation?"

She scoffs, gesturing to the organized chaos around her.

"You should know by now that I always have everything in order."

It's true. My sister is an absolute warrior. She's raising two kids practically on her own, runs this bed-and-breakfast like a well-oiled machine, and still finds time to create beautiful pottery. She's nonstop, a force to be reckoned with.

Taryn starts explaining the changes she's planned, walking us around as she points out how the wall is coming down between the dining room and the little sitting area so she can move the check-in desk over there. I don't really pay attention, checking a construction truck as it pulls up. A guy in a Moretti Co. T-shirt makes his way up the back with an easy stride. He's tall and broad and opens the door with a clipboard in his hand. "Hey, I'm looking for Miss Stone. I'm Dante Moretti, the contractor for the reno job."

His gaze sweeps over the bare space, landing on Ian, me, and then our sister, who freezes between us.

This Dante guy's eyes widen like a deer in headlights.

Neither one of them makes a move or speaks, and I glance at Taryn, frowning. On the other side of her, Ian juts his chin at her, elbowing her side to get her moving. "Yeah, you've found her."

Taryn stumbles forward, and I'm not sure I've ever seen my sister speechless before. The contractor sticks out his hand with an amazed "Hi."

Taryn stares at his hand like it's a tentacle then reaches for it, but she has the coffee in her hand and ends up spilling it on the floor.

"Shit," she mutters, crouching to pick up the cup, and the contractor springs into action, grabbing a bandanna from his back pocket to clean up the dark liquid.

"I got it. I got it," he says, pushing her away, and it's like watching a car crash.

I can't take my eyes off it. *Them.*

Taryn drags her hand over her face, exhaling a harsh breath as he stands, holding the soaked rag in his hand, staring at my sister like she's the best thing he's ever seen.

I don't know what to do and shoot a look to my brother, who clears his throat. That makes Taryn shake her head. "Uh, thanks."

"Yeah." Moretti smiles. "No problem. I'm gonna toss this back in my truck," he says, referring to the bandanna, "and then you wanna walk me around the property? I got the list, but I'd like to make sure we're on the same page."

She nods, her voice sounding strangled when she says, "Mm-hmm. Yep. Sure."

He leaves, the screen door slamming shut behind him, and I swing around to Taryn, eyebrows raised in silent question. *What in the fuck was that?*

She squats down, hands on either side of her head. "Oh my god."

"Taryn," Ian says, seriously. "What is going on?"

"I, uh..." She tilts her head back, face screwed up. "I slept with him."

I blink a few times in confusion, but Ian doesn't have my problem. "With the kid? He's, like, twenty."

She straightens, hands on her hips, annoyed now. "He's actually thirty."

Ian's brows rise, interest lighting his eyes. "You like him."

My jaw drops. "*What?*"

She slaps at Ian. "I do not like him."

"You do," he argues, and she pushes on his shoulder, getting him to move.

"I do not like him. I'm not a teenager. I don't like people."

"You liked him enough to fuck him," Ian points out, and she thumps his shoulder.

"Get the hell out of here. I don't have time for you. Go harass your own children."

Ian lets himself be pushed out, but I wait until she turns to me to hold out my hands. "So, uh, that was awkward."

"Please, just... Don't."

I shrug. I won't say anything. Instead, I cup the back of her head, ducking down to meet her eyes. "You got this."

She nods.

"But if you don't, you can always call me."

Her flattened lips twist up in the corner. "Thanks, brother."

I chuck her under the chin. "See you, sis."

Outside, I hop behind the wheel of my truck and pull out my cell phone to text Andi the photo I took. She replies immediately.

> **ANDI**
>
> If this is you telling me it's time to book a family photo sesh, I already did.

> **ANDI**
>
> In fact, I'm on Pinterest now looking at ideas for our matching outfits. How do you feel about corduroy?

I toss my phone down. I hate corduroy.

Which means I'll definitely be wearing it.

Small price to pay for the honor of a lifetime.

What's next?

If you want more Captain Stone and Andi content, use the QR code to have it delivered straight to your inbox!

To stay up to date with all things Sophie Andrews, use the QR code on the next page to stay in touch!

What's next?

Acknowledgments

Indie publishing is a wild ride. Thank you, reader, for taking the ride with me.

Big thank you to Skye Warren for pushing me to write this book, and Lily Bear for the amazing cover. As always, Libby and Lisa have turned my brain vomit into a pretty decent novel, which is always a miracle.

Biggest thank you to all of my readers. Thank you for your DMs and for your early reviews and for making all of this worth it. Without you, I'd literally just being writing these books and reading them out loud to myself like I used to do when I was a kid. And while that's fun, it's so much more fun to know people love these silly little books. I am forever grateful for you.

If you'd like more information about me, you can find it at https://sophieandrewsauthor.com/

About the Author

Sophie Andrews is a contemporary romance author who writes steamy books that will leave you smiling. As a millennial, she's obsessed with boybands, late 90s rom-coms, and will always be team Pacey. When she's not writing, she's most likely trying to wrangle her children or drinking red wine. Or both at the same time.

Also by Sophie Andrews

Tangled Series

Tangled Up

Tangled Want

Tangled Hearts

Tangled Beginning

Tangled Expectations

Tangled Chances

Tangled Ambition

Single Dads' Club

The Rehearsal Fling

The Nanny Tenure

The Dating Pact

The Bartender's Baby

Stand-Alones

How to Ruin a Wedding

Love at a Funeral and Other Awkward Conversations

Hart Brothers Novellas

Made Over by Meredith

Wrapped Up in Holly

Collections

Tangled Series books 1-4

www.ingramcontent.com/pod-product-compliance
Lightning Source LLC
Chambersburg PA
CBHW032246130525
26660CB00016B/129